ICE DIARIES

Lexi Revellian

Published by
HOXTON PRESS

While the places in this book are a mixture of real and imagined, the characters and events are fictitious.

Chapter	CONTENTS	Page

Chapter		Page

PROLOGUE

Morgan put one foot in front of the other, the snow crunching beneath his boots. One step at a time and he'd get there. A full moon shone blue and white on the undulating surface. Less than a mile away, City of London skyscrapers emerged from twenty metres of snow like the tombstones of a dead civilization. From a few of the nearer buildings thin smoke trailed through the clean air towards myriad stars glittering coldly above. He did not notice the beauty of the night; he had other preoccupations. Unless he reached the source of one of those wisps of smoke he would die.

Not far now, he could make it. The gash on his ribs gaped with every gasping breath, blood seeping. He battled pain, cold, thirst and exhaustion as if they were a tough opponent in the cage; keep fighting however much punishment you take, don't admit the possibility of tapping out.

The weight of his backpack dragged him down. Its contents were no good to him any more. He shrugged the thing off and let it thump to the ground without a backward glance, staggered on for fifty metres then fell to his knees and began to crawl.

CHAPTER 1

Tori

Monday, 30th April 2018 (Nina maintains I have got a day ahead so it's Sunday 29th, but she is wrong).

Today no snow fell, the first time for months, and the sun shone in a brilliant blue sky. With luck there'll be icicles, so much easier to melt than snow. Greg called, as he does most days, doing his rounds. He banged on the window, slid open the patio door and came in. I gave him a Mars bar. I once joked he runs a protection racket – we all got into the habit of giving him stuff when he arrived, because he seemed so helpless – and he took up the idea, though he interprets it his own way. He likes to think he protects us, checking up on our small community each day, carrying messages and doing a bit of trading. He put his bag on the kitchen counter and his gloves to warm over my wood-burning stove while he ate the Mars bar. The snow melted off his boots and pooled on the stone-effect tiles. I peered into the open top of his bag.

"What's that you've got there, Greg?" He took out an A4 notebook, black with a scarlet spine, and handed it to me. I opened it. Crisp off-white pages, with faint blue lines and a margin at the top. I had a sudden fancy to start a diary. I made him an offer. "A tin of sardines?"

Greg concentrated, his big moon face serious. He's got the hang of bartering now, and enjoys it. "It's new almost, nothing written in it. There was only some numbers on the first page, and I tore them out. You'd never know. Two tins?"

"Hey, what about the Mars bar?"

"That's for protection."

"Okay. One tin of sardines and a bar of soap. Imperial Leather." I'd come across eight bars the week before when I was working on my own, a lucky find.

"Soap?" He didn't sound keen.

"Time you had a wash, Greg, you're beginning to hum. Come round this evening and I'll heat you up some water. I'll lend you a towel. Can't say fairer than that."

He made up his mind. "Done."

I fetched the sardines and soap and gave them to him. He held out his hand and we shook on the deal, in Greg's view an essential part of the transaction. He turned to go, then thought of something.

"Paul says can you come over, because he thinks the baby's nearly coming."

Paul and Claire live not far from my place, in Shakespeare Tower in the Barbican, though in a blizzard it can take half an hour to get there from my flat. Bézier, where I live, is a lavish new block with a bulging glass façade like two half barrels, erstwhile home to rich City bankers. It overlooks Old Street roundabout – not that the roundabout is visible any more – but my flat is on the opposite side, facing south towards the City. The snow is so deep you can't see the street layouts, just the tops of the taller buildings, virtually all modern architecture. Most Victorian buildings are covered, apart from the odd church steeple or decorative tower (near me is a guy standing on a globe shading his eyes – he looks rather surprised). St Leonard's lightning conductor sticks up, with a bit of the spire below, the sort of feature that would make travelling on a sledge with a windkite hazardous. If I had a sledge… Even the tallest trees are buried now. You can see clusters of City skyscrapers and cranes in the distance, and to the south east as far as Canary Wharf where the light no longer pulses to warn off aircraft. There are no aircraft. The London Eye is silhouetted on the horizon to the south west like the wheel of a giant's bike; turn to the west, and the BT Tower looms, a high-tech totem pole.

Smoke trails rising from our fires are visible in the clear air. Similar threads in the far distance show we are not the only little group surviving in London. Sometimes I climb to the rooftop of Bézier and stare out at them, wondering who they are and how they are managing. Pretty much like us, I suppose. Snow laps the bottom of the balcony that runs outside my flat (I'm on the tenth floor) and I worry that next year I'll have to move all my supplies to a higher apartment, which would be a lot of work, though the others would help.

I set off through the white landscape, so bright in the sunlight I put on my dark glasses. Complete silence; no birds, no cars, no people. Just the sound of my boots and the squeak of the snow. Perhaps I can persuade everyone we should target a sports shop and get us all pairs of cross-country skis…

I dropped on to the terrace on the ninth floor, went down the emergency stairs and up three flights. Unlike the rest of us, Paul and Claire made the decision to pick a flat well above the snow, on the assumption the level was likely to rise. This means a lot more lugging of stores and firewood on a daily basis; I think it's easier to move up a storey when you have to. I can't lock my flat, but this no longer matters. I knocked on their door. Paul let me in, looking harassed. The room felt hot after the cold outside and I hastened to take my coat off. The flats don't have fireplaces any more than mine does, but Paul's fixed up a Victorian range with the flue going out through a hole in the wall. He made the hole painstakingly with a cold chisel and hammer. He's an architect, but not good with his hands. As a group, we're over-educated and lacking practical skills, which matters more than it used to. Gemma stood behind him and smiled up at me, looking a little lost.

"Hi Gemma." I got out a toy pony I'd been saving for this occasion and held it towards her. She let go of her father and took it. "This is for your collection."

"What do you say, Gemma?" Paul said automatically.

"Hank you Tori."

"Good girl. You go and play with it in the living room." He led me towards the bedroom. "Thanks for coming."

"When did it start?"

"Her waters broke last night, but nothing much happened till this morning."

As soon as Claire got pregnant, Paul brought home all the books he could find in the Barbican library on pregnancy and childbirth, and has been reading up on the subject. I'm not sure this has helped. He now knows in great detail every possible thing that can go wrong. Armed only with a St John's Ambulance course he took six years ago, he's not equipped to cope if they do. Now I was there to sit with Claire he went off to make a cup of tea.

An elderly stove made the bedroom smell of paraffin. Claire was sitting up in bed, pale, her hair clinging damply to her forehead. She wore a thick sweater over a nightdress, socks and legwarmers. For a moment she looked pleased to see me, then she shut her eyes, her face scrunched up and a moan escaped her gritted teeth. She inhaled deeply and breathed out through her mouth. I sat by the bed, trying to look relaxed and confident. A positive attitude was all I had to offer. I know nothing about childbirth. I had chicken pox when my school showed the mother-giving-birth video; afterwards my friends told me about it in gruesome detail and I was quite relieved to have missed it. The sum total of my knowledge picked up elsewhere was:

- You have to push but only when you get the urge
- In African tribes they put charcoal on the child's navel as it's a natural antiseptic
- If you can't get to hospital in time, you should sit up with your back against something and your legs apart
- You tie the umbilical cord in two places and cut between the threads with sterilized scissors (I suppose you should boil the thread too)
- It's important to get all the afterbirth out

And I know there are breathing techniques which allegedly lessen the pain. Claire has been doing breathing exercises religiously for months with the help of a book Paul gave her. I'm sceptical about this except as a distraction, because if it worked then they'd tell you to breathe to combat the pain of a headache or a broken bone, and they don't. If you have a headache or broken bone, you take aspirin, paracetamol or morphine because unlike breathing, they actually work. But I kept this opinion to myself.

"How are you feeling?"

She grasped my hand, her eyes wide. "Don't ever have a child, Tori, it's terrible."

"Chance would be a fine thing. Fond though I am of Greg, he's not quite –"

Understandably in the circumstances, Claire interrupted my comment about the desert that is my love life. "I didn't realize, last time they gave me an epidural. What was I thinking? I must have been crazy. I thought a brother or sister would be nice for Gemma…"

I patted her hand. "So it will. It'll be over in a few hours, then you'll have a new baby and you'll forget all about it. Probably decide to have six more."

"Paul wanted to get Nina here. Can you imagine? I told him over my dead body."

"Oh my God. Well, that's something to be cheerful about."

Nina is okay I suppose, but she has a view on every topic and expects you to agree. If you don't, she assumes you haven't understood her, and explains all over again, more slowly and in greater detail. Sometimes I want to brain her with a brick. I was really pleased when a bad back stopped her coming on our group forages, because without her, dividing the spoil takes no time at all, and it used to take the best part of an hour with Nina present being nitpicky. She's the last person in the world you'd want to split a restaurant bill with – if there still were any restaurants. Me and the guys, Paul, Greg and Archie, have a swings and roundabouts approach to share-outs. So do Charlie and Sam.

Claire began another contraction. I glanced at my watch and wondered if I should time them – was it a good sign when they got more frequent? The pain must have been worse because she yelled. Afterwards I wiped her face with a flannel from the bedside table, feeling inadequate.

"Tori...supposing I can't get the baby out?"

There were tears in her eyes. A stab of fear went through me – what an appalling way to die, and poor little Gemma would have to manage in this hostile new world without her mother. Women often died in childbirth before the invention of modern obstetrics; Mary Wollstonecraft died of septicaemia, slowly and agonizingly over days...I spoke robustly.

"You'll be fine. Loads of women do this every day – well, not the same women, obviously, different ones. But it can't be that difficult. Anyway, they say it's easier the second time, and you've been practising the breathing, and you're healthy. Plus you've got me here, and I won't let anything bad happen. Hey, I'm really good at boiling water..."

Claire smiled a scared smile and gripped my hand.

I wouldn't want another day like that in a hurry. Far too terrifying, and it just went on and on. I am now entirely certain that if God exists, he is male; he could so easily have designed women better. I'd be in favour of laying eggs myself – small ones, about the size of quail eggs. But it was all right in the end. Soon after dusk Claire delivered a healthy baby boy. Paul and I dealt with the umbilical cord between us, and it was obvious even to the uninitiated – i.e. us – that the afterbirth was all there. We opened a bottle of wine and drank to the baby, shaky with relief and triumph. Claire had a cup of tea and couldn't stop smiling and admiring their new son, her face radiant. They both kept thanking me, though I'd done hardly anything except turn up. A little later I said I must be going.

"Stay here tonight," Paul said. "It's dark outside."

"There's a full moon and no snow falling." These days I always know what the phase of the moon is without looking.

"Let me see you home, then."

"No, you stay with Claire and the children. I'll be fine."

The night was beautiful, in a slightly sinister way. Dark sky-scrapers loomed on the horizon. Not a breath of wind; a sky of the deepest possible blue, an enormous moon and countless stars. Even the worst situation has some good, and seeing the Milky Way over London is a treat that never dims, even while it brings home to me the world I knew is gone forever.

The wine had made me feel cheerful in spite of my weariness, and I was happy for Claire and Paul. The trek home seemed to pass in a flash. I neared my balcony, looking forward to bed, and paused for a final look round. A few hundred yards away moonlight broke on the mounds of snow from our failed excavation on Old Street, the only disruption of the ubiquitous smoothness; beyond Bézier, candlelight from Greg's window showed he was still up – he'd missed his wash, we'd have to reschedule. To the north a white carpet interrupted by tower blocks and the odd crane stretched to the horizon.

That's when I saw something moving.

CHAPTER 2

The stranger

A long way away, dark against the expanse of white to the north a small shape crept, stopped, moved again. A person crawling on hands and knees, and not one of us, because we seldom go out at night, and when we do, we go to each other's places. A crazy hope lit up my heart and made me shake all over.

It's David, come to find me. Please God, let him be all right.

I hurried to my flat, stepped over the glass wall of the narrow balcony, through the patio door and into the dark interior to get my sheet of tough plastic. I climbed once more over the balcony railing and headed as fast as possible into the night towards the distant figure. A man for sure, I could see as I got nearer, inching agonizingly along, his strength almost gone. He had stopped moving by the time I reached him, and lay face down in the snow. I turned him on his side with trembling hands.

"David?"

Not David.

For a moment my disappointment was so great I wanted to lie down and howl and thump the snow with my fists. I took another look. This man was in his mid-twenties, with a short beard not much longer than stubble, taller than me, wearing dark padded trousers and a jacket with a fur-lined hood. I crouched beside him, fatigue replacing my former excitement.

"Hi, wake up."

Nothing. I shook him but he didn't respond. I'd have to roll him on to the plastic. I've got a trailer made out of the top of a car roof box – we all have – for dragging supplies home, but the plastic sheet, originally used to wrap a double mattress and now with holes cut for handles, is useful for things I can't lift over the box edge. I rolled him on to the middle of the plastic where he settled on his back. His eyes half opened and he muttered something inaudible.

"What?"

"Rucksack."

I looked back along his tracks, and saw something dark in the distance. I went to fetch it – the bag was surprisingly heavy, I had to drag it – and dumped it on the plastic beside him. Getting going was hard, but once moving the plastic slid fairly easily over the surface in spite of the combined weight of the man and his belongings.

Back home, hot and sweating, I lumped the backpack over the railing on to the balcony (what on earth was in it?) and tried to lift him. I have crates there so it's easier when I'm carrying stuff, but getting an inert man over was a different matter. I struggled and heaved. No chance. Having got him this far, I didn't want him dying outside my window. I could have built ramps out of snow to drag him up and down the other side, but that would take as much time as the alternative option, fetching Greg – twenty minutes at least, and the man would get frostbite if he hadn't already. I shouted in his face.

"Wake up! *You've got to help, damn you*. WAKE UP!"

He didn't. I took off my glove, pushed his hood out of the

way and slapped his cheek a stinging blow. He grunted and his eyelids flickered. I went to slap him again and found my wrist trapped in an iron grasp. Furious eyes met mine. His voice was a snarl.

"Stop that."

"Fine. Stay out here and die of hypothermia, then."

He glanced around, still gripping me. "Where's my bag?"

"On the balcony."

He let go my wrist and after a moment pulled himself to his feet, hanging on to the edge of the railing, and stepped over painfully slowly as if he were in his eighties. I followed with my plastic, grabbed his bag, slid the door open and we both went in. I lit a tea light lantern. The stove had gone out, and the place was icy; most of the snow in the buckets round the walls still unmelted. Greg would have topped the stove up for me, if I'd thought to ask him. Sometimes I long for radiators and a timer and no smell of wood smoke in my hair. I was down to my last few sheets of newspaper for fire lighting. I glanced at the headline before scrunching the paper into a ball: *PM sets out three point plan to halt spread of SIRCS* above a photo of Boris Johnson looking sombre. I opened the stove door and dropped it inside, added kindling, wood, and a handful of coal, then lit the paper from the tea light so as not to waste a match.

The man had slumped on the stone-effect tiles and was leaning against the kitchen island, head down, face half hidden by straggling hair, pulling off his gloves with a visible effort. Irritation swept over me at finding myself lumbered with this uncouth man and his problems – my compassion appeared to have been all used up on Claire with none left over for this random stranger. I picked his gloves off the floor and hooked

12

them over the stove. He was probably dehydrated, so I scooped him a glass of water out of the nearest bucket. He drank it in one go and I gave him another.

"Is there anything wrong with you?" This came out impatient rather than sympathetic. "You haven't got frostbite?" The best treatment for that is body heat, which I was not going to volunteer, or warm water, and I didn't want to use up my water on him; it's a lot of work, melting enough snow for daily drinking and washing. And the stove was cold. I was tired and wanted to go to bed.

"I'm all right."

He didn't look all right. By the lantern's dim glow I could see a dark red bruise on his left cheekbone, and his skin was ashen and sweaty in spite of the cold. He was clearly dead beat. But there were no white patches on his face, and his hands weren't discoloured, swollen or blistered; assuming his feet were okay he had no frostbite.

"D'you want something to eat?"

"No, I want to sleep."

"You'd better sleep on the sofa." The opulent plum sofa that came with the flat would not be my choice of furniture, but there's no denying it is large and comfortable. Also it's leather, so easier to clean. It faces towards the stove and away from where my bed is, and is the warmest spot in the place when the stove's going.

He struggled upright, picked up the rucksack, made it to the sofa and lay down as he was, eyes shut, one foot still on the floor, dead to the world. Reluctantly, I unlaced his wet boots and pulled them off, because the flat was freezing and boots can restrict blood flow, making frostbite more likely. He didn't move while I did this. I got out two spare duvets and a couple of blankets and dropped them over him, and put a glass of water to hand on the coffee table. I didn't much like the look of him, but at least he wasn't in any state to pose a threat. I washed my hands and face and cleaned and flossed my teeth – in a world without dentists anyone with sense does this with religious zeal. I adjusted the stove's air intake to last overnight, went to my bed corner and took off some of my clothes, and snuggled into my sleeping bag under the duvet.

I woke as it began to get light, thinking about Claire and the baby. Then I remembered the man and slipped out of bed to check on him. He'd turned on his side, facing inwards, and still slept, the duvet moving almost imperceptibly with his breathing. He must have taken his jacket off during the night, as it lay across the rucksack beside his boots. The water glass was now empty, and I refilled it.

I dressed in the privacy of my bed corner. The man didn't stir as I raked out the stove, added fuel and put porridge to cook. Usually I dress by the stove. When I moved in, I dragged one bed into the living area and partitioned it off with neat stacks of firewood from floor to ceiling, so I only have to heat one room. The flat is seldom really warm, since a wood-burning stove needs constant feeding and when I'm off foraging I have to turn it right down so it doesn't go out. More wood is stored against the walls; I'm paranoid about running out, and work hard to keep supplies high. I live in the spacious living room/kitchen, and keep the bedrooms and two of the three bathrooms for stores. I've stacked heavy stuff on my toilets – after the sewers froze rats came up through the pipes to basements and ground floor flats, and though I'm probably too high I'm not taking any chances.

I watered my spider plant and removed a few dead leaves. It's an offshoot of Claire's enormous one, and doing quite well. They are the only plants left in this part of London. Sam used to have some cacti, but they didn't like the cold. Though there's not much difference between a dead cactus and a live one, eventually she had to admit they had shuffled off this mortal coil and were now ex-cacti.

I'd planned to go foraging today. There's this block of flats I found on my own, only the top floor above the snow, and I'm working my way down it, collecting everything of use – wood, paper, food, clothes, blankets. There are bodies, but not too many; I work fast in those rooms and avert my gaze, careful to shut the doors behind me to keep the rats out. The worst ones are where there are several people, huddling together, especially children. I try not to think about their last hours. I don't worry about catching SIRCS, because I reckon I've got natural immunity or it would have killed me when the pandemic raged. Probably most of them died of cold, anyway. One flat had a fireplace, which got me excited, but apparently they relied on the radiators and the fire wasn't often lit – there was only a single bag of coal, which I'm using up bit by bit for keeping the stove in at night. Wood burns much faster.

I decided to start my journal and simultaneously melt a load of snow to top up my water supplies, so I'd be around when the man woke. I could forage the next day.

Greg interrupted my writing mid-morning. I've started to worry too much chocolate will rot his teeth, so I gave him a musical snow globe from the flats. It was a particularly nice one. He wound the brass key carefully, shook the globe and set it down. We stared into the tiny perfect world; a village on a snowy hill, a church and snow-covered houses around a central Christmas tree. A miniature train ran on its track through tunnels while a cheerful tune tinkled and snowflakes swirled.

Greg was very taken with it, though you'd think he'd have had enough of snow. I certainly have. I said, "Imagine if we were tiny and lived there."

"I wish we did." Greg pointed. "I'd have that house, with the ivy. You could have the big one opposite. We could ride on the train."

A snow globe and London have a lot in common these days; both are perpetually snowy and limited in scope. I put water to boil. Greg had already called on Paul and Claire and admired the new baby, and told me they've decided to call him Toby. Greg was in favour of calling him Bart (he was a great Simpsons fan, and misses them). I said the name wouldn't suit him as his face wasn't yellow. Greg said Bart Simpson probably wasn't yellow in real life, just in the cartoons, then he noticed the man.

"There's a man on your sofa, Tori."

"I know. I found him in the snow last night and dragged him here. He's been asleep ever since."

"Is he staying?"

"I don't know. Perhaps he's passing through, and will leave once he's had a rest and some food."

Greg walked across to the sofa. "He's got blood on his jacket."

I joined him. He was right – how did I miss that? A big dark patch on the quilted lining. We stood for a few seconds, gazing thoughtfully. Greg picked up the jacket for a closer look, and the man erupted from the bedding and pulled a knife on him. The sunlight flashed off a short business-like blade. He stared at us in turn, bloodshot eyes narrowed, breathing fast. He was bigger than I'd realized. His sweater was soaked in blood. We edged away.

After a moment, Greg bent forward and dropped the coat back where it came from. "Sorry."

I suddenly felt annoyed. After all, I'd saved this person's life. "There's no need to act like an idiot. You're making me wish I'd left you face down in the snow. Put that away." Slowly, he clicked the knife closed and pocketed it, eyes still wary. "Is that your blood on you?" He nodded. "Are you hungry?" He nodded again. Clearly I was on my own with this conversation. I asked him something he couldn't answer with a nod. "What's your name?"

"Morgan."

"Morgan what?"

"It's what Morgan, but Morgan will do."

Greg screwed up his face. "*What* is a funny name."

I said, "I don't know, what about Wat Tyler? He was called Wat. The Peasants' Revolt, 1381. He was stabbed by the Lord Mayor of London."

"Claire could call the baby Wat."

"Oh, I don't think that's a good idea. Whenever people asked him his name, he'd say 'Wat' and they'd ask him again only louder."

"They wouldn't do that if he was called Bart."

"Good point. Maybe you could use that argument to persuade Claire. Unless the baby's already answering to Toby."

Conversations with Greg often have a surreal quality I no longer notice. The stranger gazed from one of us to the other, frowning slightly, as if we had suddenly started talking in Ecclesiastical Latin. He felt in an inside pocket and held out a coin. "I can pay for food."

I took it, curious. A Krugerrand, heavy in my hand. There's an ounce of pure gold in a Krugerrand, but they aren't beautiful coins. They could easily have made them much nicer, but their purpose was to make money from the global gold coin market so they didn't bother.

"This is no good to me." I handed it back. "We have a bartering system. Anyway, I wasn't going to charge you for breakfast. Or for lugging you here, or letting you spend the night. You'll just have to live with being in my debt for now."

He gave me a long look. "All right."

"Not at all, don't mention it." I turned away and scanned the rows of tins. "Scotch broth with corned beef?"

He nodded. While I opened the tins, they both sat on the sofa and Greg told him our names and about our little community, and asked him questions which Morgan answered without giving much away. Greg didn't appear to notice his caginess.

"Where did you come from?"

"Up north. A fair way."

"I slept on Tori's sofa when I first came, too. Then everyone helped me to find things for my own place."

"Who's everyone?"

Greg counted on his fingers. "Paul and Claire, they've just had a new baby, and they've got Gemma too. Then there's Charlie and Sam, they've got a cat. The cat's called Simone de Beauvoir, she's black with one white foot, and sometimes she scratches you when you're not expecting it, so I don't stroke her in case she does. It's because people weren't nice to her when she was a kitten, Sam says."

I scraped the contents of the tins into a saucepan and roughly chopped the corned beef with the spatula. I was never a great cook; now I'm a lousy one.

"I wanted a pet rat, but Nina said I'd get a disease. I still might get one, though. A rat, not a disease. You can train them. Tori says I don't have to do what Nina tells me. She needn't know I'd got a rat, it could stay in my pocket. They didn't let you have pets at Wingfield Gardens. I can have whatever I like where I live now."

"Where's that?"

Greg pointed through the window. "See the building with the blue bits on it? I'm at the bottom there. If I need Tori, only really badly though, not just to talk to or something like that, then if I hang my red blanket out of the window she'll come over. And the same if she needs me. You could have a flat there too. Have you got a pet?"

"No. D'you have any petrol?"

"We don't need it, we haven't got any cars. They wouldn't work on the snow."

"You can use petrol for other things than cars. Generators, for instance."

"We haven't got a generator."

I tipped the corned beef/broth into a dish and put it on the counter with a spoon and a glass of water. Morgan moved to a stool and ate, emptying the bowl in two minutes flat. Maybe I should have opened more tins. He looked up at me.

"Have you got any hydrogen peroxide? There's a cut I probably should do something about."

"I've got Dettol and bandages. Take off your top and let's see." I went to fetch my book of medical advice and the first aid box from the storeroom, had a thought and went back for my biggest sleep tee and sloppy sweater. He couldn't go on wearing his blood-soaked clothes.

When I returned, Morgan was pulling a tee shirt over his head, displaying powerful shoulders and narrow waist, a black tribal tattoo across his upper back, and a couple of round dog tags on a chain. There was also a lot of blood, dried and oozing, and a gaping three inch knife slash on the left side of his ribs. Greg and I both did a quick intake of breath. I felt queasy.

"How did you get that?"

"In a fight."

"Who with?"

"Just some guy I annoyed."

While Greg took up this topic without eliciting much in the way of concrete information, I opened *Home First Aid*.

Wash the cut with soap and water and keep it clean and dry ... hydrogen peroxide and iodine can be used to clean the wound. Apply antibiotic ointment and keep the wound covered ... change the dressing two or three times a day. Seek medical care within six hours if the wound needs stitches ... any delay can increase the rate of wound infection.

I washed my hands and tipped hot water in a mixing bowl, added Dettol, opened a new sponge from its cellophane and a new bar of soap and sat on the stool beside Morgan. There was a lot of him, all of it muscle. Stupidly, I felt myself blushing. It was a year since I'd been this close to a man who wasn't wearing at least three woolly layers of clothing. When I bent to examine the wound my head brushed his beard. I could smell his sweat and hair and blood. I busied myself cleaning the cut, then the area round the cut, guilt taking over from embarrassment. This should have been done last night. I'd known something was wrong but had been too tired to pursue it, and if he got an infection and died of blood poisoning it'd be my fault. He sat unflinching, though it must have hurt a lot. I got fresh water and washed the cut again, twice, dabbed it dry with tissues, applied Neosporin cream and looked at it dubiously.

"D'you want me to try to bring the edges together with plasters?"

"That might make it more likely to go bad. Leave it, just tape some lint over."

"How do you feel?"

"I've felt better."

"You should drink lots of water to flush out the germs. I've got a random collection of antibiotics, but I don't know which ones would work for this. But we can try them if you get a fever."

"Whatever. I'm going to sleep. Wake me for meals."

21

CHAPTER 3

You might not want to read this

I suppose I should write a bit about the two great disasters that happened – not that this is an attempt to be a historical record or anything, but my story doesn't make much sense without knowing, and someone may come across this notebook years in the future when it's all been forgotten. I'm not going to dwell on it, just give the outline and get on with other things. You can skip this part if you like. Here goes.

First the pandemic struck; I heard about the early victims on the radio, and didn't take much notice. I thought it was another media-fuelled scare, like bird flu. I was wrong. People got ill, and died within two days; later their relatives and flatmates and work colleagues and people who'd been on the same bus with them got ill. I remember the moment when I took on board this was something major that would affect people I knew. Deaths were counted in hundreds, then thousands, then millions. Those who had a holiday home abroad left the country, taking the disease with them as often as not.

The government told everyone not to panic, and put their best scientists into finding out what the disease was – easy – and working out what to do about it, which proved too great a task for the time remaining to them. They called it SIRCS, to the annoyance of several organizations with the same acronym: severe immune response coronavirus syndrome. A Chinese businessman called Guozhi Ng had brought the infection from Asia; later every single passenger and crew member on his plane died.

SIRCS was a hybrid disease as deadly as bubonic plague and as infectious as the common cold, and became a global problem within a week. Fear and chaos took hold. The government declared a state of emergency, and asked everyone except essential workers to stay at home. Cinemas, theatres and restaurants closed. Tubes and buses didn't run. Face masks were delivered to every door and we all wore them, while doubting their efficacy. The power cuts started then, as key workers failed to turn up for work. There were bodies in the streets. The army moved the dead in trucks to makeshift burial grounds in the countryside. Friends of mine died, but not the two people I cared most about, David or my mother. Some people didn't seem to catch SIRCS; but most did.

Then it started to snow in the north.

The weather had been weird for some time – we kept having the driest month since records began, the wettest, the windiest, the hottest, the coldest – and experts reassured us that these unseasonable variations were all within normal parameters. But in May 2017 temperatures dropped and snow fell and didn't stop.

At this point everything broke down. Metres of snow covered Scotland, and spread inexorably down the country. There was talk of a new ice age, that Arctic seas had warmed and turned off the Gulf Stream. People who could headed south. Electricity was more off than on, there was no gas, phones worked intermittently, television went off the air and only the World Service remained on the radio. Some sites on the internet worked and others went down as servers crashed. Roads were blocked, so transport couldn't bring food to the shops, but as the snow levels rose, people couldn't get to the shops anyway. Homes were being buried under snow. The cold began to kill those who had so far survived the pandemic. The hastily formed coalition government, consisting of only about a dozen MPs, decided to get everyone out of the country, a mass exodus to warmer parts of the world using every helicopter, plane and boat available. Southern European countries volunteered to fly mercy missions to the UK. It was assumed our people would be welcomed by countries that had lost ninety per cent of their population.

David and I agreed we'd each go to make sure our parents were okay. Before the phones stopped working, I rang my mother. They were evacuating her part of London. I told her I was on my way, and not to worry about me if they arrived first; to go with them, but leave a note telling me where she'd gone. I'd follow.

It took me two days to reach Mum's flat in Hampstead. I hadn't realized how difficult the journey would be. Blown by a high wind, soft snow had drifted and eddied into hills and dips around the buildings. I broke into a house when it got dark to sleep. When I reached the right street, the whole area appeared deserted; I didn't see another soul. The helicopters had come and gone. I climbed through a fourth floor window and went up the stairs and let myself in.

The flat seemed icier than outside. She was in bed, blankets, towels, clothes and even a rug from the floor piled over her. I saw at once she was dead. Beside her a note, the writing straggling down the page.

Dearest Tot,

I don't think I am going to last till they come, I'm sorry.

Don't be sad. That is the last thing I want for you. I had a good life and am hugely proud of my beautiful clever daughter. I hate the thought of you being sad over me. Take the greatest care of yourself for my sake. I'll be really cross, wherever I am, if you don't.

All my love, always,

Mum

XXX

After a bit, I went back home. Except that when I got there, my building had disappeared beneath the snow, and everyone had gone. David never returned from going to find his parents. Eventually I ran into Paul and Claire, and stayed with them for a while. There were dogs roaming in packs back then, and now I wish I'd kept one, but at the time I was barely able to keep myself.

In the face of disaster, you can either give up or get on with life. I decided to live.

CHAPTER 4

No other business

Wednesday and Thursday were much the same as always, apart from the presence of Morgan, either hunched fast asleep under the duvets on the sofa, only the top of his head visible, or bolting quantities of food at the counter, monosyllabic. A bit like having a teenager living with me; but not talking suited me fine. Somehow I doubted we'd have much in common to chat about. I wasn't keen on sharing my space, but there wasn't anywhere else for him to go, and I assumed he'd be off as soon as possible. He must have been going somewhere when I found him. I did my best to behave as if he was not there, and get on with the things I had to do. Survival is arduous.

I was out of the flat a lot. I dream of getting away from London and going south to where the snow stops. Everyone shares this dream, even if we seldom talk about it. A means to get south is like Rick's letters of transit in Casablanca, universally desirable. And I've worked out a possible way to do it: a powerkite. I had a friend from uni who was into them, and I've got his four-line kite and control bar. Back in the early days, before the snow was as deep as it is now, I went to Tom's home, painstakingly working out the street with an A-Z – you could do that then, enough buildings' roofs showed – and dug down to his flat. It was strange, seeing the place so different from how I remembered it; cold, dark and silent like an excavated tomb. I was afraid his body would be there, but the flat was empty. I hope he got away.

Tom used the kite on water with a special surf board, which is no good for snow, so I'd have to make some sort of sledge. Ideally with a steering mechanism, because otherwise I'd spend too much time waiting for a north wind, whereas with steering, most winds would do. If I found a go-cart or something similar I might be able to fit skis instead of wheels – if I could find skis – but I don't have the engineering skills or tools to make one from scratch. It needs to be light and able to hold provisions as well as me, and has to be reliable to take me all the way. It's a matter of getting lucky while scavenging. Meanwhile I take the kite out regularly and practise controlling the lines. I'm determined to master the darned thing. The others have seen me with the kite, but don't know what it's for. Nina takes it as evidence of my frivolity.

Sometimes I think it's evidence of my futility, because the task is beyond me. Which may be all to the good, because going south and leaving Greg and Claire and the rest to a fate I'd evaded might give me survivor's guilt for the rest of my life.

I worry about the future. Surely the others must too, but they hardly ever mention it. A month ago we ran out of tinned raspberries. No big deal, you may say, we've still got pineapple, pears and peaches. But what happens when we run out of other things? What happens when we run out of everything?

Our monthly meeting is always held at Nina and Archie's flat in Cromwell Tower, the next building along from Claire and Paul, at ten o'clock on the last Wednesday in the month – that is the last *Thursday*, if like me you've kept correct track of time. (I've got to stop thinking this, as we all operate on Nina Time these days; henceforth I'll use her, wrong, dates. Except for important ones, like David's birthday.)

On impulse I popped in to see Claire on my way there. Paul had already left for the meeting. Toby was asleep, and Gemma was practising the recorder in a corner. Claire looked bright-eyed and pretty and I told her so.

"It's the relief – I'm just so happy it's over and Toby's fine, I feel like dancing round the room. I hated being pregnant, quite apart from knowing the birth was coming up. I never got that bloom you're supposed to. I feel much better now."

"Well, you look terrific."

"I put a bit of makeup on this morning, and that helps. I look washed out without it. I'm not like you, Tori. It's so unfair." Her eyes ran over me. "Even when you've got straight out of bed and your hair needs washing and your clothes are all baggy, you still look like a model. It's those cheekbones."

"I don't, I look a mess." I twisted a neglected lock round my finger. "It's such a business washing my hair. I should do it more often, but I'm lazy."

I stayed to chat longer than I meant. Claire wanted to hear all about Morgan, not that there was much to tell, then Gemma wanted to play me her latest tune. So I was the last to arrive – I could see the others through the windows as I climbed on to the terrace, a big space which must have been lovely for eating outside in summer. The roof juts out so they aren't always having to sweep the snow from the tiles as I am at my place. I took off my jacket in the warmth of the living room – Nina is home more than me, so can keep their stove fed – and said hello to everyone.

The flat has a similar layout and dimensions to Claire and Paul's; a generously sized three bedroom apartment with dining room and study, but tidier, with no indication of the daily struggle to survive in hostile circumstances. Nina is house-proud. The big round carpet is spotless, every surface free of fingerprints and dust – though there is very little dust these days. My theory is a lot of it used to come from car tyres wearing away. Once inside, the place gives the illusion that civilization is still going strong, and if you went and looked over the terrace wall, far below you would see traffic and people hurrying by on the pavements. They don't have children, something which is I think a regret to Archie, but just as well for the children. (I'm being unkind, but I wouldn't want Nina for a mother, she's far too bossy.)

They sleep in one of the bedrooms, and the firewood is stacked in another room, even though this arrangement means a lot of fetching and carrying for Archie. He never complains. Archie is probably the nicest person I've ever met, always looking for the best in people, and finding it. He's a Church of England vicar, although this is not necessarily the secret of his niceness. I don't know what he's doing married to Nina. There's a big carved crucifix on the wall Archie salvaged from his church before it disappeared beneath the snow. On Sundays he celebrates Holy Communion there. I'm afraid most of us don't attend, being unbelievers.

Though I don't share his beliefs, I find his faith oddly comforting. I once asked him why God had let billions of people die miserably. His brow furrowed. "I don't know. God moves in mysterious ways. We are like moths living in a carpet, unable to see the pattern. One day we will." He smiled. "That includes you, Tori, when to your surprise you come to glory."

Archie called me over and I joined him and Paul. "Paul was telling me he doesn't know what he'd have done without you while little Toby was being born."

"He's being kind. Claire did all the work. I mostly watched and tried not to panic."

Paul said, "You stopped both of us panicking."

Archie nodded. Nina insists he shaves, so he is the only beardless man here; with no running hot water or electricity it's a daily chore the other men see no point in. He smiled at me, shifting his head a little to get a clear view. The left lens of his spectacles is cracked across, and of course he will never be able to get it replaced. "And I hear she rescued a stranger lost in the snow on her way home."

"Hey, I can't help being awesome. It's just the way I am."

Nina had put sheets of paper at the head of the polished wooden dining table ready for the meeting, glasses and a carafe of water. She is chairman – she'd be interrupting all the time if anyone else did it, so we've taken the line of least resistance and her tenure of the post is permanent. She tapped a glass with her pen.

"Can I have your attention? We'll start now Tori's arrived, if you'll all sit down."

We took our seats round the dining table. Silence fell, and Nina picked up her agenda. She read the minutes of the last meeting, which we approved by a show of hands. Every time, this clinging to ancient formalities amid the wreckage of civilization strikes me as slightly bizarre.

"First on the list, congratulations to Claire and Paul on the new addition to our little community." Murmurs of good wishes ran round the table, and Paul thanked us and said mother and baby were doing well. "Next, Morgan. You all know we have a stranger in our midst as of last Sunday, staying with Tori. Tori, perhaps you can tell us a little about him and his plans?"

"There's not much to tell. He's slept most of the time he's been here, just waking to wolf down food and going back to sleep. He was exhausted and had lost some blood from a cut on his side when he arrived."

"Do you know if he's staying or passing through?"

"I think he's on his way somewhere, but he hasn't said much. I really know very little about him."

Nina gazed at me over the tops of her spectacles, waiting for more. Greg helped out. "He's got a big black tattoo on his back. Tori said it's called a tribal tattoo."

"Thank you, Greg, but that's not really the sort of information I was after," Nina said repressively. "I was actually wondering when he'd start to contribute to joint projects. Which brings me to, if that's really all Tori has to offer, the subject of firewood. How are everyone's stocks lasting? Should we schedule a Firewood Day?"

We agreed we'd have one next Wednesday, and talked a bit about where to scavenge the wood from, and whether there was any prospect of laying our hands on another axe. The discussion wandered off-topic, and Nina glanced at her watch and brought us back to order.

"Let's move on. Rats in the shops. Charlie says their numbers are building up. Any ideas for how we can deal with this?"

Greg opened his mouth, and I think was about to volunteer to lessen their numbers by taking one home, but in the end he kept quiet. Nina suggested Sam and Charlie's cat might help out, but they shook their heads in unison. She wasn't used to hunting and might get bitten. Charlie fetched Nina's Argos catalogue to look for traps, but they only had plug-in Rodent Repellers, no good without power. None of us were enthusiastic about looking for nests and hitting rats over the head, a solution tentatively proposed by Paul. Dissatisfied, Nina switched topics.

"While we're on the subject of the shops, may I remind everyone that we agreed we'd only use them as a group? There are plenty of other places you can go to do personal foraging, or you can wait for our set days. I expect everyone to behave responsibly about this, else it's not fair on the rest of us."

Expressions round the table were carefully bland and innocent; only Greg looked shifty and hung his head. Nina has a bee in her bonnet on this subject, and it's easier to humour her. The fact is, we all go on our own if there is something we need – I even saw Archie in Argos on one occasion. Nina suspects we don't keep to the rule, and it irks her that she has no way of enforcing it.

"Now, contacting other groups of survivors."

Every so often, we talk about travelling to check out Londoners like us who are living in scattered enclaves. Greg is keen on this; he fancies having more people to trade with, and Archie feels it his duty to reach out if at all possible, because there might be people needing a priest. Charlie dreams of moving into a larger community where there would be a bigger audience for literary events and it would be possible to start a writing group – maybe even set up a micro-publishing business. The problem is, travelling on foot is arduous and although the smoke from their fires seems deceptively near, it would take the best part of a day to get to them. And we don't know what our reception would be like, or whether they'd put us up overnight which we'd need if we weren't to walk solidly for a day and a night. Tantalizingly, below ground is the tube network, reaching out like a spider's web throughout London. Once in the tunnels, you could walk anywhere without getting lost. The difficulty is access; most underground stations are in low rise buildings. You'd have to dig down to them, and dig up when you reached your destination. Our nearest, Old Street, is beneath twenty metres of snow. So for practical purposes, those other settlements might as well be on distant planets. As ever, we decided to postpone a decision.

"Moving on. The book club. Tori, what have you got for us?"

We take turns to choose a book to read and discuss; it has to be one the chooser can find several copies of. The last novel we read was Charlie's choice, *Madame Bovary*. Charlie said it was a seminal work and a masterpiece, and is no doubt right, but I found it depressing. Nina objected to the dislikeable and immoral heroine, and Claire said the ending when poor little Berthe went to work at the cotton mill made her cry. I don't think it was Archie's cup of tea either, but he said you had to admire it as a fascinating study of nineteenth century French provincial life. (We've yet to read a book he didn't find something nice to say about.)

I dug in my bag. "*Can You Keep a Secret*, Sophie Kinsella. I've got four copies." I handed them round to a certain amount of eye rolling and lip pursing from Nina. She prefers more literary works, though she has a weakness for family sagas. "It was that or *Bleak House* – I found six copies – but I thought we could do with something frothy and feel-good next."

There was no other business; Nina reminded us there was a group forage on Friday, and a ceilidh on Saturday, and we all went home. A typical meeting.

That evening Greg came over for his postponed wash. He could do it at his place, but I suspect he'd be tempted not to bother, and anyway, he's in the habit of coming here. Greg is my nearest neighbour. His flat is in a council block not far from me, just off Old Street. It's not particularly nice; the rooms are small and the ceilings are low – though admittedly this makes it easier to heat – and the windows are UPVC with those ugly thick glazing bars. Nina told him he should move into the Barbican, Bézier or the office block where Charlie and Sam live above Liverpool Street Station. Not so he'd have a nicer home, but because she thinks he needs keeping an eye on. But he chose this flat himself, and likes it, which is all that matters. Like the rest of us he lives in one room, and uses the two bedrooms to house his collections, arranged on shelves he has found and installed all round the walls. He keeps his stores in the flat next door. Greg is the only one of us – possibly the only person on the planet – who prefers life after the collapse of civilization. He used to live in sheltered accommodation, with rules and restrictions, being told what to do all the time. Even choosing his clothes was done under supervision. Now he is his own boss, and has friends and things to do that keep him busy every day. He has blossomed. He's actually happy.

Baths and showers are a thing of the past, but as Florence Nightingale said, with two pints of water and privacy any woman may be clean. Morgan's presence forced me to take my hot water and soap and strip off in the icy bathroom, but Greg didn't have this problem. I heated the water then disappeared into my bed corner and read a book to give him privacy. When he'd finished I trimmed his hair for him. He told me he wouldn't mind getting a tattoo like Morgan's because it was cool. I got a black felt pen and inked him a small tribal tattoo on the inside of his wrist. It looked rather convincing. He was enchanted, and made me promise to renew it when the ink wore away.

Before lunch the next day Morgan surfaced and said he felt better. He looked it, too; more alert, his face not as drawn, younger. The thought crossed my mind for the first time that Morgan was reasonably attractive, his features actually not at all bad under the short scrubby beard and unkempt hair; his cool assessing eyes, a mouth both firm and sensuous, those hard muscles; if the clichéd tough guy type seen in a thousand movies was your bag, here was the real thing. He went to the windows and scanned the view, and asked me where we were. When I changed the bandage, the cut was less red and swollen, its edges closer together as if the fight was going out of it. I cleaned the area and taped it up again.

"I got these for you." I dumped a selection of men's sweaters, tee shirts and jeans from Peacocks in front of him on the counter. I'd chosen an assortment of sizes. Clothes are one of the easiest things to find, which is lucky as washing and drying anything bigger than underwear is a huge task. It's simpler to throw them away.

He shuffled the pile warily, and looked up at me through his tangle of hair as if there was some catch. "I'll pay you back before I move on."

"I can always do with more firewood if you're offering. As

long as you don't overdo it and open up the cut just as it's healing. You need to take it a bit easy. There's a group forage all day tomorrow if you want to come and help."

"I'll take a look."

CHAPTER 5

Solar tulips and a Tardis

A heavy weight of misery was waiting to pounce when I woke Saturday morning. The 5th May is David's birthday. He would be twenty-six today. We celebrated his twenty-fifth together, just as people started getting sick; it seems a long, long time ago. There is a remote chance he is still alive, but I don't think so. He'd have come looking for me if he was.

David. Tall, skinny, dark eyed, laughing, intellectual, words spilling out of him in an effort to keep pace with his mind, a doctor fascinated by his work, hopeless with anything mechanical, the last person to get involved in a fight; my sort of man. We had barely a year together. I found the man I loved, and I lost him. Thinking about him is so depressing, I do it as little as possible. I keep the photo of him on holiday in Kos – the solitary one I have left – in a wooden box in a drawer, and only take it out on his birthday, the anniversary of the day we met, Christmas, New Year's Eve and my birthday. He looks so happy, sitting on the sand in the golden light of the sunset. It makes me smile, but I always end up in floods of tears.

Morgan had gone off somewhere, rather to my relief, so I ate breakfast alone, feeling glum. It was lucky I was meeting the others for the group forage mid-morning; it would take my mind off David. I've never told them about him, not even Claire. I couldn't bear their sympathy.

When Morgan reappeared just before it was time to go he was stripped down to jeans and a tee shirt with dark patches of sweat on it. He'd found the gym in the basement and been working out with weights by candlelight. Ten minutes later after he'd changed we set off in a light snowfall, me wearing my old black ski suit and holding the rope of my roof box trailer, which slid along behind like a faithful hound. I told him about the excavation on the way. He listened, pacing beside me without saying much, scanning the area as watchful as a commando on patrol expecting trouble.

Nearly a year ago, we'd researched and discussed the best place to dig. Old Street west of the roundabout won, as it has a chemist, a clothes shop, Argos and a supermarket. Nowhere else nearby had as useful a mix close together. Even Nina agreed without arguing. Then we started digging. We kept at it for two days of gruelling slog before we came to our senses. Paul turned up on day three with a piece of paper covered in figures and diagrams. He'd worked out we would need a trench two metres wide and over twenty metres long to accommodate stairs reaching to ground level. Approximately 420 cubic metres of snow would need to be removed, meaning that if seven of us shifted two cubic metres each per day, it would take sixty days. But he doubted we could move that much; just getting the snow out of the excavation would get more and more laborious the deeper we went. We'd spend most of our time hauling buckets of snow up the stairs.

We stood around, crestfallen. Paul diffidently suggested a

better idea would be to break into the block of flats above the shops, at the western edge of the building where a sort of tower sticks out of the surface, find a way down to the ground floor, and from there, work from shop to shop, making a short tunnel through the snow where necessary. There was a long thoughtful pause while each of us wondered why we hadn't come up with this two days ago. When we investigated, we found a door leading to stairs which ran right the way down to another emergency door at pavement level, next to the Co-operative supermarket.

Still, once the plan had been put into action, we entered a new era of comparative luxury. Before, we relied on supplies from homes we broke into, which was a lot more hit and miss. Now, I explained to Morgan, we just do that independently, as an extra, and to give us stuff to trade.

"So who's in charge? Who makes the decisions?"

"We all do. We decide things together."

"And you reckon that works?"

"Mostly. Especially if Nina's not there. Archie, that's her husband, is fine on his own, but if she's there he generally feels he has to support her."

One of the few times he hadn't supported her was when she got everyone to a meeting without Greg, and said he shouldn't have a vote. None of us agreed to this. Archie said gently that he felt one person, one vote was fair; we were all in this together. And honestly, Greg's views are generally as sensible as anyone else's.

We'd arrived at the entrance. Before we went down the stairs, I pointed out the flat roof of the block of flats above the shops we were about to visit, which sticks out less than a metre above snow level. We cleared this of snow, and painted a huge sign, white on the black surface, saying HELP PLEASE RESCUE US. This was one of the first things we did as a group. The idea is to attract the attention of any aircraft flying overhead, though it seems obvious to me things are in a mess down south, and rescuing UK survivors is not high on the agenda, if indeed it figures at all. Still, the others think it's a possibility; one which helps to give our current life the illusion of transience. We have a rota and go in turns each morning to sweep the snow off, a job that takes twenty minutes and seems particularly futile when it's actually snowing and the letters get covered up even as you clear them. Yellow paint, or red, might have been a better choice. But we all go on doing it faithfully. It's a habit now.

Morgan raised his eyebrows. Now and then when the light catches his eyes you can see they are ice blue like a sled dog's. "When was the last time you saw a plane or helicopter?"

"Nearly a year ago, when they were evacuating. Before we had the sign painted."

"Bit of a waste of effort, then."

"There's a chance a plane will fly over. You never know."

"There's a chance Father Christmas and his reindeer will fly over too, but I wouldn't hold my breath."

Morgan was right, of course. We're wasting our time. Rescue won't come.

I led the way into the tower, torch at the ready, though I didn't need it yet. Whoever gets there first lights tea lights in glass holders positioned at intervals down the stairs with a communal Bic lighter. It's there because none of us wanted to use up our own matches or lighters, though we all carry them. (Sometimes people forget to bring the lighter to the top again, and the first arrival the next time gets ratty and holds an inquisition to find out who was responsible. Most of us can be quite petty on occasion, I think because of the strain of our isolated circumstances.) Today they were lit, meaning someone was already there. We went down the eight flights of narrow staircase, each darker than the last, snow pressed against the windows. At the halfway mark we passed my favourite notice, written by a now defunct Nina-type, asking the person who had been spitting into the chute hopper to desist as it could spread TB, also the person who had been smoking on the stairs to stop this practice with immediate effect. At every other floor doors lead to a lobby with lifts, and long dingy corridors that access the flats. I've broken into all of them over time, looking for a go-cart or other useful items.

It's strange when you get to street level as it's so very different from how things used to be. The shops are dark, enclosed and claustrophobic. The lack of light makes it seem even colder than on the surface. I wear a small torch on a chain round my neck which is surprisingly effective, lighting my feet so I can see where I'm treading. We passed through an emergency door to a passage hollowed out of compacted snow, and stepped into the supermarket via a large hole smashed in the plate glass. Dim lights glimmered at the back, and we went towards them. Rats chirped and squeaked, skittering away from our torchlight. At the entrance to the stockroom Sam was stacking boxes ready to take out. A candle in a lantern enabled her to see what she was doing. She looked up and smiled at me.

"Hi Tori."

"Hi, how's it going?"

Morgan had wandered off, poking round the displays (he had

his own torch) and now he joined us. His gaze went to Sam, and stayed there. For a moment I saw her through his eyes. Petite, curvy, blonde and immaculate in a white ski suit, she glowed against her surroundings like a Hollywood star on a post-apocalyptic film set. She's the only one of us who bothers with her appearance on a daily basis. Me, I stick with basic hygiene and practical clothes except for our parties once a month when I make a bit of an effort. Sam is pretty, and makes the most of it. She streaks her hair with Charlie's help, always wears makeup, and puts polish on her nails. At home she even wears skirts and high heels. You have to admire her attitude.

Morgan moved in like a leopard who's spotted a gazelle. "Hi. I'm Morgan. Who are you?"

"Sam. Greg told us all about you. Including your tattoo. He was very taken with your tattoo."

"Any time you want to check it out for yourself, you have only to ask…"

Sam batted her mascara-ed eyelashes. "I might just do that one day. We have to make our own entertainment round here."

"I'm in favour of that."

"Are you coming to the ceilidh tomorrow?"

"Is that an invitation?"

Charlie materialized in the doorway, dumped a couple of boxes on top of the pile and put a proprietorial arm around Sam's shoulders. She gave Morgan a straight look. "You're Morgan," she told him. "I'm Charlie. I see you've met my other half."

Charlie couldn't be more of a contrast to Sam. She is thickset, with cropped hair, and noticeably lacks any form of personal vanity. She used to be a research assistant to a Labour MP whose name didn't mean anything to me, but she said he was a rising star. She's hardworking, bright, and devoted to Sam whom she spoils rotten. Watching Morgan's reassessment of the situation made me grin irrepressibly. He shot me a glance and I tried to straighten my face.

"What are you collecting?" I asked. "I forgot to look at the list."

The list is sellotaped to the wall at the bottom of the stairwell. Now and then it falls off because of the damp. We worked it out together ages ago, as soon as we'd accessed the shops. It's designed to make us more methodical by focusing our group forages on basics we all need, and stop us being distracted by inessentials. We can go after those on our own.

"The list says dry goods," Charlie said. "But the rats have got what's left of them. It's a real mess."

Morgan raised his eyebrows. "Might have been a smart move to shift the stuff the rats could get at first."

"Some of us wanted to." Charlie sounded defensive. "Personally, I thought we should come every day till we'd cleared things like biscuits, spaghetti, rice, and flour. They'd be safe in our homes. None of us have rats."

"Why didn't you then?"

"Me and Sam and Tori were outvoted. The others thought we should take a mixture of things, just in case something happened to stop us getting down here."

"You could have come on your own. For fuck's sake, it's the end of the world, and you're counting votes like you're a borough council."

Charlie bridled. "We happen to think a democracy is fairer. We all work together. That's got to be more efficient than each of us doing our own thing."

43

Sam chimed in. "Anyway, why should we do it if the others won't? It's not much fun, lugging boxes about alone in the dark with the rats under twenty metres of snow."

Morgan shrugged and walked away. Charlie turned her back on him and said to me, "We're doing mainly tins and a few toiletries, as we haven't done them for a while."

Greg, Paul and Archie turned up together, and we stood around chatting before we started a relay to move boxes to the surface. Greg's only qualification is a Level 2 NVQ in Warehousing and Storage, which sounds more useful in our current situation than it is. He's told me so much about the units he took I can recite them; Maintaining Hygiene Standards in Handling and Storing Goods, Moving Goods in Logistics Facilities, Maintaining Health, Safety, and Security in Logistics Operations etcetera etcetera. If unimaginable circumstances called for me to take that exam I'd ace it.

Morgan had gone missing, and we weren't sure if he was going to help or not. He reappeared lugging a car roof top box from Argos, and asked if there was any objection to him taking it. We said no. They were one of the first things we took, and we all had our own. I gave him a hand carrying the box up the stairs. It was a lot heavier than I expected. At the top I plonked my end down and said,

"Okay, what have you got in there?"

"Supplies. Stuff I need. I thought it would save time not to have it approved by the People's Democratic Dictatorship."

I hadn't expected him to reference Mao Tse-Tung, but he had a point. If he'd said he wanted a lot of things, there'd have been a discussion; whatever conclusion it came to completely pointless, as there was nothing to stop him coming on his own and taking what he liked. It didn't belong to any of us, after all.

Below ground again, we got organized. Greg, Paul and Sam brought boxes of tins to the foot of the stairs, Morgan took them up two flights to Charlie, she took them two flights up to me and so on. We're all pretty fit because the life we lead is strenuous. Charlie prides herself on being as strong as any of the men, and this is probably true amongst our lot; but Morgan was in a different league. He could carry two cases to our one. Working next in the line to him and trying to keep up half killed her. I didn't worry if the boxes stacked up on my landing, but for Charlie it was a matter of pride not to fall behind. Her face got redder and sweatier and her breath shorter till by the time we stopped for lunch she could hardly speak.

While we were eating perched on the Co-op's steps, Morgan told me he'd got things to do that afternoon and wouldn't be staying. Clearly, he'd failed to Develop Effective Working Relationships with Colleagues in Logistics Operations like the rest of us. Archie came over and sat down next to me to eat his tin of beans and pork sausages. With his hair badly cut by Nina he looks like a cheerful medieval saint from an illuminated manuscript. Archie has a particularly innocent smile that beams goodness. He held out his hand, and after a moment Morgan shook it.

"Welcome. It's nice to see a new face among us. I expect Tori's warned you I'm a God botherer by profession. I don't suppose you're a believer…?"

Morgan shook his head.

"Tori will tell you you needn't be worried I'm going to try to convert you or anything alarming, but if you ever want a private chat – any subject, doesn't have to be God – and think I could be useful, I'm always available."

"Right," said Morgan. Archie smiled again and chatted for a while about other things. He's a sensitive soul and never intrudes where he feels he's not wanted. Morgan didn't speak to anyone else during the break except Greg who did most of the talking; Paul tried to strike up a conversation with him but Morgan's responses were so brief and unforthcoming it petered out. After Morgan left Greg asked where he was and I said he'd gone. I could see the others thought it a bit off. An extra pair of hands had speeded things up. Charlie muttered, "Typical," looking pleased. Later, when we were working side by side, she brought the subject up again.

"Where did he come from?"

"He hasn't said."

"Honestly, Tori, why haven't you asked him? He could be anyone. He could be a serial killer escaped from prison."

I realized I'd been put off by Morgan's guarded manner; I'd respected his obvious desire not to talk about himself. This was absurd. Not that he'd tell me if he was a murderer. It's the sort of thing you'd keep to yourself.

"I'll ask him tonight."

He strolled back again late afternoon and took his place in the line, everyone except Greg and Archie looking askance at him.

By seven o'clock we'd got everything to the top and decided to call it a day. The wind was getting up, blowing a light powdering of snow into the sheltered corner where we sort the stuff into shares. My gaze travelled over the motley assortment arranged in our six roof box trailers. As we couldn't stick to the list we'd strayed from the straight and narrow, and all grabbed things we wanted. Apart from the tins of food which we'd split as usual, Paul had got loads of nappies for the baby and toys for Gemma, Sam had hair spray, perfume and what looked like the chemist's entire stock of highlighting kits, and I'd gone overboard for solar lights; several sets of upright ones to line the edge of my balcony, strings of stars plus twelve in the shape of tulips. Greg had added to his Doctor Who collection with an Expanding Tardis Tent, and Archie was highly delighted with a pair of National Geographic Porro Prism Binoculars for star gazing. Charlie had half a dozen cushions and two throws chosen by Sam.

Nina turned up just as we had nearly finished and gazed in disbelief at our haul.

"What happened to the list, people?"

Charlie explained.

"But…you could have just gone to the next item! Tinned food, if I remember rightly."

"We did get some."

"This was more fun, though," I said.

"Fun? You're not here to have fun! We need to divide goods systematically like we decided, else it's not fair."

"We're all happy with what we've got, Nina," said Paul, reasonably. Morgan leant back against the wall, not getting involved, watching, arms crossed and expression sardonic.

Nina took a closer look at the nearest box and tutted. "Greg's got a child's tent!"

"It's a Tardis," Greg said. "I know it's not the real one."

"What good is it? You can't use it for anything. If you were going to go off the list you should have stocked up with clothes, then maybe you could change them more often."

I hate it when Nina gets bossy with Greg. She makes him

lose confidence. He stared at his feet, visibly deflated. I said, "Lighten up, Nina. We don't have to be deadly serious the whole time. If you like, I'll nip down and get you some solar tulips like mine."

Nina turned on me. "Solar tulips? That's typical of you, if you don't mind me saying, Tori. You never take anything seriously, everything's just a laugh to you. Maybe one day you'll grow up a bit and realize life isn't just a long series of jokes."

I was tired, I wanted to get home, I could do without Nina snapping at my ankles like a demented Chihuahua. "Whatever. I'm off. You coming, Greg?" Greg nodded and picked up his trailer rope. Morgan slouched over to us. "Bye, everyone." I grabbed my rope and the three of us headed east together. At the roundabout Greg said goodbye and peeled off towards his home.

When we reached the flat I turned. The sun was setting, burnishing the skyscraper windows; the snow glowed gold and blue, breathtakingly lovely. I opened the door – the beastly stove had gone out. While Morgan lifted the boxes over the balcony railing I riddled the ashes, tore pages out of a Mills & Boon and scrunched them, added firewood and got it going again. (Two and a half million Mills & Boon paperbacks were mixed with the M6's tarmac to absorb sound, so they are resigned to abuse.) The stove takes a while to heat; supper would have to wait. It was too cold to take off my jacket or even lower its hood. My breath steamed in the icy air. God, I HATE the cold. I tidied away my solar lights, except for the tulips. I ripped off the packaging and stuck them in a jar on the windowsill where they would get plenty of light. Without being told, Morgan turned the trailer upside down so it wouldn't fill with snow and started to bring the boxes inside. I let him get on with it. I fetched two glasses and a bottle of Bollinger – one of the few advantages to the end of civilization is the survivors get to drink classier wine – removed the cork and curled up on the sofa.

I raised my glass and whispered, "Happy birthday, David."

Without warning my eyes swam with tears.

CHAPTER 6

Morgan's past – or part of it

Morgan finished stacking boxes inside, shut the door and came to see what I was doing. I offered him a glass of champagne, and he joined me on the sofa. He kept his jacket on, but put his hood down. Snow crystals sparkled in his beard.

"Celebrating? Cheers." He had a swig, took a closer look at my face and frowned. "Are you all right?"

"I'm fine," I said, my eyes filling again. I sniffed. "I think I'm getting a cold."

"No you're not. No one gets colds any more." There was a silence while I mopped my eyes and he stared at the flames in the stove's window and drank. He hesitated then said, "You can tell me about it if you like, but I should warn you I'm pretty useless at this sort of thing. I'll probably say something insensitive and you'll get furious with me, but that might be good because it would take your mind off whatever's upset you. So go ahead. If you want to, that is."

That made me smile in spite of my dejection. "Oh, it's nothing really. I know I'm lucky. So many people have died and I'm alive. It's just, sometimes it gets to me, being stuck here and snow day after day, and it's always freezing, and no trees or birds or animals apart from rats, and no eggs or bacon or bread or proper milk in tea or fresh fruit or hot baths, and having to work hard just to survive, and no prospect of anything getting better ever."

Morgan picked up the bottle and refilled my glass. I was tempted to tell him about David, and paused to decide whether I'd regret it. Sometimes it's easier to talk to a stranger about personal matters. Morgan was passing through, he didn't know me, plus he didn't strike me as the type to really appreciate how awful it was, which if he did, would make it worse. And I might feel better if I told someone.

"The other thing is, today is my boyfriend's birthday, and I think he's dead but I'll never find out. David, he was called." Tears slopped out of my eyes and down my face and I wiped them away. "*And* the bloody stove went out."

There was an awkward pause. "At least you've got the stove going again," he offered. "Told you I was crap at this."

I laughed wryly through my tears. "You did. You were right. Let's have some food."

I was too hungry to wait to eat, so I fetched the camping gas cooker which I save for emergencies so as not to use up all the gas canisters, opened two tins of curry and a tin of sweet corn and got out rice. While the curry heated up over the rice, I opened a tin of peaches and doled the contents into two dishes for dessert. I put the tubs of vitamins out. Say what you like about our monotonous diet, it's certainly quick to prepare; but I do miss fresh meat and vegetables. It was better when we had frozen food, but frozen food doesn't stay good forever, and in a world without hospitals, food poisoning is best avoided.

I laid the counter with cutlery, glasses and paper napkins, and lit a candle. It looked quite festive. On the window ledge my solar tulips were already glowing faintly. I still had a lump in my chest, but felt better, less desolate. That would be the alcohol. Morgan brought the champagne over and filled our glasses while I dished up.

We were both ravenous, and hardly spoke until we'd finished. I made coffee and poured brandy, and moved to the sofa. The stove was roaring away and the room was finally a little warmer; not warm enough to take off my jacket, though. I put my feet up, pleasantly mellow. Morgan stared out of the window, let the curtain fall and came and joined me. He seemed more approachable tonight, less forbidding. I felt suddenly curious about him, quite apart from my intention to take Charlie's advice and ask him whether he was a serial killer. He was so different from everyone else I know; tougher and meaner, as if he came from a harsher world where people were not to be trusted. Of course the world we live in is harsh for everybody these days, but my little group retained on the whole the manners you'd find at an Islington dinner party in the old days. I tried a dinner party-type opener.

"You never said what you were doing when I found you."

"Trying to find shelter."

"Yes, well, I kind of assumed that. I didn't imagine you were on your way to post a letter. Where did you come from, where are you heading?"

He gave me one of his long looks, and I thought he was going to tell me to mind my own business. But in the end he said, "I was with a group north of here. Not a people's republic like yours. Run by a man called Mike. Eight of us. We…we had a disagreement, and parted company. The journey was harder than I expected. I'd just about had it when you found me."

This raised more questions than it answered. "What were you and the group doing?"

"Looting, basically. When the government decided to evacuate the country, Mike came up with this idea: we'd stay behind a bit, then make our own way south, but stop on the way and collect valuable stuff, from jewellers and museums. When we got somewhere civilized we'd be rich, because gold only gets more valuable in a crisis. He reckoned what was left of the world would go back on the gold standard."

"Who is Mike? Did you work for him?"

"He used to run FreeFight before the snow, that's how I knew him. MMA."

"MMA?"

"Mixed Martial Arts. Cage fighting."

"You were a cage fighter?"

"Yeah. Mike had a finger in lots of pies. Didn't know he was a psycho back then, though. He got hold of the Semtex."

"*Semtex?*"

"Plastic explosive. For blowing up safes."

"I know what Semtex is!" A thought struck me. "So is it gold in your backpack?"

"Gold and diamonds. Krugerrands, other coins like Britannias and sovereigns, bit of museum gold, and 18 carat jewellery."

"No wonder it's heavy. Was that your share of the loot? Wow."

He gave me a dark look, as if there was more he could have said, but had decided not to. I wondered what he was concealing. He stared into his glass, drained it and changed the subject.

"So what about you? What are you doing here with this bunch of losers?"

I thought this rather unkind, and said so. "I wouldn't call them that. They're just ordinary people, coping with an extraordinary situation they didn't bargain for."

He laughed. "They're going to be dead in five years, and they're squabbling over solar tulips."

"They won't necessarily be dead in five years. They haven't done too badly so far."

"Their skill sets are about equal to running a charity car boot sale. In nearly a year none of you have set up a generator. You could have electricity, the petrol's there for the taking – all those underground car parks full of cars. Why haven't you got solar panels for melting snow and heating water? Look around a bit and you'll find them. Set up a greenhouse, you could grow fresh vegetables. Another thing, what happens if a more enterprising neighbourhood gang decide to drop in and co-opt your supplies, all neatly stacked up waiting for them, huh? You haven't even got a lock on your door. Got any defence plans? Weapons? I thought not. Two men with baseball bats could walk all over you."

Call me naïve, but this had genuinely not occurred to me. It's so isolated here in the middle of London, I'd never thought of people who might harm us turning up. I'd sometimes reflected how nice it was, not to bother with locking the flat when I was out – so different from the old London, where lock it or lose it was the rule. My balcony door only locks from the inside, anyway. When I'm out anyone can walk in. Obviously Morgan was right; there was no law left in England, nothing to protect the weak from the strong; it could happen. The thought of raiders beating me up and taking my food and firewood was scary. I could at least have hidden my reserves in different places, not kept them all together in my flat and the flat next door. I started to ask him how his gang interacted with people they came across as they moved around; but he hadn't finished.

"And what strategy have you got for when it gets worse? From what I've seen, you lot are working your butts off just to maintain the status quo. You're none of you risk-takers – maybe with the exception of you, Tori." He eyed me speculatively. "My guess is under those nice middle-class manners you're a carnivore like me, even if you don't know it, and that lot are herbivores."

"That's an insulting way of saying they're kind."

"No, just soft. In my experience, no one does anyone any favours. Everyone's out for himself."

"Possibly you've been mixing with the wrong crowd. Anyway, I'm not sure I like being called a carnivore."

"What I meant is, they're not gamblers, they're risk-averse. To get lucky you have to take a risk and maybe fail. It's fear of failure that'll kill them. Yes, they're managing now, but in the end the ice will get them because they're living off finite resources. What will you do when you've chopped up the last scaffolding plank or office desk for fuel, burnt the last book? What will Paul's kids do? There's no future in this country, not till the climate changes again."

"I know."

"If you know, what are you doing here? You seem smarter than the others. The only future's in the south. I want to get there and have a life again, live instead of just surviving, feel the sun on my skin. This whole country is like some Arctic research unit, but with no supplies in and no helicopters out and no long-term future. What's your five year plan, Tori? Where do you see yourself in ten years, twenty years? Before the power went down, you couldn't turn on the TV or the radio without hearing people arguing over whether this was a Little Ice Age or the real thing, or just something weird and transitory to do with global warming. Whatever it is, it's not going to get easier here; it's going to get a lot harder."

I wasn't going to tell him about my project. I didn't entirely trust him not to steal my powerkite, though that I have got hidden in a safe spot – after all, like me he wanted to go south, and needed transport. I decided not to practise for a day or two in case he saw me, and focus on finding materials for the sledge. On the other hand, if as I sometimes suspected it was a dumb idea, I didn't want him to mock me.

"I'll work something out. What's your plan, then? You're no better placed than me. That gold won't help you."

He smiled to himself. "Like you, I'll work something out."

I eyed him. He'd got something in mind he wasn't telling me. Perhaps he'd got a powerkite concealed somewhere too. I sipped my brandy, and started to think about weapons. I quite forgot to ask him if he was a serial killer.

CHAPTER 7

Ceilidh

Morgan left early the next day without saying where he was going – the gym, maybe, or running in the snow. While washing up I thought over what he had told me about himself the night before. He was the first cage fighter I'd ever met. I don't mix in the right milieu for cage fighters, whatever that may be, nor do I see the appeal of watching two men beat hell out of each other. On the other hand, with no police force or justice system, civilized behaviour was optional and if it came to it, might was right; martial arts experts had an advantage over the rest of us. Morgan had made me appreciate how defenceless we were, and I decided I must do something about that, however small. It was my day for sweeping the rooftop help sign clear of snow, and once I'd finished I made a lone trip to Argos.

It's seriously creepy down there on your own. The darkness, the maze like quality of the abandoned aisles in the storeroom, the rats' faint scuffles; the disagreeable dank odour, like an ice rink but with the added smell of decay and rat droppings. The light from my torch illuminated only a small circle at a time, making it slow work to find what I'd chosen from the catalogue. I kicked myself for not bringing a lantern. But I found them in the end; Sabatier twelve-piece knife block sets. I opened two boxes and took the knives, leaving the wooden blocks, and put the knives in my backpack. I found the quality pair of Olympus binoculars I'd selected, compact but powerful. The baseball bats were right at the back in a far corner, and I'd just reached them when my torch began to dim and flicker – foolishly I'd forgotten to bring a spare. I grabbed two boxes and headed for the exit, afraid of having to find my way out in the dark. When I got to the top and examined them, the bats were junior ones, only twenty-six inches long; considered as a weapon, they didn't look all that fearsome. I took them anyway.

Back home a thought struck me as I unpacked the bats to hide them beneath my bed. I went to rummage in the kitchen bin and retrieve the empty champagne bottle from the night before. Early champagne bottles tended to explode, so the manufacturers kept making their glass thicker to contain the pressure caused by secondary fermentation – 90psi, three times what you get inside a car tyre. This makes them heavy. I swung the Bollinger bottle experimentally. Given a choice, I'd opt to be hit with a junior baseball bat rather than a champagne bottle. I put it to hand under the bed as well as the bats.

The knives I laid out on the kitchen counter. They were razor sharp and well made, with triple-riveted handles; a good weight and balance in the hand. I chose a medium size knife and made a sheath for it with cardboard and black duct tape, cutting the card to the shape of the blade, then winding duct tape round. It took me three goes to do it to my satisfaction, so that the fit was close but not too tight for me to be able to withdraw the knife quickly. On my third effort I incorporated a neat loop for it to hang by.

I threaded my belt through and re-buckled it so the sheath was on my left hip, and practised whisking the knife out in front of the mirror in the bathroom, trying to look menacing, a person not to be messed with. Alas, my acting lacked conviction; I was about as scary as one of Doctor Who's female assistants. I once read that soldiers have to be trained to overcome their reluctance to harm a fellow human, information I found heart-warming. I could not imagine sticking the knife in anyone; could only hope that in dire necessity I would find the necessary courage.

The next day I split between scavenging and cutting up wood. I made a rewarding if not terribly useful find; a flat with a wardrobe full of new designer clothes in my size. I stood in the cream-carpeted bedroom by the mirrored doors and gasped over the labels: Alexander McQueen, Vivienne Westwood, Dior, Dolce & Gabbana, Emporio Armani. Even the shoes fitted: Manolo Blahniks, Jimmy Choos and Christian Louboutins. There was some fabulous costume jewellery, too. The owner must have been a rich woman with good taste and a packed social life. I took a selection home, wishing I had the occasions to wear them to.

Later, while sawing and chopping chairs into firewood, I wondered what Morgan did all day after he'd finished exercising. The day before he had not returned until dusk. When asked he'd said he had been foraging, but without giving any details – I'd never met anyone so good at not answering questions. He hadn't brought anything back with him. I decided to find out what he was up to. That evening was the ceilidh. Next morning I'd follow him.

I washed my hair and sat head down in front of the stove scrunch-drying it. Nothing short of a miraculous return to a normal climate would persuade me into a skirt, but I wore a brand new pair of skinny jeans under ski trousers and an Oscar de la Renta lacy silk top under my sweater for when the dancing had warmed me up. I put on makeup, earrings and a necklace and studied myself in the mirror; not bad. It's reassuring to know I can still look good when I want to.

We all get together once a month on the last Saturday for a party, at a different flat each time; we play games, dance and chat, and do an assortment of turns of varying entertainment value. Each of us brings candles, food and drink. None of us are Scottish, but ceilidh seems to cover the mixed activities of the gathering better than any other word, and one of the most fun things we do is Scottish country dancing. Paul has a wind-up gramophone and some old 78s with Scottish dance tunes, and Archie found a couple of books, *Scottish Ceilidh Dancing* and *The Swinging Sporran*. We had a hilarious time teaching ourselves how to dance, and now we're quite good at it.

This ceilidh was at Claire and Paul's, to make it easy for them with Toby. It was really my turn to host it. Morgan hadn't returned by seven-thirty when Greg called to walk over there with me. I wrote him a note:

Yo Morgan,

I'm at the ceilidh at Paul and Claire's in Shakespeare Tower in the Barbican...

Would he know it?

...it's one of the three brutalist towers southwest of here, less than a mile away, the one in the middle. If you get back in time, do come if you'd like to. You'll see the lights from close to. It's the most fun you'll have around here with your clothes on.

Tori

I reread this, had second thoughts, and wrote it out again without the final sentence before setting off with Greg across the snow.

I unlaced my mountaineering boots, slipped out of my ski trousers (my skinny jeans were underneath) and into the Balenciaga ankle boots I'd brought with me. The room looked its best in the light of a dozen candles, the cushions' bright colours glowing cosily. In daylight it looks a bit the worse for wear. It's difficult to keep a room immaculate when you have a child and no running water. Nina and Archie were on the sofa talking to Gemma, and Greg went to join them.

"Hi Tori," said Claire. "Morgan not with you? I was looking forward to meeting him. I'm the only one who hasn't."

"He's out, I left him a note. Maybe he'll come later." I showed her the two tins of soup I'd brought. "Shall I open these?"

Paul came and took them. Claire poured me a glass of wine. "Will you be godmother to Toby? Archie's going to christen him."

"I'd be delighted – as long as you don't mind me not being very religious."

"I'm not either, but it'll please Archie and anyway, the ceremony will be nice."

"Who are the other godparents?"

"Greg and Archie. It'll be a little tricky for him conducting the service as well as making the responses as a godfather, but I'm sure he'll rise to the occasion."

Claire looked well; she seemed very happy. She told me you could tell Toby was intelligent already by the way he squinted at you and waved his hands. I thought she was joking, but realized in the nick of time she was entirely serious. As I was lighting my candle Gemma came over. She wore a pink tutu over her jeans, and Mickey Mouse ears on a headband.

"My tooth came out." She opened her mouth and pointed to a gap in her front teeth. "I'm having to lisp till my tongue gets used to it."

"Then you should be getting your first visit from the Tooth Fairy tonight."

"That's what Mummy said. But I want to keep the tooth, it's my favourite tooth, so I might not put it under my pillow."

Once Charlie and Sam had arrived and everyone had admired Gemma's tooth, we settled down to play Monopoly, sitting on the rug between the two big sofas, the board in the middle. We play a fast and ruthless game, cheerfully bankrupting the vulnerable and taking advantage of any inattention to get away without paying rent – something that gets a good deal likelier as the game progresses and we are collecting food from the buffet between moves. When Sam was fetching steak and kidney pie, she missed me landing on her Mayfair with a hotel on it – something I gleefully pointed out once Paul had had a turn and her chance had passed.

Gemma is as merciless as the rest of us, but we go a bit easier on her as she is only six and gets upset if she is first out. She always has the boat as it's her favourite token. With eight players there are generally early bankruptcies and the game doesn't string out too long. Greg won. People got to their feet, stretched, helped themselves to drinks and chatted. The room had warmed with people and candles, and I took off my sweater.

Archie topped up my glass. "I hear you're going to be little Toby's godmother. I thought we'd have the baptism Sunday week. Claire will be more rested by then and with any luck Toby will sleep through it. Always a good idea to get it over with before they get to the wide-awake wriggly stage. A pleasing choice of name – did you know Tobias means 'God is good'?"

Charlie produced several sheets of paper, which I hoped was a short story. I prefer these to her poems, as I only like poetry which rhymes and scans. We all settled comfortably on sofas and chairs. A respectful silence fell, and Charlie glanced round the room.

"This poem is called *Consummation*. It's one I've been working on for some time, but it only really came right yesterday." She cleared her throat and began, in a droning, emphatic monotone.

"Take me
To the snow
The virgin snow
The sure, pure, candid snow
The snow that cures, kills, fills the planet and my mind…"

Frankly, I've had enough of snow to last a lifetime; I don't need to hear odes to the darned stuff. Charlie's delivery, waving a hand in the air for emphasis, intermittently closing her eyes, her voice rising to a shriek and falling again, embarrasses me; to her this is art, and she has no worries about looking or sounding ridiculous. She is in deadly earnest about her poetry. This seemed to be one of her longer pieces. I glanced around the room. Archie and Paul were gazing at their knees. Nina was picking with her nail at a mark on her sleeve. Claire wore an encouraging smile, the sort she has when watching Gemma try to juggle or do magic tricks. Sam fiddled with her hair, but then she'd probably heard it before. Gemma lay on the floor, walking her tooth over her stomach. Greg had his eyes shut tight, concentrating.

A bang on the door; Morgan had arrived, and Paul tiptoed to let him in. They stood by the doorway, waiting for Charlie to finish. Morgan took off his jacket and slouched broodily against the jamb, hair in his eyes, eclipsing Paul, making him look tame and domesticated. I noticed Sam sit up, glance at him and slip off her cardigan, revealing a low-cut top. Maybe he made her nostalgic for one of the disastrous boyfriends in her past. Several more long minutes elapsed, and Charlie's voice slowed for the final lines.

"*Take me to*
The earth
The dark earth
The cold, black, waiting earth
That lies forever coupled with the snow."

She halted, head bowed. A brief silence to be certain that was the end, then an appreciative murmur ran round the room.

"Well done, Charlie, one of your best, I think," Archie said. He could not possibly mean this. He poured her a drink while she talked earnestly to him, no doubt about *Consummation*'s subtext.

Paul wound up the gramophone and put needle to shellac; the Ink Spots crooning *Do I Worry*. Morgan strolled across the room, sat briefly next to Sam eyeing her cleavage and flirting with her until Charlie noticed and stood over him to reclaim her place. He settled beside me on the sofa holding a bottle of Beck's Claire had given him. He turned my way and his eyes flicked over my new look, lingering here and there.

"I kind of assumed you had a figure somewhere under all those layers, but it's nice to know for sure."

"Did you have a good day?"

"So so. You didn't warn me there'd be poetry."

"Only Charlie's. Don't be worried you'll be called on to recite a limerick of your own composition. She used to be big in a sort of alternative writer group – she actually had her first novel published by a small press, quite an achievement." I added sotto voce, "What did you think of the poem?"

"Crap. And lengthy crap, too."

He didn't lower his voice. Nina, passing with bowls of soup, overheard him and bristled, though I've heard her cast aspersions on Charlie's poetry more than once. Morgan drained the beer in one go, put the bottle on the floor beside him and wiped his mouth with the back of his hand. He got a band out and scragged his hair into a short pony tail. Gemma joined us and sat on his other side, barely coming up to his shoulder, feet not touching the floor, big brown eyes fixed on him. Eventually, compelled by the force of her stare, he swivelled to look at her. She fished in her pocket and held up her milk tooth.

"This is my tooth, it came out today."

Morgan eyed her warily. "It happens."

Gemma waited, not realizing that was the sum total of his reaction.

"Some people just don't appreciate teeth, Gems," I said. She got up and went to find a more receptive audience. The Ink Spots finished on a falsetto wail, the needle crackling repeatedly until Paul lifted it off the record. I was pleased he didn't turn it over – a little of the Ink Spots goes a long way, in my opinion. I was about to suggest Morgan fetched himself some food before something else started, when Paul moved to the centre of the floor, unfolded a spindly music stand and got out sheet music.

He looked around the room, screwing his flute together, and the chatter faded.

"If you'll bear with me, I'm going to try your patience with a few extracts I've been working on from Mozart's Flute Concerto in G Major. It's a bit of a work in progress, but at least it's brief, you'll be pleased to hear."

I couldn't help darting a look at Charlie to see if she took this personally as a comment on her interminable poem, but she was smiling and opening a can of beer, chatting to Sam and Gemma. I like the flute (Paul has a Bach Partita in his repertoire I love) but Mozart is not a favourite of mine; I find him twiddly and repetitive. Paul's rendition was surprisingly piercing, and a bit breathy. No wrong notes though, as far as I could tell. Towards the end, little Toby woke and started yelling, drowning the last bars and ensuing scattered applause. Perhaps he doesn't like Mozart either. Claire took him into a corner to feed him.

As Paul folded the stand, Morgan muttered, "Are we done now?"

"Sam sometimes sings…karaoke was one of her favourite things, apparently."

"Jesus." Morgan shifted his weight and picked up the book he'd been inadvertently sitting on, Giles Brandreth's *Great Party Games: Over Two Hundred Games for Adults of All Ages*. He shook his head. "You're all a bunch of weirdos, you know that?"

Greg approached holding a pack of cards. He's been teaching himself conjuring tricks from a book. Some of them are quite impressive when he gets them right.

"I've got a new trick."

"Go on then. Show us."

He fanned the cards and riffled through them, frowning with

66

concentration. "Tori, can you pick a card from anywhere in the pack, anywhere you like. Tell me when to stop."

I said, "Stop," and took one. The card was the four of diamonds.

"Now Morgan, you do it."

Morgan said stop and took a card.

"Look at your cards, but don't say what it is and don't show each other, then put it back in the middle of the pack." We did this. He shuffled the cards and fanned them, carefully. "Tori, you pick a card and show it." I did. "Now, that's not the one you chose before?"

"No." It was the Jack of Clubs.

Greg turned to Morgan. "But is it the one *you* picked?"

"No."

Greg paused, disconcerted. "Are you sure?" Morgan nodded, gravely. "Oh. Then in that case something's gone wrong…" Greg took back our cards, walked across the room and sat on an out-of-the-way chair to work out what had happened.

I was suddenly suspicious. "*Was* it the one you picked?" Morgan's expression was non-committal, but his blue eyes glinted at mine. He was laughing. "You bastard! That's not very nice."

"Like Sam said, you have to make your own entertainment round here."

I fixed him with a cold eye. "Listen to me, Morgan. Never do that again. I don't care who else you take the piss out of, but lay off Greg. Is that understood?"

He stared at me for a moment. "Okay."

I got up and helped the others move the furniture ready for the Scottish country dancing. Morgan didn't stay for it. He sloped off alone to the flat in Bézier. Nina said, "Of course I can see you had to take him in, Tori, and naturally we'll all do our bit to help him, but I can't say he's much of an addition to our community. I for one won't be sorry when he goes."

When I got back a couple of hours later feeling warm all over, relaxed and cheerful – country dancing always has this effect on me – he'd drawn the curtains. I slid open the patio door. Morgan said, "Hi," and turned away again. He was lounging on the sofa in the glow of a lantern. Several empty beer bottles stood beside him on the floor. He did not look like a man who'd remembered to minister to the stove.

As I riddled, emptied the ash pan and added wood I said over my shoulder, "You should have stayed. It was fun. You missed the best part of the evening." I adjusted the air intake and straightened up, brushing off my hands, ready for bed.

"Not necessarily."

He stood, reached out and grasped my hand. His hand felt warm, dry and strong. My body overreacted to his touch after its year of celibacy; a shiver shot up my arm and fizzed through my blood like electricity. He drew me gently towards him, staring into my eyes, his other hand sliding across my shoulder and beneath my hair on the back of my neck, giving me goosebumps. He smiled a lazy smile at me that took years off him.

"Hey, Tori…" he murmured. His head bent towards mine.

A sudden unbearably vivid vision of David made me want to cry. I couldn't speak, just shook my head.

He let go of me.

I went to bed.

CHAPTER 8

Trails

I woke early the next morning to a pale grey sky and the sound of Morgan moving stealthily about. One way and another I didn't want to talk to him. I lay doggo until I heard the patio door slide open and shut again, then leapt out of bed and flung on my clothes. Today I would follow him and discover what he was up to. No time for breakfast, so I put a tin of baked beans and a spoon in my pocket and gulped some water before leaving the flat.

There had been a blizzard overnight, the first snowfall for days. I'd woken in the small hours and heard the wind howling, sculpting the snowscape into new undulations. As I stepped outside, a stiff breeze, brilliant sun and icy air made my eyes water. I hitched my scarf over my nose and put on my dark glasses. Morgan had headed left, following the balconies round. I stayed well back. He glanced over his shoulder two or three times, and I shrank against the building. He didn't see me. Then he turned to his right and set off across the snowy waste in a straight line south. For the best part of a mile in that direction not much is tall enough to show above the snow, then you come to a group of City high rise office buildings rising from a scurf of roofs, as monolithic and functionless as Stonehenge, casting enormous shadows on the snow. Taller still, the Shard arrogantly spikes the sky, but that's beyond the frozen Thames. Morgan was making a bee line for the Gherkin. If I went after, he'd see me in that wide open space when he checked behind him. Better to follow his tracks later. I wanted to surprise him.

I walked back home and made myself porridge and had a wash. I realized virtually nothing of Morgan's was in the flat; not his backpack, no spare clothes, none of the things he'd scavenged – just a toothbrush and a few tee shirts and boxers. Half an hour later, I set off again toiling through the soft new snow which made the going hard, keeping far to the left of his trail. From where I was, the Gherkin peeks out from behind two taller rectangular buildings on the left; my approach would be hidden by the office block next door. I wanted to sneak as close as I could before coming out from cover.

The Gherkin is enormous. I hadn't really appreciated the fact, having only ever seen it on the skyline back in normal times; you didn't get a clear view from the streets. Since the snow, it stands like a monument to a lost civilization, but I'd never had occasion to go near. Close to, the diamond glass panes and criss-cross girders are massive, overwhelming, on a giant scale. Eat your heart out, Ozymandias.

I have a natural affinity for facts and figures, and they stick in my mind; I miss the ability to satisfy my curiosity on Google more than is rational. (I've brought encyclopaedias home, but it's not the same.) I know that the Gherkin is 180 metres tall, so most of it – 160 metres – still sticks out of the snow. It made me feel puny and ant-like as I trudged nearer, abandoning thoughts of concealment as I followed Morgan's footprints. One triangular window at snow level was not reflecting light like the others. As I got closer I saw the glass was missing. I stepped into the building and through another inner window, this time rectangular and floor-to-ceiling, but also glassless. A vast empty floorspace, a hushed secular cathedral, light because of its white floor and ceiling and the huge windows; the air surprisingly temperate; a faint smell I identified as petrol. To the right, a lobby with a steel staircase. Sunlight slanted in from the east. Occupying only a tiny part of this grandiose space was a modest pile of human clutter; a neat yellow generator, a few boxes of tins, toilet rolls, a compact tent and sleeping bag, a typist's chair and several twenty-five litre water cans, the type from Argos we all use.

And right at the front, shiny black and silver, was a snowmobile.

I put my hood down, staring, and walked round the machine. It resembled a two-seater motorbike, but with short ski-type runners at the front and a caterpillar track at the back. I got on the saddle to see what it felt like. On the dashboard were LCD display panels; a speedometer, rev counter, mileometer, engine thermometer, and compass. I've never ridden a motorbike. How difficult was a snowmobile to learn? At least you wouldn't need to keep your balance. I clicked an inviting red rocker switch on the handle, searched around for what to do next and noticed an ignition like a car's. No key.

Feeling it beneath me, gleaming and raring to go, I had a sudden doubt my powerkite idea would ever come to anything. I ran my hand over the glossy paintwork. This was what I needed – a snowmobile would get me to the south, no problem. *This* snowmobile, if I stole the key while Morgan was asleep. Not that I'd do something so…unethical.

A change in the light made me look up. Morgan stood between me and the view, unsmiling. For such a powerfully built man, he moved quietly.

I said, "You didn't tell me you'd got a snowmobile." He said nothing, just stared at me. "Why not? What's so top secret about it?"

"You followed me here." His surprise was giving way to righteous anger. To my mind, Morgan had no business to be righteous about anything.

"That's right. So, are you going to tell me what you're up to?"

His eyes narrowed. "And I should do that because…?"

"Because you are living in my flat, sleeping on my sofa and eating my food. And because you don't want to sleep in the Gherkin tonight."

There was a pause while he thought this over. Then the tension went out of him. He drew up the chair and sat down. "What do you want to know?"

"Where the snowmobile came from, for one thing." Perhaps he had found a snowmobile shop beneath the snow, and there would be one each for all of us and we could go south together…or perhaps the Snowmobile Fairy gave it to him.

"I was travelling on it. I ran out of petrol and had to walk, that's when you found me. I collected it yesterday."

"Why didn't you bring it to Bézier? Why hide it here?"

"In case I was followed." I raised my eyebrows. "By Mike and the gang. I didn't want to leave a trail to your door."

"Why would they follow you?"

"It's kind of involved. I guess there's no reason not to tell you. Mike threw me out. He gave me a clapped out Lynx with a full tank and told me not to come back. I didn't go quietly."

"Why did Mike throw you out?"

Morgan paused before saying, "We had a disagreement."

"Is that how you got the knife cut?"

Morgan's eyes became opaque for a moment. "Yes. After that, two of his goons went with me for a couple of hours, to make sure I left. I was mad as hell. When they'd gone I waited till dark and turned around – I had enough petrol to get most of the way back. I took Mike's snow machine."

"This one?"

"Yeah. It's a 600 ACE Ski-doo, the best one we had. And I drained the petrol out of the other machines, and emptied the spare cans on to the snow. We were in the middle of nowhere, camped in a church bell tower. They'd have had to go on foot back to the last place we found petrol to fetch more. I figured by the time they'd done that, my tracks would have been covered by fresh snow."

I was getting a bad feeling about this. "It's hardly snowed for the past week, till last night."

"No. Unlucky, that."

"But even if you took his best snowmobile, is that worth Mike chasing you to get it back? He's presumably found the Lynx where you left it. Okay, I can see you gave them a lot of trouble with the petrol and he wouldn't be pleased, but the sensible thing for him to do would be to say good riddance, cut his losses and move on."

Uneasily, I remembered Morgan saying Mike was a psycho. Maybe he didn't do sensible. Maybe he had really, really liked his 600 ACE Ski-doo. It was a nice machine. Morgan sat there, silent, and I had a disagreeable feeling there was more, and it was worse, and he was deciding whether to tell me. I waited, unreasonably apprehensive, reminding myself it wasn't my problem. Finally he spoke, avoiding my eyes.

"It's not just the sled. I took the gold too. All of it."

Silence fell while the significance of this information sank in. "So – there were eight of you…and you'd all worked for the best part of a year amassing this gold. Digging down to jewellers, blowing up safes. And you stole the lot." I stared at him. "Were you insane?"

He darted a look at me. "I was angry. I wasn't thinking straight."

"That has to be the understatement of the century. Because those seven men –"

"Six men and a woman."

"– whatever, those seven are going to be in total agreement about tracking you down to get back the stolen gold. They'll probably agree about beating you to a pulp afterwards, too. If you'd just taken your share, okay, Mike might have wanted to get his Ski-doo back, but he'd have had trouble getting the others to care. As it is, they'll all be thirsting for your blood. And any minute now, they could be here."

I looked out of the window to the north, half expecting to see seven ominous and growing black dots on the horizon. I didn't want any of us to get caught up in a showdown between Morgan and Mike's gang, and that seemed a real possibility if – when – they turned up in a London with no law. I didn't want them to know we'd been harbouring him for fear they got nasty with us. Morgan appeared to guess my thoughts.

"I was going to leave tomorrow. But I'm nearly ready, I'll go today – this afternoon. Get out of your way. I've just got to find one or two other things I need, rope up the trailer and I'll be off.

Okay, it's bad luck about the snow, they'd have been able to follow my tracks until the blizzard, but there's no reason for them to bother you. If they pick up my trail they'll follow me out of London."

"I bloody hope so." I had an idea to defuse the situation. "Why don't you count out the gold and leave seventh eighths with me? If Mike turns up I can give it to him, and then he probably won't chase you."

He laughed, as if I'd made a pathetically transparent attempt to trick him that he wasn't going to fall for. "I don't think so."

"Honestly, Morgan, you are a fool. Not everyone is as venal as you and your mates. I'm not after your beastly gold. You can't eat gold, or warm your hands at it, or ride south on it. I think the whole scheme you and Mike had is stupid. For all you know, it'll be worthless where you're going, like it's worthless here. You lot had snowmobiles, you could have got out of this country and spent the last year in the warm, somewhere where there's a future. I think you're all crazy. Still, it's up to you." I swung my leg over the Ski-doo and stood. "I'll be going. Things to do."

Morgan got to his feet and came close, pale blue eyes meeting mine. "You were thinking of stealing the ACE, weren't you, when I turned up? I could see it in your face. You're not as different from me as you'd like to think."

He'd read my mind. How did he do that?

"It's been nice knowing you, Tori. Shame we couldn't have got to know each other better. I'll miss you telling me off." He put a hand on my arm, bent forward and kissed my cheek, his beard softly scratchy on my skin. My body did the electric shock thing again. He smiled. "I'll miss you."

❖

I walked back to Bézier in Morgan's footprints. To my surprise, I felt sorry he was going. I would miss him, too. Nothing to do with my meaningless physical frisson – but I suppose our group is so small, any addition makes a welcome change, and he was certainly different. Though from the point of view of not wanting to tangle with vengeful psychos it was all for the best.

CHAPTER 9

Expect the unexpected

B ack at the flat, I tidied up and swept the snow off the
balcony. Slightly grumpily, I put away Morgan's duvets and
beer bottles. Then I went up five flights of stairs to the top of
Bézier, traversed dark corridors, and climbed to the roof garden.
The curved walls are filled with snow blown level by the wind,
and I didn't go too near the edge. The view offers a panorama of
London, an edited version where only the tallest buildings exist. I
got out my binoculars and trained them on the broken window
of the Gherkin, which was ridiculous, nothing to see, because he
wouldn't be leaving for hours.

I'm foolish about partings and find them unduly poignant;
they are like a mini form of death which is the final and
irrevocable parting. I'd never see Morgan again, and this must be
why I was up on a snowy roof hoping to get a last glimpse of
him. I wondered how he would cross the Channel, and how long
it would take him to reach the point where the snow stopped,
and what it would be like when he got there. I imagined warm
sun on bare skin, a balmy breeze, a seashore, greenery... I pulled
myself together. For once, I decided, I'd take a day off; mess
around, achieve nothing. I'd go and see Claire.

Claire was pleased to have an excuse to stop the half-hearted tidying she'd been engaged on while Toby was asleep, and have a cup of coffee with me. She put water to boil. Gemma was doing a jigsaw at the table with great concentration, watched by a row of toy ponies. She looked up as I took off my jacket and said,

"Tori, why have you got a knife stuck with tape to your belt?"

"In case I have to suddenly peel a lot of potatoes unexpectedly."

"There aren't any potatoes except in tins, and they're already peeled."

"Course I realize that *now*, but I'd already made the sheath and didn't want to waste it. Good, isn't it?"

Gemma contemplated it, then said critically, "It's a bit black, with the black handle as well. You could stick on gold stars. Or sequins."

"I'll consider your suggestion."

Claire and I flopped on opposite ends of the sofa and put our feet up. They had made fridge cakes, which were delicious. I told her about Morgan's snowmobile, and that he'd be leaving today. I didn't tell her about the gold – I didn't want to alarm her about Mike the Psych. He'd probably never turn up.

"You'll miss Morgan."

"He's only been here a week! It'll be nice to have the flat to myself again."

"He's quite good looking, didn't you think? I thought you made a nice couple, sitting together at the ceilidh."

I laughed. Claire was way off beam. Morgan was not the sort of man I go for. Of course, I hadn't told her about David; she had no idea what my taste in men was. "You old romantic, trying to pair me off. We've got nothing in common."

Claire said shrewdly, "As if that ever made any difference."

"If he'd been interested, he wouldn't have gone home early from the ceilidh." For some reason I didn't tell her about him making a pass afterwards. His last year might well have been as monastic as mine. No doubt he'd jump with gusto on any female; he hadn't chosen me for my niceness, wit and beauty, I just happened to be around. I remembered how his eyes had lit up at the sight of Sam, and how he'd sat by her last night before being moved on by Charlie. And he hadn't told me he'd got a snowmobile, which meant he didn't trust me any more than I trusted him. I like a man you can trust. "Anyway, I'm not interested in Morgan. He's not my type."

After the coffee, while Claire fed the baby, Gemma and I went outside and had a snowman building contest. She won, because I over-reached myself and made a snow sculpture of a tooth which, though topical, turned out completely unrecognizable. Claire brought Toby outside to see.

"Okay, I've finished. What d'you think?"

Claire walked in a circle to view it from all angles. "What's it supposed to be?"

"Can't you tell? I'll give you a clue; the real thing is that colour, or nearly."

"It's a snow Ku Klux Klan member?"

"No! Gemma, I bet you can guess. It's to do with you."

Gemma stopped putting finishing touches to her snowman, and stared thoughtfully at mine. "It's a snow ghost."

"Huh."

After I told them what it was, Gemma said it looked much more like a snow ghost than a tooth, and I should give it eyes. Then she and I played snowball-bowling with wine bottles, which is a good game with flexible and inventive rules.

I got back to Bézier thinking about lunch and intending to spend the afternoon curled up on the sofa by the stove, reading. As I approached, I saw Greg at the window. He must have had something particular he wanted me for, to wait for me when I was out. He waved. I stepped over the threshold removing my sunglasses, my eyes taking a moment to adjust to the dimness of the flat after the brightness outside. A movement in the shadows startled me. Greg was not alone; there were two men sitting on stools at the kitchen counter. They were built like Morgan, on a large scale. I guessed they were cage fighters too. A third man standing by my bookshelves put the book he'd been looking at back on its shelf and came forward.

Greg said, "Tori, this is Mike. He's friends with Morgan. And the others are Big Mac and Eddie."

Mike did not look remotely as I'd imagined him. A tall slim black man with shrewd eyes and a sunny smile that showed perfect teeth. His hair was cut short to his scalp, and he was clean-shaven. Young – at a guess a year or two younger than Morgan, but with a certain natural authority. He looked as if he'd be more at home in a suit than the parka he wore. He held out his hand and I shook it, my initial alarm subsiding somewhat.

"Mike Shand. Nice to meet you, Tori. Is that short for Victoria?" His voice was deep and pleasant, the sort that made you think he'd have a good singing tenor; his manner was engaging. I nodded. "Sorry to barge in on you like this. Greg said you wouldn't mind."

"No, that's…er, fine. Would you like a tea or coffee?"

"No, it's okay. The others are setting up the generator. I just thought I'd better introduce myself to the neighbours."

"Are you moving in to Bézier?" I wasn't keen on this. I regard it as mine.

"Just for a little while, then we'll be moving on. We're in a flat on the other corner this side."

I was still recovering from Mike not being at all what I'd expected, finding it difficult to adjust. From the little Morgan had let drop, I'd picked up a vivid mental image of an overweight middle-aged white guy with mean shifty eyes, a shaved head and a Northern accent; a villain straight out of a run-of-the-mill cop series on TV. The only thing that fitted with my preconception was the presence of the two muscular men who, by the way they stayed in the background and said nothing, seemed to be bodyguards.

Mike picked up a solar tulip, smiled and put it back in its jar. "I was hoping to have a word with Morgan. He's living here, Greg said."

"He was." Amiable as this man seemed, I'd only just met him, and was not going to tell him anything till I'd worked out what was going on and who to trust. "He left this morning."

"On a sled? A snowmobile?"

I paused. "No. He hasn't got a snowmobile. He arrived on foot." I'd mentioned the snowmobile to Claire. I must go back and tell her to keep quiet about it.

Greg said, "We all have to walk everywhere. It's all right, though, because we've got trailers for moving supplies."

"He left us on a sled." Mike frowned slightly. The smile had vanished from his eyes. He was suddenly dead serious. "My sled, to be precise. Maybe he didn't tell you about it. He plays his cards close to his chest. I'd like it back. That's one of the things I want to talk to him about."

"He was heading south," I said. "I expect you'll overtake him easily enough."

"I expect so." He stood, his pleasant smile in place once more. "We'd better go and give the others a hand. I'll be seeing you."

He got a pair of dark glasses from an inner pocket, unfolded them and put them on. The two men rose and followed him. Perhaps they were the men who'd escorted Morgan when Mike threw him out, to make sure he didn't come back. Greg and I watched them walk to the door and out to the balcony, swing their legs over the rail and head away to the left.

"What did they say to you, Greg?"

"Big Mac and Eddie didn't say much. Mike was asking about Morgan, because they're friends and he wants to see him. And I told him about you and the others, and he was interested. He wasn't interested in Doctor Who, though."

"Did you meet the other people with him?"

"No, but I saw a woman. She was being cross about something, I don't know what. When they've settled in they might want to trade with me."

A loud revving noise penetrated the double glazing, and two snowmobiles ripped past the windows, spraying snow.

Greg watched them out of sight. "I wish I could have a go."

Greg stayed for ten minutes more, before going to call on Charlie and Sam in their office block above Liverpool Street Station. I made myself wait another five minutes, as long as I could bear, then left, pulling my trailer and not looking behind me. I went to the Old Street shops and as quickly as possible raced down and brought up four big packs of disposable nappies.

I didn't see anyone hanging around when I came up. When I got to the Barbican, Claire thanked me for the nappies, rather surprised.

"You shouldn't have. Paul can do that."

"They were just camouflage, in case anyone was watching." Her eyebrows rose. "Morgan's old gang has turned up, they've moved into Bézier. Mike, that's the leader, seems very keen to find Morgan. I said he hadn't got a snowmobile, so don't tell anyone, will you, if they come sniffing round? That's what I came over for. Morgan wasn't going to tell any of us, so I thought I'd better play dumb."

"Is it a secret?" said Gemma. She'd gone back to doing her jigsaw.

"Yes. Act shy if they ask any questions, and don't say anything. They may be nice, but we don't know yet."

I said goodbye and headed for the Gherkin, to tell Morgan Mike had arrived.

I crossed over one of the sled tracks, a distinctive double ribbon, its centre churned and lumpy. Halfway I heard a buzzing like furious wasps and caught sight of the snowmobiles in the distance kicking up spray, making deep scars on the fresh surface of the snow. I was careful to keep against the buildings to stop their riders noticing me. Were they letting off steam or hunting Morgan? I made a wearisome detour behind the neighbouring office blocks west of the Gherkin on the off chance someone in Bézier was watching me through binoculars. Paranoid maybe, but you can see a person for miles on the snow, standing out like a spider walking up a white wall.

The surface outside the triangular window was smooth and

undisturbed apart from my earlier footprints. I stepped inside, pulling my trailer after me, and left it between the inner and outer façade. Morgan was crouched beside the snowmobile, stripped down to his sweater in the comparative warmth of the building's energy-efficient ventilation system, hair tied back, working on the engine.

He glanced up. "What are you doing here?"

"Hi to you too. I came to tell you Mike's arrived."

"Yeah." His concentration went back to what he was doing. "I saw the sleds racing around. D'you know how many people were with him?"

"No, don't you? You said there were seven. I only met Big Mac and Eddie." He didn't answer, just reached for a spanner. "I want to talk to you about Mike." I came closer to get his attention. He had taken the engine casing off; bits of engine lay on the floor around him. He was unscrewing something, swearing under his breath, intent. "What are you doing?"

"It won't start. It's not the spark plugs or the fuel line, the wiring or the crank seals. I'm checking the fuel pump…" He eased a component free. "Oh shit."

"What?"

"There's a puncture in the fuel pump diaphragm. I don't have a spare." He stared at it. "Fuck."

"Can you mend it? Or find a spare somewhere?"

"No and no. The nearest spare parts are in Mike's baggage. Second nearest, Scotland under a load of snow. You didn't tell Mike you'd seen the sled?"

"No."

"Or get followed here?"

"I came via Claire's and round the back."

"That's something. Don't come here again unless you have to." He started work on the engine once more, putting it back together fast, his expression blank. He was thinking. I didn't interrupt. I don't know why I felt I had to help him – possibly just because he'd been staying with me for a week, and I'd got to know him a bit. And I'd saved his life, so had an interest in keeping him alive; I didn't want my initial effort to be for nothing. When he had finished, he stood and wiped black grease off his hands on to a tee shirt. "You can help me hide it. We'll have to bury it round the other side of the building. Go and find a curtain or something big enough to cover it. And a broom."

"Bury it? Is that really necessary?"

"Yes. Because else Mike will find it and take it. Then I'll be stuck here with you lot."

"I can see you wouldn't want that."

Ignoring my sarcasm he gripped the handles on the front of the sled's skis and pulled it over the threshold. Catching his sense of urgency, I dumped my jacket and ran to the lobby and up a flight of stairs. The next floor had been occupied and was full of partitions and work stations. One could believe that, come Monday morning, phones would be ringing, computers glowing and office personnel busy at their desks. The only clue no workers would be back, ever, were large dead plants in steel planters, their leaves brown and brittle. The executives' offices all had blinds. I tried the next floor, with the same lack of success, and the next; there seemed a consensus curtains were out of place in this futuristic building. I was just beginning to think he could maybe use his trailer instead when I came across an office abandoned in the middle of redecorations. I folded a couple of groundsheets, grabbed the dustpan and brush lying on the floor, and went to find Morgan.

At the south-facing side of the building, close to the windows, he had already dug a deep hole and was standing in it, his shovel moving like a machine, snow flying on to a growing heap. I threw a dustsheet over the sled which was glittering in the sun – no point letting our activities be too eye-catching from a distance if the sleds came round this side. The cans of petrol were there, too, waiting to be interred.

"Where did you get the shovel?"

He kept working as he said, "Folding one I carry on the sled. Essential kit. Dig a ramp that end."

I started to scoop snow. I'd get him to talk later. The top layer was easy, but it got harder lower down, and the dustpan was bendy, being plastic not metal. Morgan did most of the work. As soon as the hole was deep enough, he dragged the ACE into it, arranged the petrol cans around the sled and spread the dustsheets over, tucking them in underneath. We shovelled back the snow, stamping it down and artistically spreading the excess about so there was no trace of a bump. Morgan levelled the tracks and our footprints with his shovel, and I backed out, sweeping the surface. It looked pretty smooth from a few feet away, if you weren't looking for it.

Back inside, he wiped the sweat from his face with his sleeve, and said, "Let's hope it snows."

I thought of something. "Did you mark where it is?"

"No. I counted how many windows from here."

"How many?"

I could see him debating whether to tell me.

"Thirty-three."

"Is that the real number?"

86

He laughed and chucked his supplies into his roof box trailer, then asked me to take one end. The backpack with the gold wasn't there. Even without it the trailer was heavy. We headed up the stairs.

"You're going to stay here, then?"

"I can't stay with you now Mike's living next door. And this place only gets really cold at night, and I've got a sleeping bag and a tent."

We went up the next flight, and the next. My legs were getting tired and the edge of the trailer was digging into my hands. "How far are you going?"

"High enough to get a good view. High enough for anyone searching the place to give up before they get there and go away."

"How high is that?"

"A few more."

He stopped eight floors above snow level, not even breathing hard, in a smart coffee-making area tucked behind a wall; all grey, white and steel, with upholstered banquettes and a clear view of Bézier to the north. I'd started to worry he was going all the way to the top. I flopped on to a bench to get my breath, rubbing my sore fingers and gazing at the panorama. Morgan rummaged among his stuff, looking for something.

"Mike wasn't how I expected. From what you told me, I imagined his knuckles dragging along the ground. But he wouldn't be out of place in a boardroom."

"That figures." Morgan spoke without looking up. "He's a smooth operator. He's got a lot of confidence, he carries people along with him. The family business was motorbikes – they dealt in snowmobiles too, but he wanted something of his own."

"How did you meet him?"

"In a Manchester nightclub. Some drunks were hassling him because he was with a white girl. I told them to get lost and he bought me a drink. I wasn't doing much at the time, casual manual work while I concentrated on getting my Jiu-Jitsu black belt, and he said I could do better than that. He'd pay me more to work for him. That was two years ago."

Morgan had found what he was looking for. He took the lens caps off binoculars and leaned on the double rail, focusing on Bézier.

"Mike had issues with his parents, maybe because he was adopted. His father was a self-made man, very successful, and didn't let anyone forget it. Mike wanted to prove himself, he was determined to make more money than his dad. He started by setting up events after he left uni, fights, illegally at first in empty properties. He made a packet running a book on the side. Then he went legit, got licenses, hired venues. Finally he made enough to rent his own building and do it up; ritzy bars and restaurants and dance floors on different levels, and in the middle the cage fighting arena. Somewhere different for the rich kids to go. He'd have set up a chain of FreeFights if civilization hadn't crashed on him."

I leaned on the rail next to Morgan and got out my own binoculars. I focused them on the windows of my flat, then swung along to Mike's, easily identifiable by the row of sleds. There weren't any people about. "Were you with him from the start?"

"Yup. I helped him break into empty buildings and sort out the space, fly-post the area, act as bouncer when I wasn't fighting. I needed the money at the time."

So Mike had started with an acknowledged debt of gratitude

to Morgan, and they'd worked together for two years, then had a blood row of some sort.

"What did you argue about when he threw you out?"

Morgan gave me a sidelong look. "A logistical matter." He raised the binoculars again.

"What does that mean?"

Silence. It was clear he had said all he intended to. I abandoned that line of enquiry for the matter in hand. In the current circumstances it was in both their interests to settle, surely. "Why don't you strike a bargain with him, hand over the gold – their share of the gold – in exchange for the spare part? He struck me as quite civilized and reasonable."

"Civilized and reasonable. Yeah, I can remember when I thought that."

"But he has everything to gain by coming to an agreement with you. Aren't you going to at least try?"

"Maybe. But he wants the ACE, and the gold, and I got the better of him in front of the others. He doesn't like me, and he'll want to show the gang you don't mess with him and get away with it."

He lowered the binoculars and turned to face me. His voice was matter-of-fact.

"I think I'll have to kill him."

"You can't just kill people!"

"You're right – I'll send him a solicitor's letter. Oh wait – can't do that, no solicitors. I'll have to kill him. Tori, you aren't being realistic. I could go round tomorrow morning and give Mike all of the gold, the whole lot, keeping not even a half sovereign for myself, dig out the ACE for him and fix the fuel pump diaphragm, then make a grovelling apology for the nuisance I've caused. He'd still want to drag me behind his sled till I was dead, or push me off the top of the Shard, or break my legs and leave me in the snow."

CHAPTER 10

Hidden depths

I walked back home, disturbed. Morgan's reaction was so extreme. You couldn't just *kill* someone because you thought you would not be able to come to an agreement with him, and he didn't seem to see this, there was no convincing him – he refused to discuss it.

I've disagreed with a lot of people in my life, and if it weren't for SIRCS and the snow they'd still be around. Nina still was, case in point, and we failed to agree on a daily basis. Again the thought occurred to me that he lived in a tougher, harder world than I did, where they did things differently. Then there was the fact that for the first time in many centuries, it was possible to murder without legal consequences; the police no longer existed, and nor did the criminal justice system. Morgan could kill Mike and go on his way, the only penalty a guilty conscience. Had he been misleading me, and he rather than Mike was the psychopath? Perhaps I ought to warn Mike, put him on guard. But doing that would betray Morgan, and anyway, Mike had three strong men to protect him.

Uneasily, I decided to do nothing. I realized I was starving – I still hadn't had lunch. I got out some tins.

❖

In the afternoon I lay on the sofa, reading. The sun went in and the sky became a luminous light grey. Thick flakes of snow began to fall. By teatime, several inches had settled. Had his sled been working, it would have covered Morgan's tracks as he made his escape. Every so often I stared out of the window, but could barely see the Gherkin in the white-out.

Archie called, which reminded me it was Sunday (Nina Time). I made him a cup of tea. He had just been round to call on Mike. Apparently Mike is a Christian and told him he was sorry to have missed the service that morning.

"He said he'll come next Sunday if he's still here. Nina bumped into Mike this morning and was very taken with him, they had quite a chat. One of his friends is a male nurse, which is a stroke of good fortune. Perhaps Claire would like him to take a look at Toby – not that there's anything wrong with him, but she might find it reassuring."

A nurse passing through – it seemed a waste we were all quite healthy.

Archie got an envelope out of his pocket and handed it to me. "We're going to have a dinner party for Mike and his friends, Wednesday evening. You'll come, won't you, Tori?"

I opened the envelope. An invitation card with a picture of deep red roses, a silver bow on the corner, and my name inside. It said the theme was crimson and silver, and would guests dress to match. Nina seemed to be going all out to impress the newcomers.

"Let me see," I said. "I'm going to the opera tomorrow, then there's the private view at Tate Modern Tuesday, and Thursday I'm seeing a film…but yes, I've a window on Wednesday. Who else is going?"

"Everyone, I hope. It'll be quite a big party. Mike's got four friends and his young lady with him."

"So six of them…" One fewer than Morgan had said there were. I wondered what had happened to the seventh man, and what Mike's girlfriend was like.

Archie said, "It's a pity Morgan's no longer here."

"He wasn't very sociable when he was."

"No, I think perhaps he was a little shy. I'd have liked to get to know him better. I feel he had hidden depths."

I didn't tell Archie I was currently worrying over Morgan's hidden depths, anxious about what sort of predator might emerge, covered in mud and slime, from their murky waters.

I'd just settled down with a book after Archie's departure when there was a rap on the window. A woman slid the door open and came in.

"Hi. I'm Serena." Her gaze darted over me, taking in every detail. I became aware my sweater was stained and my fingernails grimy and my fringe could do with a trim. By contrast, she was immaculately groomed; shiny hair, discreet makeup, manicured nails. She smiled. "You must be Tori. Mike said he'd met you."

"Hello." I offered her tea ("Ooh, tea, lovely,") and put the water to boil. I waited to find out why she'd come. Serena perched on a stool, opened her jacket and looked around her. Improbably, she had the air of a wholesome English rose in Val d'Isere after a good day on the slopes.

"This *is* nice. You're very well organized. I *love* your tulips! And the stove…we have boring old generators and electric kettles and fan heaters as we're travelling around."

She slipped off her jacket. The soft pink sweater underneath had the expensive sheen of cashmere. "So who else is there I haven't met?"

I ran through the list. "But you'll meet them all at Nina's party the day after tomorrow."

"You've got a nice balance of numbers. The last place we stopped was all men."

I laughed. "Charlie and Sam are women. Paul and Archie and Greg are outnumbered."

"Oh." Her face clouded and she didn't say anything for a moment. "How old are they?"

"Not sure exactly. Sam's a bit younger than me, Charlie a bit older I'd guess."

"Oh. Well, I'll see them soon. Mike said Morgan stayed with you while he was here."

"That's right."

"But you didn't go with him when he left."

I laughed. "No. Why should I?"

"No reason really, I just assumed…he's terribly attractive, and I thought maybe…"

Why did everyone think Morgan was so attractive? "I only knew him a week," I said, coolly, getting out the tin of biscuits.

"I'm sorry, I didn't mean…it's just most people want to go south. How was he?"

"How do you mean?"

"Was he okay? He was bleeding from a cut when he left. I was a bit worried about him."

"He was fine. The cut wasn't much." I was not sure why my instinct was to play this down. I put teabags into mugs and got out a tin of biscuits.

"Oh good. I'm fond of Morgan, in spite of everything."

"Everything…?"

"I don't suppose he told you. He stole from all of us when he left. Mike's team had spent a year stockpiling stuff, collecting valuables on the way south so we wouldn't arrive poor – and after all, none of it belongs to anyone anymore – and he took the lot. All except for this because I was wearing it." She felt below the neckline of her sweater and lifted a heavy gold chain round her neck. I leaned closer to see; like Sam she wore perfume, a subtle floral scent with hints of jasmine, roses and lilies. Set at the front of the necklace was an ancient Greek coin with a warrior's helmeted head. "Nice, isn't it? It's Bulgari."

"Why did he take your…things?" I'd nearly said gold, and the less I appeared to know the better.

"There was a row. Mike told him to go. But he came back when we were asleep and stole our stuff."

"What was the row about?"

"Oh, they'd been drinking a lot, that was what caused it," she said, vaguely. I was beginning to get curious about this row. No one wanted to talk about it; they all got evasive whenever the topic arose. She leaned towards me and lowered her voice. "Has Morgan really gone?"

"Yup. He packed his bags, said goodbye and everything."

"Mike said there aren't any sled tracks leading out of here."

I poured the boiling water. "That would be because he went on foot."

"He had a sled when he left us. Maybe he hid it somewhere and didn't tell you."

I didn't want to pursue this line of conversation. "Sugar? Milk powder?"

"No thanks."

"So how long are you staying?"

"That's up to Mike. Now we're here he'll probably want to look for gold."

"The Bank of England's not far away. It's got four hundred tonnes of gold."

Serena laughed. "We'd need a nuclear bomb to get inside the vault. Anyway, Mike reckons the government took it out – to pay for the evacuation, for one thing. No, more likely he'll go for the British Museum or Bond Street."

Movement on the balcony caught my eye. It was Big Mac, a bull of a man with short ginger hair. His ears were lumpy and didn't match, his neck as wide as his head above massive shoulders. He knocked on the glass, opened the door and stood there letting in a blast of cold air. He looked at me.

"The boss says, could you come round if it's convenient. He'd like a wee word."

"What about? We're just having a cup of tea."

"He didnae tell me."

Why would Mike summon me like this? All my apprehension returned. I looked at Serena; she'd got to her feet immediately as though what Mike wanted, he got, and this request was perfectly normal. Perhaps it was. If I didn't go he'd no doubt come round here. Anyway, I was curious to meet the rest of his entourage. I picked up my jacket and went outside with Big Mac and Serena, outwardly calm but inwardly agitated.

The wind had got up and a fine snow blew in my face as we followed the curve of the building. The six snowmobiles outside the balcony of Mike's apartment were covered by a tarpaulin. Once inside, I didn't take in the details of the room, just saw Mike sitting on a sofa with four men. One of them was Eddie, one looked Chinese, the other…I stared; for a moment he looked so like David with a beard; the same bright eyes, gangly build, the way he sprawled on the sofa…he must be the male nurse. At a closer look the resemblance diminished; his face was narrower and less intelligent. The fourth was Greg, looking bewildered.

"Greg… Hi."

At a glance from Mike Serena went past us and settled behind the counter in the kitchen area out of the way. Mike got up and came towards me, beaming. "Thank you for coming round, Tori, I apologize for disturbing you. Take off your coat. Do take a seat. You know Eddie and Mac, this is BJ and Hong."

I sat on the sofa opposite, dumping my jacket beside me, feeling as if I was about to be interviewed. Or interrogated. Mike leaned forward.

"Greg has told me he saw Morgan today."

Damn Morgan. How could he have been so careless, letting himself be seen? I turned to Greg. "I expect that was before he left, was it, Greg, this morning?"

Greg shook his head. "No, it was about an hour ago. Near Claire and Paul's."

"In the distance, was it?"

"Yes. I waved at him and he waved back."

I addressed Mike. "Greg can't have seen Morgan an hour ago, because he left this morning. He must have seen Archie or Paul – even Charlie. We all wear quite similar jackets with the hoods up. It's easy to get confused from a distance. I do myself."

Greg said, "I wasn't confused, Tori, he –"

I interrupted, fixing my eyes on Greg meaningly. "D'you remember that time you mistook me for Nina? You were absolutely certain I was her." Greg's forehead crinkled as he tried to recall this fictitious episode. He started to say something, then stopped. "We had the same colour parkas for a while. Not that we're at all alike really." He blinked. He'd grasped I was trying to get some message to him. He just had to work out what it was. "We had a good laugh about it afterwards, you remember, Greg? I think this is like that time – you just thought it was Morgan when it wasn't."

Greg's face cleared. He'd got it. "That's right, Tori. I thought it was Morgan at the time, but thinking back, perhaps I made a mistake and it wasn't him at all."

Mike considered us for a moment, nodding his head. "My feeling is you two have got friendly with Morgan over the past few days, am I right?"

I shrugged. "We haven't known him long enough to become friends. He seems okay."

"Nina told me how you rescued him in the snow. Saving a person's life forms a bond between you. I can see you wouldn't want to be disloyal. Did he say anything about me while he was here?"

"No." I thought this the answer least likely to cause trouble. "He said very little about anything. He was asleep most of the time."

Mike hesitated. "This is awkward. I don't want to blacken Morgan's character, and I can see you've no reason to trust me more than him. You don't know me from Adam. If, as you say, he's moved on, then it doesn't matter anyway. But I feel I have to give you a warning. If by any chance he is still around, please do be careful. Don't necessarily believe everything he tells you. Watch your back. He can be very plausible."

"Thanks. But I doubt we'll see him again."

Mike stood. "I'll let you go now. I'm glad we had this chat. Let Mac walk you home."

I smiled. "We can walk ourselves, thanks. Come on, Greg."

The tea had gone cold. I put water to boil to make us some more. I felt unnerved and also uncertain. Was it possible I'd got Morgan wrong and that Mike was the injured party?

"You know, I did see Morgan this morning," Greg said. "I didn't make a mistake. It was definitely him."

"Yes, I know. But Morgan doesn't want Mike to know where he is. Best not to mention him if possible." Greg nodded. "Thanks for backing my story up, Greg."

"Mike got quite excited when I said I'd seen Morgan," Greg said, thoughtfully. "He really wanted you to tell him where he was."

I remembered what Morgan had said; two men with baseball bats could walk all over us. My improvised dagger was still at my side, but it didn't make me feel any safer.

CHAPTER 11

Serena

That night I set my alarm for 4.35. The next morning, an hour before dawn, I sloped off to the Gherkin by a roundabout route to tell Morgan about Nina's dinner party. If Mike and his gang were at Nina's, that would be the perfect opportunity for him to steal the spare part for the ACE. I climbed the stairs cautiously, following the tiny circle of light my torch made in the inky blackness. At the entrance to the eighth-from-snow floor I called out his name, which was just as well since he turned out to be standing round the corner with a lump of wood waiting to brain the intruder he'd heard.

He stepped into view, making me jump. His eyes shone through his hair, looking me up and down. "It's you again. Why don't you just bring your toothbrush and move in with me?"

"Very funny. I came for a reason."

"Because you can't keep away?"

I rolled my eyes and told him about the party. That done, I didn't hang about, though he said now I'd woken him I might as well stay for a coffee. I wanted to return while it was dark and no one could see me. I got home and back into a cold bed as the sky began to lighten, and lay there sleepless, thinking. Either Mike was the baddie, or Morgan, and I was still unsure which was which. I was not at all convinced I should have told Morgan about the opportunity to steal from Mike, when he'd already stolen his gold and his sled. On the other hand, if he got the spare part he'd be able to repair the snowmobile and leave, rather than stay and kill Mike. Not that I could believe he actually would...

That day was our scheduled firewood day. All of us except Claire and Nina met up in the office block next to Bézier. It's more difficult than you'd expect to find timber in a modern office, since most furniture these days is made out of veneered chipboard, MDF or ply and doesn't burn well. There is too much glue in its composition. We'd discovered a massive conference table made from solid wood, not easy to break up but worth the effort. We attacked it with our motley collection of saws and our one axe, and by the end of the day had reduced it to five satisfyingly neat piles of fuel.

Pleasantly tired, I traipsed home with my share and heated some food. I'd eaten supper, spent a couple of hours curled on the sofa with a book, and was beginning to think of bed when a bang on the window startled me. I went over and drew the curtain. Serena stood outside, holding a bottle of Moët & Chandon. I let her in. She looked different from the day before, less composed and sleek. Her eyes were slightly unfocused, her face flushed and she held on to the edge of the door as she stepped over the threshold. Serena was drunk.

She smiled a brilliant smile. "Hi, just thought I'd drop in for a chat. Is that okay?"

"Sure. Make yourself at home. Would you like a coffee?

"No, I'm hitting the champers." She plonked herself on the

101

sofa with her champagne and wrestled with the wire fastening, swearing.

"Shall I do that?"

I took the bottle, fetched glasses and eased out the cork. Foam spurted into the flutes and I filled them with champagne.

"Cheers." Serena knocked hers back in one go and reached out to pour another. "Mmm, lovely, that's better. D'you ever just feel like getting ratted? I hope you don't mind me coming round here like this. I couldn't stand that flat one minute longer. Mike's playing poker with the boys, they'll go on till the small hours."

"Don't you play?"

"Me? Good Lord no, I might lose."

"What are they playing for? It can't be money."

"Forfeits. You wait, any minute now there'll be someone running round the building just wearing his boots. That's why I won't play any more. It's all right for Mike, he never loses." She looked towards the window then around the room. "Don't you get fed up stuck here, nothing ever happening?"

"It's not so bad – could be a lot worse. Of course if I got the chance to go south I would."

"That's what I thought when Mike offered me one of his sleds." She nodded. "Anything to get out. All this fucking snow! I'm so sick of it. And I thought he was quite sweet. But I wish we were going straight there. It could be months till he thinks he's got enough gold, longer if he doesn't get back what Morgan took. And I know he'll dump me if he meets someone prettier." She stared into my eyes. "I can tell you this, Tori, because you're my friend and I know even though you want to go south, you wouldn't go after Mike –"

"No, I wouldn't."

"– and anyway, you're not his type, you're too scruffy, he likes women who bother with their appearance, not like you, anyone can see you don't give a damn."

"Thank you."

"Nothing personal, but s'true, isn't it?" She was having to take care not to slur her words.

"Yup. I don't give a damn."

"S'not easy, keep looking like this with no hot water or hairdressers or manicurists, you know. If I let myself go even a tiny bit, don't do my hair or makeup, have an extra glass of wine, whatever, this kind of shadow comes over his face and he gets all cool… Mike doesn't drink, that's 'cause he wants to stay in control. He won't let me smoke, even outside. I say, d'you mind if I do? I'm gasping for one."

"Go ahead."

"Thanks." She got out a squashed packet of Benson & Hedges, lit a cigarette and inhaled. "He doesn't like it if I swear, either. He's allowed to but not me. And I'm in trouble if I even *glance* at another man, and he checks out every girl he meets, I see him do it. D'you know, sometimes I get so sick of him I could scream." She gulped more champagne. "He's obsessive about having everything just so, he's neurotic about germs, always sniffing at food in case it's gone off. So irritating. Plus he's a total hypochondriac, every single day he finds some new imaginary symptom for BJ to check out. He can be really horrible, too. I liked Morgan better. I was hoping he might take over from Mike, and everything would be much nicer. But then there was that row and he left."

"You never said what the row was about," I said, hopeful she'd tell me now she was on transmit not receive.

"Him and Red fell out… I fancy Morgan, don't you?"

"No." I was firm about this. Firmer than I felt. "Not my type. Who's Red?"

I didn't get an answer. She was dreamily focused on Morgan. "He's got lovely eyes, just like aquamarines, have you noticed? Sort of cold but warm…and that way he kind of broods…fabulous body, too, and he can beat up any of the others if he wants. Listen, I'll tell you something I haven't told anyone else. When we get to the sunshine, I'm not staying with Mike. He can't make me. Soon as we get there, that's me done, I'm off. I just need to get there first, and he's the only way I can, that's the only reason I'm staying with him. Don't tell anyone. Specially not him. You know what?" She leaned closer. "He frightens me."

Nothing much happened the next day. The weather was bright and sunny, leading me to fantasize about the snow melting and life returning to normal after a few weeks of flood, which would be all right as my flat was high up and I had lots of provisions and making a raft would be fun…

Mike's people were in evidence around the place, moving stuff in bulk from the shops (did Nina know?) and roaring about on their sleds. I wondered if Mike had been cool towards Serena when she'd finally tottered home the night before, worse for drink, hanging on to my arm. I hadn't gone in with her. I hadn't been much help, but then she'd only really wanted someone to rant to. I don't think Greg told anyone about Mike's disquieting quizzing of us, and I didn't tell anyone about Serena's visit. There were no further sightings of Morgan.

CHAPTER 12

Rat to dinner

Wednesday was the day of the dinner party. While getting ready, I felt curiosity to meet Mike and his group again and see how the evening went; we'd be an ill-assorted crowd and I couldn't imagine how we'd all get on. I washed my hair and did my eye makeup with care. I put on a Vivienne Westwood top, boned plum velvet with a zip down the middle, and Dolce & Gabbana skinny jeans. I checked myself in the mirror from all angles, added a leather cuff and diamond earstuds and smiled smugly at my reflection. I'll admit that what Serena had said about my appearance stung a little.

When I arrived a bit early, it was clear Nina had gone the whole hog, and possibly Mrs Hog and the baby hoglets too. The room was warm and smelled of lilies from scented candles. A third sofa had been brought in to accommodate the extra guests, and Nina, in a long raspberry dress with silver jewellery, was busy arranging dozens of silver and red scatter cushions. A pair of eight-branched silver candelabra decorated the table (it was longer than usual – she must have added another, the join concealed below the white damask table cloth) which was laid with enough cutlery and glassware for a banquet. There were napkins folded on the side plates, names on flowered cards by each place, and in the centre a convincing arrangement of silk flowers complete with acrylic dew drops. Archie, unlike himself in a dark suit and clearly under orders, stood by the sideboard. On it were arranged a silver bowl containing water tinted red with floating candles and more faux roses, bottles of expensive wine and a tray of canapés.

"This all looks very nice," I said.

"So do you, Tori. Champagne?" Archie fiddled with the wire on a bottle of Cristal.

Nina looked up from her cushions. "No she doesn't, not in that stained old ski suit she goes foraging in every day. Tori, do take it off before anyone gets here and sees you."

I peeled off my scarf, jacket and trousers and changed my shoes. Nina whisked my outer garments out of sight, holding them well away from her. Archie poured me a glass of champagne and I helped myself to a canapé. Belatedly I said through a mouthful of caviar, "Is there anything I can do?"

"I think everything's under control. Nina's been working hard for days."

I bet Archie's been doing most of it, under direction. "Well, it's certainly paid off. The last dinner I went to this grand was when my godfather took me to the Savoy to celebrate my eighteenth birthday."

I told Archie about it. I'd ordered roast quail because I'd never had it before. To my surprise, it turned out to be as round as a canon ball and slippery. When I tried to cut it up, the darned thing shot off my plate on to the carpet. I was mortified, but my godfather thought it hilarious, and the waiter fetched me another one in the most charming manner, and told me deadpan not to worry, he'd got several more lined up in case they were needed.

I've wanted to go back to the Savoy ever since. Too late now.

Paul, Claire, Gemma and little Toby, asleep in his cot, arrived. Gemma was wearing her dressing-up Renaissance Queen outfit; red with gold lacing and handkerchief sleeves, plus matching crown. It was getting a little short for her, as it dated from before the snow. She started at once to turn a chair into a throne using the silver cushions. Nina had set up a screen for Toby's carrycot so she could pretend he wasn't there, with a seat so Claire could feed him discreetly without being seen. I think ideally she'd have liked to tidy Gemma away behind it too for the evening. She eyed the disarranged cushions.

"As soon as you get tired, Gemma, you can have a nice nap in our bed until it's time to go home."

"I won't get tired," said Gemma. "I'm good at staying up late."

Claire said quickly, "That's very thoughtful of you, Nina." I caught Claire's eye; the corner of her mouth twitched and I turned away before we got the giggles. Paul reappeared from the bedroom wearing grey trousers and a corduroy jacket. None of us looked like our normal selves. Like Gemma, we were in fancy dress. Claire had put her hair up which she never does. She wore a long skirt and a low-cut draped top with a dramatic necklace.

"I haven't had a cleavage like this since I fed Gemma, so I'm making the most of it. Lucky Nina's is always so warm. Get you – is that Vivienne Westwood?"

"Yep."

A movement on the terrace caught my eye. Greg was swinging his leg over the wall. I realized Nina had got us all here half an hour before Mike's lot, in order to check our hands were clean and our hair brushed and have us sitting neatly in a row for when he arrived. He must have made quite an impression. Greg wiped his feet carefully on the mat, and removed his parka revealing a new red cardigan. He offered Nina the plastic bag he was holding, and she took it and peered inside.

"I'll put it away with your coat. You didn't have to bring supplies. This evening isn't one of our usual get-togethers."

"Will we be playing Monopoly?"

Nina pursed her lips. "No."

"Scottish dancing?"

"No. I don't expect Mike and his friends know how to."

Greg's brow wrinkled. "What will we do, then?"

"We'll make conversation in a civilized manner on topics of general interest." Nina bustled off to the kitchen.

Archie gave Greg a drink, and went to help Nina with the food. Greg came and sat between me and Claire.

"Cheers." I clinked glasses with the others. "Shall we practise a bit of civilized conversation? What topic do you fancy?"

"I nearly came as Minnie Mouse," Gemma announced, sitting on her throne and swinging her legs. "The dress has got white spots but it is red and has a black top, and there's a bow at the front and between the ears, and you wear black tights. It's got a petticoat with frills."

"That is the most amazing coincidence! I nearly came as Minnie Mouse too. But on reflection, I thought I wasn't quite mini enough to carry it off."

Gemma was not deceived. She gave me a disapproving look. "No you didn't, Tori. You haven't got a Minnie Mouse costume, or I'd have seen it. You've only got ordinary clothes."

"Yes, and it's not fair. I'm going to make a formal complaint. I see Toby came as a baby. Cheating a bit. Must have a word with him."

"He can't talk yet, Tori. You're being silly again."

"Darn. Have to watch that." I turned my attention to Greg. "Nice cardigan." I peered closer. "I don't wish to alarm you, but your pocket appears to be moving…"

Furtively, Greg shot a look over his shoulder towards the kitchen; Nina's voice and the chink of crockery could be heard through the open door. She'd be a while. He put his hand carefully in his pocket and got out something small and furry. A baby rat; soft grey fur, pink nose and feet and ears, with long whiskers and black bead eyes. Claire exclaimed and Gemma jumped off her seat and came over to have a look.

I said, "He's so sweet! Can I hold him?"

"She's a she," Greg said, putting the rat in my hands. "I found her in Argos. She was lost. I don't think Nina would like her at the dinner party, so don't let her see. I couldn't leave her behind on her own all evening."

"We won't tell," said Gemma.

Paul hovered. "Careful, Gemma. She won't bite, will she?"

"No, she's very friendly."

Claire said, "Did you wash her?"

Greg nodded. "I heated some water and used Head and Shoulders. She wasn't nearly so fluffy when I found her."

Claire did not look totally reassured. The rat felt warm and light in my hand, and her claws tickled. I could feel the beat of her small heart. Her blunt nose snuffled at my fingers, then she sat up and groomed her whiskers, quite unafraid. I stroked her behind the ear with one finger and she shut her eyes as if she liked it.

Greg smiled proudly. "I'm going to teach her tricks when she's bigger."

Gemma was practically hopping up and down. "Can I hold her?"

I handed the rat over. "What's she called?"

"Rosie. After Rose Tyler." His favourite of Doctor Who's companions.

Gemma laughed, delighted. "She's nibbling my fingers! Shall I get her something to eat?"

"She's had her tea. I've got some muesli in my other pocket in case she gets hungry. You can try her with a bit."

Rosie took the proffered almond flake and held it with surprisingly hand-like paws, turning it round and audibly crunching, little furry jaw working.

"Aaah… Mummy, can I have one?" I knew how she felt. I wanted one too.

"No." Claire's voice was firm.

"Why not? I'd look after it."

"Because they're wild creatures…except for Rosie who's …adopted."

"But if I had one it would be adopted too. Please, can I have one?"

Nina's voice became more audible. Greg took Rosie from Gemma and pocketed her. Her worm-like tail hung outside briefly, then vanished. We all sat back as Nina walked past us to the table.

Gemma hissed, "Please, Mummy, can I? I want one."

"Ssh, we'll discuss it later. Go and wash your hands."

I went too. Their bathroom is nice; they have a proper commode, and an old-fashioned bowl and jug for washing, with a matching soap dish, and a hanging lantern.

I could hear the snowmobiles' engines getting louder as we

rejoined the others. Team Mike had arrived. They lined the sleds up the far side of the terrace wall. Mike walked into the room, all smiles and compliments and introductions, and Nina fussed over him, taking his jacket. Beneath it he had on a smart suit and tie. So, improbably, did Big Mac, Eddie and Hong, giving them the air of bouncers outside a flash casino. BJ wore a suit with a shirt open at the neck while Serena, once changed out of her ski suit, was elegant in a long dress with a ruffled neckline. Sober she was back to normal; I was no longer her best friend. They'd all come. Morgan had thought Mike might leave a couple on guard duty at Bézier. Mike handed Archie a boxed bottle of Rémy Martin XO Excellence Cognac, and Nina a bottle of Jean Patou's Joy.

Nina was delighted. "Mike, you shouldn't have!"

"It's nothing. I'm sorry not to be able to bring you flowers."

Mike greeted me like an old friend, holding my hand and kissing both cheeks. He stepped back so he could survey me. "Tori, you're looking amazing tonight."

Nina moved him on to the drinks. Mike refused champagne and had a glass of orange juice. He shook Gemma's hand and said he'd always wanted to meet the Queen, made Claire glow by admiring Toby thoroughly and convincingly, briefly discussed the design of the Barbican with Paul, then charmingly evaded Nina's clutches and came and sat next to me.

"Tori." He lowered his voice to an intimate level. "I've been worrying a little about our conversation the other day. Perhaps I should have kept quiet."

"Don't worry, I didn't take it too seriously." From across the room, I saw Serena's eyes straying in our direction, computing Mike's interest/lack of interest in me. More to needle him than in the hope of being told anything, I said, "Though I have been wondering what you and Morgan fell out over."

He smiled and leaned forward. "You just want me to badmouth Morgan so you can get angry with me. I bet you're beautiful when you're angry." Having delivered this cliché, he settled back against the sofa, smug as a panther lolling in a tree, irritating as a raspberry seed between the teeth, regarding me under half-closed lids. "I've got an almost overwhelming urge to pull that zip, and Nina wouldn't approve. Quick, tell me something, take my mind off it. Something that's not corsets or bodices or bustiers." He shut his eyes for a moment. "Or velvet or zips."

The stare I gave him was as cool as the weather. "I'll make it easy for you." I got up and joined Greg and Archie over by the drinks, keeping my back to Mike.

Charlie and Sam arrived late – on account of Sam fussing over what to wear, if past form was anything to go by. Nina introduced them to the guest of honour. I saw Serena notice Mike's eyes flicking over Sam the same way they'd flicked over me, but she didn't have anything to worry about; Charlie always puts people in the picture at an early stage.

"This is Sam and Charlie. Charlie was a published author, as well as being P.A. to Harry Carrington."

"A published author, I'm impressed. Tell me, what books have you written?"

"Book. Just the one, *Carapace*. My pen name is C.J. Hewitt. I don't expect you'll have heard of it, it's rather niche."

"*Carapace*? But I bought it for my sister, it was the last present I gave her." He looked sad for a moment then rallied, as if determined not to let his loss cast a pall. "I thought it sounded her sort of thing, and it was, she loved it. I'm honoured to meet

112

you. Are you writing something else?"

I didn't believe Mike. The guy was a creep. He was making friends and influencing people tonight, and in my opinion this was just part of his charm offensive. Clever of him to say he'd bought it as a present; too easy to be caught out if you say you've read a book when you haven't. But Charlie glowed just like Claire had, happily taken in, and chatted about *Carapace* and Jeanette Winterson and Sarah Waters until Nina called us to sit at the table.

Archie sat at one end and Nina at the other, with Mike in the place of honour on her right, BJ on her left. Mike chatted to Claire on his other side, but mostly to Nina. From what I overheard, they seemed to be talking about foreign travel and music. I was in the cheap seats next to Archie, opposite Greg and Serena. When she told him about the labradoodle she'd had as a child, I could see he longed to boast about his new pet, but after a glance at Nina he evidently decided it was not a good idea. The three bodyguards said little, and when they did speak it was to each other in a sort of guttural shorthand. Hong sat on my left. He was younger than Mac, shorter and Chinese, but with the same Chesterfield sofa build. English wasn't his first language, I discovered when trying to get him into conversation. I have a theory that most people have one subject on which they are interesting, if you can only discover what it is; but if Hong had one, I failed to find it. So I leaned across the table and tried Mac.

"Tell me about cage fighting."

He regarded me curiously. "What d'you want to know?"

"Well, everything, really. I don't know anything about it."

He gave a short laugh. "You and everyone else. A mate of

mine's wife asked me, 'Is it to the death?' I said, 'Yeah, and I've only lost twice.' Mind you, she was pissed at the time."

"I suppose it's because not many people have met a cage fighter."

"No. There's a lot of people say they're MMA when they've never been in the ring. The sort of meathead who used to say he was SAS to impress the lassies. Got the ink, some of them, that's all."

"Ink?"

"Tattoos."

"Did women do MMA?"

"Oh aye. There were some good Scottish girls coming up."

I sipped my wine while deciding what to say next. Archie on my right, unaware he was interrupting, said my top was quite Elizabethan in style, apart from the zip of course, which got us talking about royalty and Shakespeare and Tom Stoppard and circuses... When I next looked, Mac was involved in some ponderous and incomprehensibly Scottish teasing of Eddie.

Every so often snatches of conversation from the other end of the table reached me. Mike's deep voice, "One would like to help more, but we have to be realistic..." "Not wanting to be sententious, but civilization is more important than any individual." "The Magic Flute is a great favourite of mine, I envy you." And Nina, "No, I entirely see that. Anyone would do the same in your position..." "Oh absolutely, I couldn't agree more..." "Ah, Mozart..."

BJ was regaling Sam and Paul with funny stories about when he was training to be a nurse and was the only male in the group. Serena strained to hear, clearly wishing she was the other end of the table. I tried to picture Morgan at the dinner; if his behaviour at the ceilidh was anything to go by, he'd be scornful about Nina's efforts, uninterested in social chit chat, and rebuff people who tried to start a conversation with him. In a word, ungracious. Whereas I had to admit Mike was making the occasion go like a rocket. Part of me would have liked Morgan sitting by my side, bad manners and all.

The meal was leisurely, with several courses and a different wine to accompany each dish. Even had Nina thought them appropriate, we wouldn't have had time for board games or dancing. The wine was rather better than the food – no fault of the cook, Nina had done well with the materials available. I began to feel pleasantly chilled out. My mind ran on Morgan's raid on Bézier, wondering whether it had been successful. Over tinned fruit and cream with Muscat de Beaumes de Venise, Nina asked Mike about his plans, and how long he'd be staying. There happened to be a lull in the buzz of conversation just then, so even from the far end of the table I could hear Mike's answer.

"Well, you know we're practically pirates." An amused, deprecating murmur rose from his neighbours. "So while we're here we're doing some pirating, looking for gold. We're digging down to the British Museum. Unfortunately it's a low-rise building."

"But that's stealing!" Gemma stared at him, scandalized. "It's not your gold, it's the Museum's, you can't take it. And anyway, pirates have ships and you don't."

Nina and Claire both said, "Gemma!"

"It is, though."

Mike smiled. "I'll get a ship when I need it to cross the Channel, Your Majesty. And I'm not sure anything left behind under twenty metres of snow belongs to anyone any more, unless you dig it up, at which point it belongs to you."

Gemma thought about this. "So have you got a lot of treasure?"

"No." His voice was grave; all laughter had left his eyes. He'd done one of his disconcerting mood flips. "We did have, but someone took it."

"Who?" said Nina. All heads were turned towards Mike.

He took a sip of his dessert wine. "I think you've met Morgan?"

Nina nodded, her eyes bright with curiosity. "Yes. I know he was with you. But he never told us anything about his past. He never talked much at all."

"That figures. Before the snow he used to work for me. When I first knew him he was earning peanuts loading trucks, and I thought he was better than that. He's not just muscles, he's got a brain when he chooses to use it. But he's his own worst enemy. I gave him a job in my organization, then when the snow built up I said he could come with me. We were friends, or so I thought. He went off one night with my sled – my snowmobile – and everything we'd spent a year collecting. I was hoping to catch up with him and persuade him to give us back our share."

"That's terrible! What made him behave like that?"

Mike shrugged. "Greed." He smiled down the table at Archie. "One of the seven deadly sins. And a bit of envy, that's another."

Nina shook her head, deploring Morgan's low behaviour. She was enjoying herself. "I can't say I'm surprised. I didn't take to him while he was here. He had no manners, and I know that may sound trivial, but I find it's often indicative of deeper personal flaws."

"He didn't have a snowmobile though, did he Tori?" Charlie said.

"No."

Mike said, "Maybe he just didn't let you see it."

Without meaning to, my next remark came out hostile and rather loud, so that all eyes slewed in my direction. "He did have a knife cut on his ribs, though. How did he get that?"

"He lost his temper and tried to stab Eddie. Eddie defended himself."

Eddie nodded, not meeting anyone's gaze. I said to him, "So you're a better fighter than Morgan? You surprise me. Because he's bigger than you and a Jiu-Jitsu black belt."

Eddie went a dull red but didn't say anything. Serena's gaze was steadfastly on her lap. Mike said, "There's more to fighting than Jitsu. Eddie's a boxer."

"But good with a knife as well apparently."

"Morgan's knife – but I'm not defending either of them. It was a dispute that got out of hand, an ugly brawl that shouldn't have happened. If you want to blame anyone, blame me. I'm in charge, and I failed to stop Morgan getting hurt."

Nina rushed in to forestall an awkward silence. "I'm sure whoever's fault it was, it wasn't yours. From what I've seen of –"

A piercing scream interrupted her. Serena jumped to her feet, chair clattering to the floor behind her. While we were disagreeing over Morgan, Rosie had woken up unnoticed and decided to explore. Paws gripping the rim of Serena's dessert dish, her nose twitched as she busily investigated its contents.

CHAPTER 13

Civilized and reasonable

"She made an awful lot of fuss," Greg said thoughtfully, as we walked back together through the snow. "Rosie wouldn't have hurt her."

"Suddenly appearing out of nowhere made it worse, I suppose. But Serena didn't have to be such a total wimp about it, especially after we'd told her Rosie was a pet. D'you want to come in for a coffee? It's still quite early."

The party had broken up not long after Rosie's unscheduled appearance. The last part had been taken up with people fussing over Serena on the sofa, soothing her and fetching glasses of water and commiserating. On the other side of the room Nina was ticking Greg off in a furious undertone, accusing him of wrecking her party, while I simultaneously told Nina to get a life, and if that was the worst that ever happened to Serena she was a very lucky woman. Nina started doing that thing of closing her eyes when talking to me as if to shut out my viewpoint, which never fails to irritate. Archie came over and said the party hadn't been spoiled, that no bones had been broken and it had provided an interesting finale to the evening. Before we left I overheard Nina tell Mike that Greg had learning difficulties and was a cross we had to bear. I glared at her. Luckily Greg didn't hear as he'd gone to get changed for the walk home.

The snowmobiles zoomed past us on our journey back. We waved. As Greg and I approached Bézier, we could see Mike's people milling about on the balcony in the cold light of a gibbous moon. Something was up. It seemed unlikely they'd caught Morgan, or noticed a small spare component had gone missing. Probably some unrelated matter. We went inside and Greg lit the tea lights while I fed the stove and put water to heat for coffee.

I was pouring boiling water into mugs when there was a noise on the balcony. I looked up as Mike slid open the door and came inside without asking. Hong, Eddie and Big Mac followed, closing the door behind them. None of them were smiling, and men that size need to smile or they look menacing. Mike's cordiality too had been left behind at the Barbican; his face was cold and hard. He walked straight up to me.

"Someone's been in my flat while we were out tonight."

My heart began to beat fast. "Well, it wasn't me or Greg. We were with you at Nina's all evening."

"I don't think for a moment it was you or Greg. I know who it was. Morgan."

I raised my eyebrows. "I'm beginning to think you've got an obsession with that man. What makes you think anyone's been in your flat?"

"Because I'm not stupid. In particular, I'm smarter than Morgan. I don't keep my brain in my muscles. I put a light dusting of ash on the floor and a black thread across the doorway so I'd know if someone called."

"Even so, and even if it was Morgan, which I doubt, I don't see what it has to do with me."

"Let me enlighten you, then. I think you told him we'd be out tonight. I believe you know where he is. I thought so three days ago and I'm certain now."

"Well, I don't."

"Nor do I," said Greg.

Mike ignored him. He came close to me, and stopped with his face inches from mine. His eyes were black-flecked amber in his dark honey-coloured skin. I could feel his warm breath on my face as he said, "You know where Morgan is, and it's not far from here. You're going to take me there."

I maintained a bold front. First rule when dealing with a bully, don't show fear. "Wishful thinking. Just because you want a lead on him doesn't mean I've got one."

He stared at me for a moment longer, and turned to Greg. "Greg, go outside with Eddie and Hong."

Greg said, "I haven't had my coffee yet. I'll wait."

"This won't take long. You can wait outside."

"You go home. I'll see you later," I said. Better for it to be just me if things were going to get nasty. Greg picked up his jacket and scarf.

"You won't need those," said Mike.

"No, I will, it's cold."

Mike turned to Hong and Eddie. "Take him outside where we can see him and don't let him run off. Mac will relieve one of you in ten minutes, if you're still out there."

Hong and Eddie put on their hats and jackets and gloves and forcibly escorted Greg, wearing only his cardigan over his trousers, outside. A blast of icy air and powdery snow came in as they closed the glass door. They stood a few paces either side of Greg, a short distance away beyond the balcony. He was saying something but they ignored him. He looked at me and called my name, though I couldn't hear him through the double glazing, then moved towards me. They shoved him back; he lost his footing and fell. He picked himself up and looked from one to the other, not fully understanding, and put his hand protectively over the pocket that held Rosie.

"Let him back in!"

"When you tell me where Morgan is."

"I can't tell you what I don't know. Get Greg back in here and let's discuss it calmly. Then maybe I can help."

"The only help I need from you is Morgan's whereabouts."

"I'm not telling you anything while Greg's out there!"

"I can wait. We'll see how you feel in thirty minutes, shall we? With this wind and a temperature of what, minus five I'd say, frostbite isn't going to take long. Half an hour out there and Greg can say goodbye to his fingers and nose. Are you going to sit here and watch it happen when a few words from you could save him?"

For a moment I felt sick, then anger flared through me.

"You evil bastard."

I lashed out at his face. He flinched away, but the punch connected. As I flung myself at him and grabbed his throat Big Mac leaped towards us. Huge hands gripped me from behind and hauled me off. I kicked and struggled until Mac got hold of my arms and bent one up my back, and pain immobilized me.

Coughing, Mike got himself a glass of water and drank it, then came and stared at me. Oddly, there was admiration in his eyes, and speculation. "You've got more courage than most of the women I've met, and I've met quite a few. You're nice looking, too." He ran a finger down my cheek and neck. I strained away

121

from him. He said reprovingly, "You should make the best of yourself every day, not go around dressed like a tomboy."

"I couldn't care less what you think, and I don't want your advice."

He ignored this, pursuing his own line of thought. "I wonder why you're covering up for Morgan? Perhaps you think he'll take you south. If he says that, he's stringing you along. He won't keep his word. You don't know him very well. But on reflection that may be in his favour." He sneered. "You just see the bulging muscles and the handsome face, you have no idea how devious, sneaking, greedy and disloyal he is. He'd sell his own grandmother, and pull out her gold fillings first."

"I'm surprised you worked with him for two years, then."

"He's good at covering his tracks. That's how he imposes on people. You're making a big mistake. I suggest you reconsider."

"Bring Greg in."

"For an intelligent woman you're being stupid." He pushed a stray bit of fringe from my eyes to get a better look at me. I hated being held there, unable to get away, while he patronized me and worse, touched me. I hated being in his power.

I spat in his face.

Not something I'd done before, or ever expected to do. There was a pause. He didn't move. I couldn't read his expression. Only my anger stopped me being very frightened indeed about what would happen next.

He wiped my saliva off and slowly licked his finger, eyes never leaving mine, creeping me out. "You have a lovely face, Tori. It's a shame to risk it. A waste. But you give me no choice." He spoke abruptly to Big Mac. "Take her outside with him, then come back here. Tell them to keep her there till she's ready to say where Morgan is."

Mac frog-marched me through the door, pushed me towards Greg and went back in. Greg looked pleased to see me, then worried. The air was very cold, and the light wind penetrated my thick sweater and velvet top with no trouble at all. I wrapped my arms round my shivering body, hands in my arm pits.

"Why is Mike making us stand out here? I'm cold. I'm worried Rosie will get cold."

I muttered, "He thinks if we get cold enough I'll tell him where Morgan is."

"But you don't know where Morgan is."

I said nothing. I tried to put my fear to one side and think. Of course, I could tell Mike he was hiding somewhere he wasn't, say Centre Point. If I did, he'd probably let Greg go. But he'd take me with him because he wouldn't trust me to tell him the truth, and when he found I'd been lying the consequences for me would not be good. He was mad and strange and fancied me, a bad combination when I was in his power. Or I could betray Morgan, take Mike to the real place in the Gherkin, and watch while his three cage fighters beat Morgan up or worse, because I could not imagine Morgan simply handing over the gold and telling where the ACE was. And even if he did, they'd still beat him up. But at least Greg would be out of it. His teeth were chattering already. Soon mine were too. I tried heating my hands on my neck, and cupping my nose to warm it.

The two men watched us impassively from several metres off, one each side; for the first few minutes Mike strolled around in my flat picking things up and putting them down again, glancing through the window from time to time, then he went and sat with Mac at the kitchen counter, talking, relaxed. I saw him laugh. My nose, ears and fingers were beginning to hurt from the cold, competing with the ache in my sore knuckles and arm. Fear came over me in dark waves, rising higher, driving out rational thought. I remembered photographs I'd seen of Everest climbers who'd suffered frostbite; I hadn't understood why they would risk something so terrible for the sake of saying they'd climbed to the highest point on earth. I imagined my nose and fingers freezing, going black; I imagined being crippled and disfigured for life. I was not brave enough to face that. I was going to have to tell him.

"Tori," Greg whispered, "Can you make them let us go home? I'm cold."

His face was white and pinched. It doesn't take long to get frostbite, it's irreversible and there is no cure; you just watch the flesh mortify. All doctors can do is amputate the dead fingers or toes. I'd have to tell Mike. Morgan would have to look after himself. I'd wait as long as I could bear in hope of a miracle. Maybe Mike was just trying to frighten us, and didn't intend to leave us here long enough for us to get frostbite. Any minute he'd send one of the men to get us.

Big Mac emerged from my flat as I thought this; but he'd been sent to relieve Hong. We'd been out here ten minutes. I'd been careful not to look in the direction of the Gherkin, but now as Mac talked to Hong something caught my eye against the moonlit snow. A figure was running, arms pumping, straight as an arrow towards us, snow kicking up behind him. He was past halfway, as far as I could judge. Morgan. I looked away, my heart hammering. The later they saw him the better. I moved towards Mac to try to distract him. He told me to stop when I was a few paces away. Eddie watched me, having nothing else to do, stamping his feet.

"Perhaps we could make a deal." My face was stiff with cold, lips numb, teeth chattering, making speech difficult.

Small eyes looked down at me from under sandy eyebrows, his head a little on one side. "You shouldn't have gone against Mike. Tell him what he wants to know lassie, okay, then we can all go in. I've no wish to go on standing around out here in the cold."

"Imagine what it's like for us without jackets."

"Why d'you not tell him then?"

"Because I don't know!"

"He reckons you do."

"I don't."

"Then you'll be out here a while."

Tedious. I hadn't had an idea for a deal anyway, I'd been bluffing. I tried something else. "What happened the night Morgan left?"

"What d'you want to know for?"

"I'm curious."

"Ask him then."

"He's not here."

"So you say."

I felt a spurt of irritation. "Do you know, this is a really boring conversation? Probably the most boring conversation I've had in the last year. You're a boring man. No wonder Mike never talks to you, just uses you as servile muscle. Does it ever occur to you he'll screw you one day too?"

"Shut it."

"When it happens don't say I didn't warn you." I turned and walked over to Eddie. "Are you any more interesting to talk to?"

Mac said, "Dinnae answer her, Eddie."

Eddie avoided my eyes and said nothing.

"Nope. Even worse. Dumb and Dumber, you two." I joined Greg, who was now shuddering with cold. "Let's keep moving, jump around a bit. That'll warm us up. Copy what I do."

I started jogging on the spot, beating my hands together, and did some camp 80s type aerobic exercises with plenty of arm movements. Greg mirrored my moves. I felt chilled to the bone and weak. Pretty stupid, too, with the two men watching – but while they were watching us they weren't noticing Morgan. After a few minutes we stopped, out of breath but no warmer. A covert glance showed Morgan nearer, still running fast towards us through the soft snow. I had an inspiration.

"Hey, Greg, let's do some Scottish dancing. The Gay Gordons."

Mac frowned, no doubt wondering if I was taking the piss. I began clapping the beat and humming. Greg joined in; we linked hands side by side, his right to my right, his left to my left, and started the dance, forward then switching backwards, whooping now and then. The men watched us. Next move; I twirled under Greg's arm for eight beats, and we polka-ed for a notional four bars, with me counting out loud. It wasn't our best performance, but not bad given we could hardly feel each other's hands or our own feet any more. We had done all the steps and started over, gasping for breath, when I realized we had lost our audience's attention. I stopped dancing. They'd spotted Morgan, nearly upon us. He wore a thick black sweater and his face was shining with sweat from the long run.

He slowed to a walk as he reached us, breathing fast. "Mac, Eddie, hi. How's it going?"

Mac said, "Mike wants a wee word with you. About the gold." His voice was unfriendly. "He wasnae happy about that. Nor us. In your place I'd be feart."

"Mike doesn't scare me. I'll talk to him now I'm here." Mac turned away and went through the patio door into the apartment, presumably to alert Mike. As we followed, Morgan stopped, turned to Eddie and said conversationally, "Who are you most afraid of, Eddie? Me or Mike?"

Eddie laughed. "Mike, no contest."

Without warning, Morgan head butted him then punched him in the stomach. "Wrong answer." He kicked Eddie's feet from under him and he crashed to the snow, blood pouring from his nose. Mike came to the window, peering into the darkness, Mac behind him. I don't know how much he could see with the candlelight reflecting on the glass.

Morgan looked at me. "Tori, you okay?"

I nodded. "Glad to see you, though." Greg and I followed him inside.

I was relieved to be out of the cold, even if it meant being back in Mike's company. He confronted us, Mac on his right, Hong on his left. After what had happened I felt revulsion just looking at him. I hoped it wouldn't come to a fight between our two groups, because though our numbers were now even, I had no experience and nor did Greg. This had not worried me earlier when I had been fighting mad, but now Greg was safe the urge to throttle Mike had dissipated. Morgan would effectively be on his own. But he looked confident enough.

Mike smiled without warmth. "Let's conduct this in a civilized manner, shall we?"

"I will if you will."

Mike turned to Mac. "Where's Eddie? Tell him to come in."

As he spoke the balcony door opened slowly and Eddie hobbled over the threshold, blood on his face and running down his neck and jacket, eyes puffy, nose askew and beginning to swell. Mike's smile vanished and he shot a malevolent look at Morgan. "Eddie, go to the flat."

Eddie left. The rest of us faced each other warily. My ears and fingers began to thaw and burn in the warmth. My feet were like lumps of ice.

Mike said, "I want the gold. I'm prepared to let you keep your share."

"That's big of you. What happened to Red?"

"He's no longer with us."

"Then my share's a seventh. And I'll be dividing it."

"I want the ACE back."

"I'll swap you for the Polaris. I'm not taking the Lynx. And I want a trailer."

"Okay. You bring the gold and the sled here, and I'll give you the Polaris."

Morgan shook his head. "No. You give me the Polaris and both keys, plus trailer, spares and cans of petrol, and I'll tell you where you can find the ACE and the gold on your way out of here."

CHAPTER 14

Red

Mike didn't argue or bargain. He said he'd think it over and left. I locked the door and hurried to check in the mirror for rigid white patches on my face, signs of frostbite. I prodded my cheeks gingerly, and the flesh sprang back. Nothing. Overcome with shaky relief and gratitude, safe for the moment, nose and fingers intact, I turned to Morgan. "Thank you for coming for us. That was an impressive run."

"You didn't tell him where I was. You could have told him and kept out of trouble." As if it cost him physical effort, he muttered, "That was nice of you. Not many people would have done that. Thanks."

I don't think I'd ever heard him say thank you before. Honesty compelled me to put a damper on this pleasant exchange. "Another five minutes and I would have. And it was your fault we needed rescuing."

Morgan grinned. "Don't spoil it."

Because of not worrying Greg, I didn't add that Mike might give us more trouble in the future. "You know he put ash on the floor and a thread across the door? That's how he knew you'd been there."

He scowled. "Fuck. I didn't see it."

Greg had got Rosie out to check on her, but she'd been fine, tucked up in his pocket in her own fur coat. He let her investigate the counter and told Morgan about her while I made more coffee. My ears burned painfully as they thawed and no doubt looked like his, scarlet and glowing enough to guide Santa's sleigh. A hot drink made me feel better. After that Greg went home. I said he could stay the night if he liked, but he wanted to get back to his own place. I told him to lock his door and not let anyone in, and he nodded.

"I don't like Mike any more. He's definitely off my protection list."

After he had gone I went to the window to watch him walk home. Morgan told me he'd be fine, Mike had no reason to waylay him, but I wanted to be sure. Greg's figure gradually diminished till he disappeared and the faint golden light of a candle shone from his windows. Morgan said we should barricade the front door just in case, so we extricated a double bed from under my piles of stores and heaved it into the hallway, leaving the frame on end at an angle against the door. Would that be enough to stop a person intent on getting in? I was glad Morgan was there to protect me. Except it was Morgan Mike had the quarrel with...

"We could add more furniture. I hardly ever use that door."

"We need to be able to get out that way if we have to. Two exits are better than one."

I still felt chilled to my core and bone weary, so got myself a glass of brandy. I needed it. I put my socks to warm on the stove top and flopped on the sofa, exhausted. My feet were marmoreally pale, and I began to rub them. Morgan joined me, heat radiating off him. He said, "Give me a foot," and massaged it. The warmth of his hands brought an involuntary smile to my face. I was telling him about the party and had reached the rat incident when a thought occurred to me and I broke off.

"I assume you got the spare part after all that?"

"No. The box with the spares in wasn't there. Either he's hidden it somewhere else, or he had it with him tonight."

This was bad news. It meant Morgan had no alternative but to make a deal with Mike; and the longer this thing went on the more likely we all were to get involved. Greg and I had already. "D'you think you can trust Mike if he agrees?"

He gave a short laugh. "No way. He's lost too much face. He'll want to get his own back."

That's what I'd thought. My heart sank at the prospect of more conflict. "Mike said it was Eddie who knifed you."

"It wasn't Eddie."

"Then why did you hit him? It seems a bit gratuitous."

"If I hadn't it would have been three of them against me instead of two. I don't count Mike." He spoke as if it was a simple matter of arithmetic. "And I didn't like what Mike did to you and Greg."

"Why didn't you hit *him*, then?"

"He wasn't standing outside on his own. Eddie was."

I thought about this, unable to decide whether a savage premeditated attack on an unprepared man was justified in the circumstances, or reprehensible. We'd needed rescuing and Morgan had rescued us with efficiency, but smashing a person in the face and guts in a world without hospitals was a brutal thing to do. He might have ruptured his spleen and killed him. The fact that BJ was a nurse and presumably able to help Eddie had not, I felt sure, entered into Morgan's calculations. David would never have behaved like that…uneasily, I recognized this was a situation he would not have been able to deal with. He'd have come to help and ended up outside instead of us – or as well as us, depending on Mike's whim. I also had to admit, reluctantly, that some primitive part of me thought Morgan's violent alpha male behaviour awesome. I changed tack.

"What do you think Mike will do?"

"Nothing tonight, most likely. He'll think it over like he said. Nothing till he's got the gold and the ACE. It's after that he'll try something. Other foot."

I swung my left foot up and put my hot sock and slipper back on my right, which felt more its old self. "Tell me what happened to Red."

"Why d'you want to know?"

"Because I'm sick of everyone being mysterious about when Mike kicked you out. Mention the subject and everyone tells you contradictory stuff, or goes all vague and clams up. It's like the Secret of Glamis Castle."

"None of us come out of it well, that's why. Okay. I'll tell you." He let my foot go, went and got himself a bottle of beer, and sat down again. He took a drink and absently resumed massaging my foot one-handedly. "We were going through a small town when Red crashed his Yamaha, snagged it on part of a building sticking out of the snow and smashed into a wall. The sled was a write-off, but he was thrown clear, not a mark on him. That left us with seven sleds and eight people. Four of the sleds take two, but with two they go slower and use more fuel, and we were hauling supplies anyway. Mike told me to take Red behind me on my Polaris. Slowed me right down, it was a drag, we were way behind the others. I had a go at him for being careless. We had a row, yelling abuse at each other as we went along. At nightfall we stopped in a bell tower, the only building above snow for miles around. Cold, no proper windows."

He gazed at the flames in the stove's little window without speaking for a bit, stroking my foot as if it was a cat, sending distracting tingles up my leg.

"I should tell you Mike and I hadn't been getting on too well. We'd disagreed over a few things. I'd always been closer to him than the rest, like his second in command, but after a while he cooled on me. I got the feeling he thought I was angling to take over, plus he didn't like to see me talking to Serena. He got less friendly, started criticizing everything I did or said. To make this more noticeable, everything Red said was clever, a really good idea. I know this sounds dumb. It was. So that evening, we were all sitting round in the bell tower drinking to keep the cold out, talking about being one sled short, and Mike told Red he could fight me for my sled. The loser got left behind. We were in the middle of nowhere – anyone left there wouldn't survive. I said no way. Did I say we'd had a lot to drink? The others were chanting, 'Fight! Fight!' Red was all for it. We'd fought back in FreeFight days, and were pretty evenly matched. He was dancing around, calling me chicken. I told him to fuck off. He hit me. I told him he was drunk, he should go to bed. He wouldn't leave it. I couldn't walk away, there was nowhere to go. I lost my temper. Mike got the fight he wanted. I'd got Red in a head lock on the floor. He had to tap out, I'd got him beat. Instead he pulled a knife and tried to stick it in my ribs. By chance I moved and spoiled his aim."

"That was the cut on your side?"

"Yes. I got mad, which was stupid. You shouldn't get angry

when you're fighting. I broke his arm, deliberately. I shouldn't have done that."

Silence while I compared his version with Mike's. Eddie had looked as if that story was untrue, the way he'd gone red and hadn't met anyone's eyes. I believed Morgan. And I didn't like it. The more I found out about Mike, the worse he seemed, and everyone else except Greg thought he was a nice guy. They'd been eating out of his hand at Nina's, all of them. Eventually I said, "Then what?"

"Mike kicked me out, like I told you. I don't know what happened to Red. He wasn't any use with a broken arm. My guess is they left him behind, with no transport, in the middle of nowhere. Mike's a cold-blooded bastard."

I didn't say anything for a while. Morgan might sneer at our little group, but it was a hell of a lot nicer than the one he'd been part of. I couldn't imagine any circumstances in which we would leave an injured man to die alone. I wondered whether he'd told me everything.

"Why didn't Mike like you talking to Serena? Was there anything between you?"

"Not really. She hadn't been with us that long."

"I thought you'd all set out together a year ago?"

"Six of us did. Mike and five fighters who worked for him. But he had eight sleds, space for two more. He thinks people are disposable; he ditches them when he doesn't need them any more, or falls out with them. Serena's the third girlfriend he's had this year. He dumped each one when he met her replacement. That's why Serena does what she's told. She doesn't want to be left behind with some random group of people existing at subsistence level like you lot. If Mike had been able to get his hands on guns Eddie wouldn't be with him, he's too thick to be a good fighter, he's only fit to be a bouncer. Mike wasted a lot of our time trying to find guns. We dug down to two police stations, but the cops must have taken them when public order started to break down. That's what you'd do with civilization collapsing round you like a house of cards. I told him at the first one that's what had happened, it wasn't worth trying another, and I was right."

The thought of Mike with a gun was chilling. I hoped he didn't come across any in London. Morgan was still talking.

"Then there's BJ; he's an upgrade on Ben, the paramedic we had before. We left him in Birmingham, and as soon as Mike comes across a doctor BJ'll be toast. Mike's terrified of catching some bug or getting hurt, a real wuss."

Morgan hadn't answered my question about him and Serena, so I went back to it. "What does 'not really' anything between you mean?"

Morgan smiled at me under his lashes. "I always knew you cared, Tori."

He lifted my foot and kissed my toes. I snatched my foot back and put on my sock. It had been thawed for a while but I'd been focused on what he was saying…plus who doesn't like having her foot rubbed?

"Serena was the only woman around, so you kind of noticed her. If we were alone she used to stand a bit too close to me – I don't flatter myself, I'm sure she did it to everyone. She knew the effect she was having all right, but she'd act shocked if you tried to take it further. It was partly to up her value in Mike's eyes, having all of the guys wanting to shag her, but I don't know how loyal she'd be to him if he wasn't top dog."

Serena had fancied him, she'd told me so. In vino veritas. Interesting he hadn't noticed. But she'd have been too scared of Mike to do anything about it. "You tried to take it further?"

"I'm only human."

I let that go. "Why was Serena the only woman? Travelling from place to place, you must have come across lots of groups of people like us."

"Yeah, there were women. Never had time to get to know them. Some of them saw us as their ticket out, but Mike didn't want passengers. He said they'd slow us down and use up supplies. He was the only one allowed to bring a woman along."

I sipped my brandy and considered all this. Morgan might not have told me everything, but what he had said I believed, and it seemed to me the situation was rife with hazardous possibilities.

"So to sum up: Mike is a psycho in a world without law, where might is right, and he has three cage fighters on his side. You tried it on with his girlfriend, and stole his gold and his best sled. Then you broke Eddie's nose. He is now living a two minute walk away from this flat. You are not possessed of superpowers. You have no way as yet of getting away from Mike," and here I fixed him with a stern eye, "and even if you did, you would not go leaving Mike dissatisfied in case he makes all of us who do not have sleds so we can escape from him stand outside till we have no noses or toes or fingers any more. Because that would be a mean and shitty thing to do, even worse than what happened to poor Red, and it would prey on your mind and stop you sleeping."

I took a breath; I hadn't finished, but before I could continue, he interrupted me.

"I'll be able to get away from here tomorrow, as soon as Mike hands over the sled. He'll do that because else he won't get his gold. When I said I couldn't trust him, I meant he'd want to get back at me. No reason for him to pick on your lot. Come with me."

He said this in such a throwaway manner I wasn't sure what he meant. "Come with you?"

"Out of here. On the back of my sled. Go south. Isn't that what you want?"

"Yes, but…" I prevaricated. "I thought you didn't like carrying people on the back of your snowmobile?"

"Depends who it is. I liked you holding out on Mike for me, and I liked that you told me you wouldn't have kept it up much longer. You're not a fool, Tori, and you're honest. And not bad-looking either." He scrutinized my face. "You scrub up well."

I paused. "Would there be a…sexual element to this arrangement?"

"A sexual element?" He laughed. "Yes. I can definitely promise you sex would be involved. But I think you might like that too."

He reached out and put an arm round me, and my skin tingled and my stomach fluttered at his touch. I didn't resist when he pulled me to him and his lips nuzzled my neck, nor when his mouth met mine in a lingering kiss. I shut my eyes. His muscles felt hard as he held me to him. His face tasted of salt and he smelled good – sweaty, but good. His fingers found the zip tag on my top under my sweater and I pulled away.

"I'll think about it." My voice sounded husky, my heart was pounding. After a year of drought, my body was waking up and flowering like a desert after rain. David came into my mind, as insubstantial as a ghost, as far away as a friend from childhood.

Morgan murmured, "D'you have to start thinking about it right now? Can it wait?"

"No. That wouldn't help me think." I got up and moved away.

CHAPTER 15

Dig two graves

I fell asleep ten seconds after my head hit the pillow. It had been a long day. In the small hours I woke to the sound of the wind howling round the building, and snow spattering intermittently on the windows. I've never got used to how black the nights are now. For most of my life, the streetlights' orange glare meant it was never completely dark; awake at night, I could see well enough to go to the bathroom without turning on a light. These days, unless a full moon shines, the blackness is absolute.

I lay rigid, eyes open seeing nothing, heart beating fast, listening for sounds of people creeping about and trying to force an entry, hating being a sitting target. Imagining how much safer I'd feel if Morgan was lying beside me, I was tempted to light a candle and go and fetch him. He wouldn't mind being woken; I was certain he'd make the move with enthusiasm, and then proceed to take my mind off my fears. That idea, and the memory of kissing him, made my heart beat in a much more agreeable way… But I hadn't decided whether to travel south on his sled, and didn't want to sleep with him then say goodbye, leaving me an emotional mess, yearning for him as well as David. And after all, he was only a few metres away over on the sofa if anyone did break in. He hardly stirred, either lacking imagination or confident in his theory that nothing would happen yet.

His proposition ran through my mind. It would be a gigantic leap into the unknown; not just because I didn't know Morgan well, but because no one knew what was happening where the ice stopped, or where that was – the Mediterranean, North Africa? It could be full of warring factions mowing each other down with machine guns. But at least it wouldn't be under twenty metres of snow… I tried to imagine what it would be like to travel south on the back of his snowmobile, camping in abandoned buildings on the way. The journey would be dangerous – we might die slowly of cold or hunger if anything went wrong, if the snowmobile broke down, for instance, or we ran out of supplies. How was he planning to cross the Channel? Would it be frozen over, or would we need a boat? I realized I no longer believed David might come to find me. I had to accept he was dead, and leave him out of my plans. I had a cautious faith in Morgan; it seemed to me, little as I knew him, that beneath a guarded, sometimes churlish exterior he had a basic decency one could rely on. And God knows I found him attractive.

I got up early and made breakfast, yawning. Morgan joined me. He didn't say anything about the night before. I brooded about how ineffectual I'd been in my brief struggle with Mike and Big Mac; how I'd hated being held, unable to move let alone get away. Realistically, I'd never defeat a cage fighter, but I hadn't even left a mark on either of them. We sat side by side, spooning porridge silently until I said,

"Can you teach me some self-defence moves?"

He gave me a sidelong look and smiled. "After breakfast."

We did a warm-up session first which left me sweaty and panting and wondering if I'd have the energy to learn to fight. Morgan was cool and breathing normally.

"I'm not as fit as I thought I was."

"You're using different muscles, that's all. You'll get used to it. Okay. Surprise, speed and ruthlessness. Remember when you're up against someone who's bigger and heavier than you your main weapon is surprise, and you can only surprise him once. So make the most of it. You need to hit him as fast and hard as you can in a vulnerable area, and don't worry about hurting him badly – that's the idea. You want to disable him. Never pull your punches, try to hit right through him. Commit to the move. I'm teaching you to fight dirty, and the only rule is to win."

Morgan stood facing me. Snow whirled past the windows.

"Let's do some basic moves in slow motion. I go to grab you." His right hand came towards my left arm. "You raise your left to knock my hand out of the way, and chop the side of your right hand against the side of my neck, carry through, bend your arm and hit me in the face with your elbow coming back."

He made me practise until he was satisfied, then moved on to what to do if someone grabbed my hand – you twist out of it and get them in a wrist lock – and also showed me how to avoid being grabbed in the first place.

"You're doing well. Intelligence gives you an edge in MMA. A journalist once said it's like chess for the abnormally tough. Oh, there's one low trick you can try if a cage fighter's got you in a lock on the floor – tap out. He's so used to it in training, he might just release you from force of habit, then you can hit him and run away."

He moved on to thumb strikes, showing me the location of the most vulnerable points. He was a surprisingly good teacher, and I told him so. Without mentioning my surprise, naturally.

"To get a Jiu-Jitsu black belt you have to teach."

"How did you get into it?"

"I went to a crap school where I got picked on. I used to bunk off most of the time. Then I came across a free Jitsu class for kids, and thought if I joined I could beat them all up."

"Did you?"

"Just one of them. Kyle Jackson. I got excluded for that. Worth it, though. When I went back they left me alone."

I wanted to ask why his parents hadn't helped, but didn't like to. I suddenly felt curious about his past. "But you kept it up."

"I'd got into it by then. I liked the discipline – it was the only place I did what I was told. When I got older I did some Muay Thai, because Jitsu's purely defensive, and that got me into MMA. Try that last move again."

We'd just about finished when a figure at the window indistinct in the falling snow made me jump. It was only Archie. Before he even stepped over the threshold he said, "Are you all right, Tori? Greg's been round and he told me Mike made you both stand outside without a jacket." He sounded shocked. "I came straight over."

"I'm fine. It was scary at the time, though. I was pleased when Morgan turned up."

Morgan nodded at Archie, put his sweater back on and went and fed wood into the stove.

"Thank goodness he was here." Archie lowered his hood,

took off his spectacles and cleaned the snow off them, peering anxiously at me. "Nina didn't believe Greg, she said there must be some misunderstanding, Mike wouldn't do such a thing."

"I know he didn't seem like that last night. But when he's not turning on the charm, he's a psychopath."

"He can't treat people the way he treated you. It's appalling. As a practising Christian, he must see he's wrong."

Over by the stove, Morgan snorted. "He told you he was a Christian? First I've heard of it. He's about as Christian as Genghis Khan."

"Dear me." Archie's mouth straightened into a firm line. "I'm on my way to speak to him. I wanted to call here first in case there'd been some mix-up."

I had to make him see this was a really bad idea. "Ooh, I wouldn't do that, Archie. It wouldn't do any good, and he might get nasty with you."

The stove lid clanged down. Morgan came towards us. "He doesn't like being told he's wrong. He'd chew you up and spit you out. Or rather, get Mac to."

"Nonetheless, someone needs to tell him."

I said, "He's probably going today. Morgan thinks he will. No one got hurt. Honestly, I'd leave it."

Archie lined his glasses up at me, concerned. "If you say so, Tori." His expression was dubious.

At that moment there was a roar of engines and we got up to look. The noise got louder, then all six snowmobiles flashed past the window in a spray of snow.

"There, you've missed him now anyway. Have a cup of tea instead."

"I'd love a cup of tea." He put his jacket by the stove. "I don't

143

like you being so near him. What a blessing Morgan's here to protect you. Oh, Greg asked me to tell you he wouldn't call in today. I think he was afraid of bumping into Mike."

I made tea and Archie sat with us and drank it, talking about the situation. Reading between the lines, Nina had thought Archie's visit unnecessary. She had totally fallen under Mike's spell and wouldn't hear a word against him, dismissing what Greg had told her, saying he must have got it wrong. Before he left, Archie said to me, "Do take care. If there's anything I can do, just ask."

He plodded off through the soft fresh snow, turning to wave. Waving back I said, "He's such a nice man. Brave, too, being prepared to tell Mike off."

"So the vicar fancies you."

I turned to stare at him. "What do you mean? No he doesn't. People can be brave and kind without fancying you."

Morgan shrugged.

I said, "He's a married man with principles. And a lot older than me."

"What's that got to do with it?"

"Don't be ridiculous."

I went and chose a book to read and settled on the sofa. Morgan stood at the windows with his binoculars. The snow had almost stopped. Suddenly he said, "They're going to search the Gherkin."

I got up and joined him at the window and took a look. The snowmobiles were lined up outside the window with the missing glass and I could see people moving about. They must have followed his trail from the night before.

"Did you leave the gold there?"

144

"Yes. He'll have a job finding it, though."

"Why? Where did you hide it?"

"I split it into seven lots, plastic bags sellotaped into tight packages, and hid it in different places all over the Gherkin. He's probably looking in spaces big enough to hide a backpack."

"It's an enormous building."

"Yup." He smiled a wicked smile. "They've got no chance. They'll be really pissed off by evening."

Morgan spent most of the day at the window. While he was sitting there, he wrote out a list of where to find six of the bags of gold and the ACE. An hour before sunset, we heard the snowmobiles return. Ten minutes later Big Mac appeared outside my balcony on a black and red Polaris pulling a trailer – a proper one, not a car roof box. Morgan let him in, and he silently handed over keys and a plastic bag. He barely glanced at me. Morgan peered inside the bag and put it on the counter, went outside and started the engine, turned it off, came back and sat down.

"Okay."

After an expectant pause, Mac said, "Mike wants the location of the ACE and the gold."

"He won't go now it's getting dark. He can have it tomorrow as he's leaving."

"He'll no be happy."

"Tough shit. I told him the deal. Call for it when you're ready to go."

Mac left. He didn't look happy either. When he'd gone, Morgan said, "That's capitulation."

"So why make him wait?"

145

"Because I can."

"I'm not sure it's a good idea to rub his nose in it."

"I doubt it makes any difference." He smiled. "If you want a practical reason, I don't want him sabotaging the Polaris before he goes. It's a pity I can't bring it inside." He looked fondly at the machine. "It's nice to have it back."

"Why did you take the ACE, then, instead?"

"Because it was Mike's."

The evening passed slowly. Given the hostility between the two men I felt on edge, waiting for something to happen, and Morgan had a watchful air. I suggested playing cards, but he didn't want to, so I read. He paced about or sat by the windows. We went to bed early. I slept well, so I don't know if he did.

The following morning we'd got up and had breakfast when we heard the whine and judder of engines. Five snowmobiles stopped a hundred yards away. Four of them towed trailers and one had two passengers. Big Mac detached himself from the group and walked across the snow to my balcony, climbed over the railing and came in.

"We're headed south," he said.

Morgan handed him the sheet of paper. Mac read it slowly, his frown deepening. He got to the end and looked up. "The ACE isnae working? And you buried it so we'll have to dig it out?" He shook his head. "Mike'll no be happy about this."

"You keep saying that, like I give a fuck."

Mac gave him a dark look before he left. "Maybe you should."

We sat side by side watching them for a bit through our binoculars. The sun shone so we had a clear view. It seemed to take an age. The sleds parked at the Gherkin, then four people walked round the building out of sight, presumably to disinter the ACE. How would Eddie be managing with his smashed nose? It must be painful, but at least he'd had BJ who would know what to do about it. The other two, whom I guessed to be Mike and Serena, went inside through the broken window on the trail of the gold. You'd think with all that glass we'd have been able to see them now and again, but the building was too vast and shiny and far away.

"Where did you hide it?"

"I put most of the packages in office drawers in the middle of big areas full of desks." He replied absently, fiddling with his focusing wheel. "I wrote details of how many paces north etcetera. He's only got to follow my instructions. One's right at the top in a microwave behind the bar, twenty-eight storeys up – that'll give him some exercise, if he didn't get enough yesterday. Amazing view from up there. Another's below the reception desk at ground level in the dark with the rats. Serena'll like that." There was satisfaction in his voice.

"Don't you have any sympathy for them? After all, you were with them for a year, most of them. I'd have expected you to be more friendly."

"Mike believed in divide and rule. He didn't want us to get on too well. He used to say, 'You have to earn your place on my team. That sled is yours as long as I say it is, it's not yours by right. Underperform and I'll leave you behind.' Each sled's got two keys, and Mike keeps all the spares on his keyring. When he invited BJ to join us, everyone was waiting to see who'd be dumped. He took his time telling us, he wanted to keep us unsure, competing with each other. That doesn't make you feel friendly."

Morgan put his binoculars down. "They'll be a while." He pulled his sweater over his head. "Come on. While we're waiting I'll carry on turning you into a lean mean fighting machine."

It was nearly lunchtime before Mike's lot left. Whenever we took a breather we checked up on what they were doing, so we saw when they brought the ACE round the building and worked on the engine. At last the whole group mounted the sleds and disappeared in a flurry of snow, heading away from us towards the south. I'd thought Mike might call at Nina's to say goodbye; the fact that he didn't bother made me hope he had no intention of coming back.

Morgan put down his binoculars. "I'll leave tomorrow morning. You've got till tonight to decide to come with me."

"*Whether* to come with you."

"That's what I said."

After lunch Morgan took me behind him on the Polaris to collect the last package of gold and his belongings. The passenger seat had a backrest and handles at the side, so I didn't have to cling on to him. I loved whizzing across the snow after a year of trudging through the damn stuff. Morgan picked up on my excitement. He dropped off the trailer at the Gherkin and we went down to Tower Bridge and east to the unbroken expanse of snow that shows where the Thames lies frozen. To the west I could see the Houses of Parliament and the London Eye.

"No worries here about catching on buried buildings," he shouted over his shoulder, accelerating. At top speed he turned and curvetted over mounds of snow, carving deep lines over the virgin surface, kicking up a spray just to show off and make me gasp. It was huge fun. I made him promise to take Greg for a ride before he left.

Back at the Gherkin he led me to an executive's office on the third floor above the snowline, and lifted a large dead plant out of its container. Beneath was a sellotaped black Primark bag full of gold. Next we went up to where he had left his things. As soon as we opened the door from the lobby I knew something was wrong from the smell. Morgan's face darkened. We rounded the corner into the coffee-making area where he had camped out. The vile stench of burnt plastic was overwhelming. Someone had piled Morgan's possessions into a big heap, tipped petrol over everything and set it alight. Above, black goo dripped from the blackened ceiling tiles, and a sticky film darkened the glass and every surface. The flames' heat had cracked the windows and buckled the steel counter. At the centre of the burnt-out pile you could make out the remains of the trailer, the generator and tins of food.

I said, "That's just unpleasant. A waste of resources."

Morgan stood looking at the mess for a moment, his eyes stony. But he only said, "Predictable. It's a drag, I'll have to collect everything all over again."

"I'll give you a hand."

Morgan crossed to a conference room on the far side of that floor. Inside was a long wood-veneered table surrounded by chairs. He ducked beneath the table. There was the sound of tape ripping, and he emerged with a plastic bag full of something.

"More gold?" But it couldn't be, they collected the other bags…

"Semtex."

"Where did you get it?"

"Mike's when I was looking for the spare part. I took the lot. I made up blocks of plasticene to the right size and used the same wrappers, so he won't know till he goes to use it. Then he'll notice it's a bit brightly-coloured for Semtex."

He'd have got the plasticene from Argos. I'd helped Gemma make animals with it once or twice. "Lucky for them you didn't leave it with the rest of your stuff."

He shook his head. "Semtex doesn't explode if you burn it, just makes poisonous fumes. You need a blasting cap to detonate it."

We descended flights of glass and steel stairs once more. So now Mike had got his gold again, but lost his Semtex. There was a lot in the bag. Morgan hadn't needed all of it; he'd wanted to wind up Mike. He'd been unable to resist; had learned nothing from the gold episode. I saw with sudden clarity that neither of those two men was ever going to back down or walk away. They hadn't got it in them. I remembered the proverb, *before you embark on a journey of revenge, dig two graves.* I doubted burning Morgan's belongings had made Mike feel he'd got his own back; merely torching a few possessions wasn't enough. I could only hope they'd never meet again. Surely once they were both out of London the chances of encountering each other would be slim. On the way down Morgan hid the gold back where it had come from, being careful not to leave tell-tale traces of compost on the floor or the edge of the plant container. He said it was better not to keep it at my place.

"What did you have, that he burned, I mean?"

"Trailer, generator, tent, sleeping bag, clothes, stores and general supplies. The problem's the generator, it's a bitch losing it. I was lucky finding that one, I'll never find another. The other stuff's straightforward." He glanced at me as we went down the stairs side by side. "It gives you more time to pack and say goodbye to everyone."

"I haven't decided if I'm coming."

"You've decided. You're just not admitting it yet."

CHAPTER 16

Decisions

I got Morgan to drop me off at Claire's. I told him I'd join him later at the Old Street shops. Paul let me in then went back to installing a stove in the bedroom, aided by Gemma. In the living room, Claire sat on her sofa cradling Toby, her dreamy, contented expression making me think of a Madonna and Child painting. It seemed a shame to interrupt her. I plumped myself down.

"Have a coffee."

"No thanks, I'm not stopping. Claire, I need your advice. Morgan's going south on his snowmobile, and he wants me to go with him. Leave here and get to where there isn't any snow. D'you think I should?"

Claire's gaze left Toby's face to focus on me. "What do *you* think? That's the main thing."

"I don't know him well enough to make a decision. I don't even know his first name."

"You could always ask. Mike didn't seem to think much of him, going by what he said at Nina's. Even before he said all that about stealing his gold and the sled and fighting Eddie."

"He was lying, I think. And Morgan's given him back the gold." I told Claire what had happened after the dinner party.

She listened, concerned. "I'd never have guessed he was like that. He was so charming. Gemma said he was the nicest man she'd ever met."

"But because Mike's horrible doesn't mean Morgan's not. They could be as bad as each other. They were together a long time before they fell out."

"True."

"And I've only known him a week. The real problem is I have to make up my mind in the next day or two. I'm settled here, all set up in the flat with stacks of wood and food and friends. The journey might be dangerous. Anything could happen. And I don't want to leave you lot, you're sort of my family now, and there's Greg…and am I crazy to even think of going with a strange man somewhere unknown?"

"What's your gut feeling about him?"

This was difficult because of the attraction I felt, which got in the way of objective assessment – my body kept interrupting my mind. I didn't want to admit this to Claire. "That he's okay…ish…but I could be wrong. He hasn't said much about his past, and what he *has* said is alarming, and he's kind of surly and defensive some of the time. And quite violent, hitting Eddie like that. Unforgiving, too." I expected Claire to be put off by this, was possibly counting on her telling me to exercise caution; so what she said next surprised me.

"Talk to him. But Tori, unless you don't trust him, or you think he'll hit *you*, go. I'll miss you dreadfully, but it's an opportunity that may never come again. We'll look after Greg. If I had the chance to get out of here with Paul and the children I would. My dream is helicopters appearing out of nowhere to take us to safety. I worry about our future. Supposing the snow keeps rising? How will the children manage? And if they do, there's nobody their age for them to fall in love with." Tears were in her eyes. "If I were you, I'd go in a heartbeat."

I didn't linger. I was desperate to get to Morgan, irrationally afraid if I delayed it would be too late and he might vanish. I walked fast then ran through the snow towards him.

He hadn't lit the tea lights on the stairs, but I had my torch. I hurried through the dank darkness possessed by a sense of urgency. He wasn't in the Co-op. I went next door to Argos, beyond the counter and through the swing doors. My heart jumped at the sight of a dim light and movement in the aisles. As I got closer I could see he was sorting through tents. Still panting from the run through the snow, I shone my torch on his face.

"What's your name?"

"Get that light out of my eyes. You know my name."

I directed the torch to one side. "Your first name."

"No one calls me by it. Why d'you want to know?"

"Because I don't know the first thing about you. When were you born?"

He stopped what he was doing and came over to me, standing close. His voice was quiet and intimate in the darkness. "Dominic. Hate that name. The twenty-third of September, 1993. What else do you want to know?"

"What happened to your last girlfriend?"

"SIRCS."

"I'm sorry. Are you a serial killer?"

"No."

I eyed him narrowly. "If you were a serial killer, would you tell me?"

"No. I'd let it come as a surprise."

After a moment I smiled, and he put his arms round me and kissed me. Suddenly it was as if everything had become simple. Going south with Morgan was meant, it was what I had to do, even at the risk of my life. He wasn't David, but he was Morgan. I wasn't sure exactly what my feelings for him were, but I finally admitted they were overwhelming and maybe I should do something about them while I had the chance. I'd made up my mind.

CHAPTER 17

Interlude

Back at Bézier I started to top up the stove. Morgan held me and kissed my neck, insistent, getting in the way. He unzipped my jacket, muttering, "Leave that. It can wait."

"It'll go out. We'll freeze."

"I'll do it then. You get into bed."

I drew the curtains to shut out the grey light and the falling snow, double-checked I'd locked the door, and lit the bedside lantern. The silence was absolute. I undressed fast and got into bed, wondering if I was insane. The sheet and duvet against my naked skin felt strange; I'm used to wearing layers even in bed, curled like a cocoon inside my sleeping bag. Now I lay propped on one elbow with the covers up to my chin, chilly, gripped with doubt and anticipation, watching Morgan in the shifting candle light. He closed the stove lid and came towards me, his eyes grave under level brows, frowning slightly, intent. I couldn't stop staring at him. He stripped, dropping his clothes on the floor, till he wore only the chain with dog tags. All his muscles were as impressive as the ones I'd already seen. The black tattoo contrasted with winter-pale skin. He'd got just the right amount of chest hair. I don't like men with bald or simian chests. He slid into bed beside me and pulled me close.

"Come here."

I shivered. "Your hands are icy."

"So are your feet, but I'm not complaining."

I stared into this stranger's eyes, so alarmingly close, then at his mouth, just beginning to smile. His stubbly beard was a shade darker than his unkempt hair. He had an L-shaped scar on his forehead I'd never noticed before. His skin against mine made me shake, but not with cold. His finger tips brushed my face. That felt good – Morgan felt good. I relaxed into his arms and ran my hand down his muscled side, lightly over the knife cut scab, round his waist and up the cleft of his backbone. He made a noise somewhere between a sigh and a groan and his mouth met mine. My toes were warming up. I was beginning to think this had been one of my better ideas after all.

Some while later I insisted on making Morgan tea, wearing his sweater over my pyjama trousers. We sat up in bed leaning against each other and sipping. He was nice to lean on, like a sun-warmed boulder. Though entirely sober, I felt happy and irresponsible and a bit drunk. I was seized by a sudden curiosity.

"What did you do before you worked for Mike?"

"I went in the army at seventeen. Didn't like it much, too regimented. No pun intended. Casual labouring jobs after that."

I reached for his army dog tags, one on a long chain, the other attached to it on a short one; steel with black rubber rims. Both said,

O POS 892058172 MORGAN D ND

"ND?"

"Non denomination. Though it's true what they say, there's no such thing as an atheist in a foxhole."

"Why d'you still wear it?"

"I got superstitious after a couple of lucky escapes."

I made him tell me about them. Then, "What would you have done if the world had gone on?"

"Not MMA for much longer. The businessmen get rich, not the fighters. I was saving for a sailing cruiser. I wanted to go round the world, see all the places off the beaten track. I'd nearly saved enough, I was starting to look at boats. If it had all happened a month or two later, I'd have been in the Mediterranean. How about you?"

"Much tamer. I worked as a copywriter for a voucher firm. You know, they do special deals to offer dinners out, spa days and tooth whitening half price." It had been my first job; I'd enjoyed it. "Talking of boats, how are we going to cross the Channel?"

"I think it may be frozen by now. It's only twenty-one miles from Dover to Calais, and it's been sub-zero temperatures for a year."

"Supposing it's not?"

"Then we'll think of something else. The Channel Tunnel, maybe."

"Right." I didn't ask how we'd get a snowmobile through the tunnel. I decided not to worry about our two thousand mile journey, but take it one step at a time. Morgan said we should leave as soon as possible. He didn't say *because Mike might come back to get me*, but that's what he meant. A shadow fell over my happiness. I suggested we started sorting out what we were taking from my stores that same evening. He agreed.

Going through my supplies I was amazed how much was there. I couldn't quite believe that in a day or two I'd be out of the home that had been mine for the last year, and never see it again; never use the food, firewood and clothes I'd put so much effort into collecting. I've always been nagged by the anxious feeling that my stockpile needed building up for fear of illness or some other disaster; however much I had, it never seemed enough. Now I realized I'd got plenty for one person to live on for a year or more, and almost all of it would be left behind, like my friends here. I felt suddenly overwhelmed by nostalgia for the life I'd soon be leaving; my head drooped and I stood motionless, on the verge of tears.

"Hey, what's up?"

Morgan came over to me. I swivelled and buried my face in his chest, sniffing. "I don't know. It's the thought of leaving everything, I suppose."

He stroked my hair. "You're tired. You'll be fine once we're on the move."

"Suppose we can't find a generator? What then?"

"We can manage without if we get the right kit. Arctic expeditions do – did. Goose down sleeping bags and high tech clothing, an extra gas stove for if one fails. We'll get up early tomorrow and do a systematic search. It'll be okay."

His arms were comforting. I'd forgotten how nice it is to be hugged by another human. After all, the others could use up what I left; nothing would be wasted. With luck we'd be on our way the next day. Morgan said, "We're nearly finished. Let's take a break. Food and drink, that's what you need. That'll cheer you up. Then I'm going to move the sled somewhere out of view."

I looked up at him.

"Just in case," he said.

CHAPTER 18

Visitor

When I woke the next morning, I was alone. Sunlight shone between a crack in the curtains. A note by the bed read,

Didn't want to wake you. Gone to get petrol.
Morgan

I lay and thought about Morgan for a bit, then stretched and got up, skirting the neat pile of all the stuff we'd chosen last night to take with us. He had filled the stove before leaving – I must have been deeply asleep for his moving about not to have roused me. I washed and dressed, then put another pan of water on to the stove top and got out the porridge. Something outside the window caught my eye. Dark against the brilliant sunlit snow, a man, skiing towards me. A new arrival; no one I knew had skis. As I stared, the tall figure looked more and more familiar. My heartbeat accelerated. He swerved to a halt by my balcony, bent to release the skis, picked them up and climbed over the rail, clumsy in shiny red ski boots. I fumbled to open the door, stumbled forwards and wrapped my arms around him as tight as I could, my eyes filling at the feel of his skinny frame through the padded jacket. David had come to find me at last. He propped his skis against the railing so he could hold me.

"I thought you were dead!"

He patted me. "I thought you were dead too, Piglet. This is unbelievable." I wanted to cling to him forever. Morgan – I'd have to tell him I couldn't go with him. After a minute David pulled away and held me by my shoulders, looking down into my eyes. I'd forgotten his were that particular shade of greenish khaki. I could have gazed for an eternity. He said, "We'll freeze. Let's go inside."

I led the way. He laid his skis on the floor and sat on a stool, one leg swinging, looking round the flat. "You're nicely set up here. Very organized." I grasped his hand. He smiled and said, "It's so good to see you. You look just the same. You haven't changed a bit."

He had always had soft hands; they still were, unlike mine which were now hard, with calluses. Or Morgan's hands... I rubbed his knuckles against my cheek, unable to stop gazing at his face. "You're thinner. I missed you so much...I've imagined you turning up like this, but never really thought you would." With my free hand I knuckled the tears from my eyes. "Did your parents get away?" He shook his head. "I'm sorry. Nor did my mother. Where were you all this time?"

"For the last year I've been living in a sort of commune – there's over sixty of us – in Strata, at the Elephant and Castle."

"The Elephant and Castle?" I stared at him. "But that's only three miles away!"

"If I'd known you were here I'd have come before."

Three miles was a long way walking through the snow. That's why our group hadn't made contact with any others. "When did you get skis?"

"Six months or so ago."

Six months. On skis, he could easily have visited every nearby settlement, if he'd been determined to find me. A lump formed in my throat. For a moment I couldn't speak. I dropped his hand, and he let me.

As if excusing himself he said, "I fractured my fifth metatarsal, I couldn't walk. I did come, as soon as I got better and got the skis. Your flat was under the snow. I thought you'd died or been evacuated."

"You could have asked around, tried all the places with smoke. I wasn't far away. Anyone here would have told you where I was." My old flat was half a mile from Bézier – he'd been so close. All that grief he could have saved me... I'd prayed for David to be alive, I'd longed to see him again, and now I had, my main emotion was pain that he'd given up on me so easily – with, I had to acknowledge, a side helping of resentment. I said, "If you'd looked, you'd have found me. You didn't bother."

"Tori, don't be like that."

"Have you *any idea* how miserable I was over you?"

"I was miserable too." He sounded defensive. This wasn't how I'd imagined our reunion, or how it was supposed to be. This was the man I loved. It was all going wrong. He said, "I came as soon as I knew you were here."

"How did you find out?"

"A group of people turned up yesterday. They fetched me because one of the men had a broken nose – quite a bad one, with displacement and bleeding that wouldn't stop. He was having trouble breathing."

"Eddie. Did you meet Mike?"

"Yes."

"He's a psycho."

162

David frowned. "He didn't strike me as a psychopath. He came across as a genuinely nice guy, anxious about Eddie, and very pleased to get a doctor to him."

"Okay, I should have said, he's a plausible psycho. Trust me on this."

He looked unconvinced. David has a good brain, and is confident about its capacities; he tends to believe his own observations where they conflict with other people's experience. I'd forgotten how annoying this could be.

He said, "What about the man who smashed Eddie's nose, is he still here?"

"Morgan. Yes."

"Seems to me he's the one who's a psycho, if anyone is. I had quite a long talk with Mike. He seemed eminently sane and normal to me. Caring, even. His main concern is to protect the little group of people he's trying to get away from this mess."

"In other words, he turned on the charm and you fell for it."

"Give me some credit, Tori, I'm not a complete idiot."

"I'm not saying you are, just that he fooled you."

"Have you considered, perhaps it's you who's got him wrong? He offered me one of the snowmobiles to go south with him. He said he'd like to have a doctor along. It's a fantastic opportunity. I'm almost sure I'll accept."

If Mike was offering him a passage south, then David had every reason to want to think well of him. Maybe it *was* a fantastic opportunity – if Mike didn't dump him en route. "Did he tell you where I was?"

"Your name didn't crop up. His girlfriend told me later while she and Mike were having a drink with me. She got quite chatty and mentioned you. So of course I came as soon as I could get away."

"That was big of you." *Now I'm channelling Morgan.*

He flushed. "I came, didn't I? Even though I got into a row with Katie over it."

"Katie? Who the fuck's Katie?"

"You never used to swear." He was being evasive.

"Maybe I've changed in the last year. Who is she?"

"She looked after me when I turned up with my fractured foot."

"And that gives her the right to tell you what to do?"

"She…she's my girlfriend. I'm sorry."

"Fine." I took a deep breath. I couldn't see how to right this nightmare conversation, everything was changing too fast. It was like watching a film on fast-forward, or being a passenger in a brakeless car, waiting for the crash as it careered along, engine screeching and juddering.

He said, "Try to understand. I was ill, she was nursing me, it just happened. Then she got pregnant…"

"So you have a pregnant girlfriend." Next he'd be telling me he'd acquired a dog, a Volvo and a mortgage.

"No, she had the baby end of March. A little girl. She's nearly two months." He smiled fondly. "We called her Tessa. I wish I had a photo here to show you, she's a sweetheart."

So he'd got it together with Katie within weeks of losing track of me, and now they were a happy family unit. In the same period, all I'd done on the relationship front was grieve for him. While I'd been crying over him on his birthday, he no doubt had been celebrating with Katie. I could hardly blame him for having a girlfriend when I'd slept with Morgan, but at least I'd waited a year before being unfaithful. And why on earth would he imagine I'd want to see photos of his child by my replacement? How crass can you get? Indignation rendered me speechless. As the silence lengthened David began to look uneasy. I'd forgotten how we used to argue – maybe it was coming back to him too.

I was still struggling to find adequate words when there was the sound of an engine. The Polaris hove into view, did a flashy U-turn in a fountain of snow, and stopped by my balcony in a sudden silence. Morgan climbed over the rail and walked in, taking off his dark glasses. He looked from me to David and back again. I wouldn't have said he was one of the world's most sensitive souls, but the tension in the room was so palpable you could trip over it.

I said, "This is David. Morgan."

I could see Morgan thinking back to locate where he'd heard that name; the flicker in his eyes as he registered who David was. He gave him an assessing glance, said hi, then deliberately came to my side, put his arm round me and kissed my cheek. I got a whiff of petrol from his clothes. "What's for breakfast?"

"Porridge." David's expression was one of shocked surmise, even anger, I was gratified to see. I wanted to tell him to leave, but maybe I'd regret it when my own anger had died. I strove to sound calm and friendly. "D'you want some?"

He dragged his gaze from Morgan and said, "No, I'd better be off. Can I just have a private word with you before I go?"

I shrugged. "Okay." I slung on my jacket and went with him to the balcony. We stood facing each other. "What?"

His voice was low and concerned. "Are you…involved with that man?"

"Yes. Not that it's any of your business."

"Are you sure you know what you're doing? Mike told me

about him. He said he was a cage fighter with a violent temper, untrustworthy, a thief."

I glared at him. "Here's an idea. Why don't you run your life, and leave me to run mine?"

"I don't want to see you get hurt."

That was rich, considering how he'd just hurt me. "Do you know, I feel the same about you. Shall I come and vet Katie for you?"

His face changed. "You've made your point, Tori. I'm sorry it had to end like this. Be seeing you."

"Bye." I stomped inside and joined Morgan. I watched David fix his skis, put on his goggles, turn and head south, my feelings a maelstrom. He didn't look back. His figure diminished in the distance.

Morgan said, "Tell me what happened, then."

I told him, my voice trembling with indignation. Near the end, when I got to David's two month-old baby Tessa and him wishing he had a photo to show me, Morgan turned away. This seemed a bit odd when I was talking to him – then I noticed his shoulders shaking. He was trying not to laugh. All at once it struck me as hilarious too, in kind of a heart-breaking way. I wailed, "I waited a year for him!"

"How long would you wait for me?"

"Ooh, a week at least."

"Hey! I'd give you a fortnight."

He hugged me. Morgan was good at hugs, perhaps because he was so large and solid; with his arms around me everything seemed a bit better. He made me feel safe.

CHAPTER 19

Shopping with Semtex

Thumbing through an old copy of Yellow Pages as he ate, Morgan located a sports shop opposite Harrods which he thought would have a block of flats above it. We hoped to collect everything we needed from one place. After breakfast he packed a couple of shovels and two backpacks in the Polaris's trailer, then turned to me.

"I'll show you how to drive it. Get on." I swung my leg over the saddle. He sat behind, holding me so he could look over my shoulder. "Feet in those pockets. Pull up the kill switch – the red button – and turn the key. Now pull the start cord here." The engine started. "Okay, that's the brake on the left, throttle on the right. Release the brake and gun the throttle. Gently." The machine leaped forward. "Don't go too fast at first, watch out for obstacles and take it easy turning till you get the feel for it. Head west southwest."

Snowmobiles have a compass on the dashboard, handy when most of the streets have vanished under snow. I drove carefully, wanting to do it right, keeping an eye on the direction and the snow surface. I couldn't stop beaming, partly because it was such fun, rushing through the snow with Morgan's arms round me, and partly because showing me how to work the sled meant he trusted me not to steal it, and he was not a man who trusted easily. I was warming to him. I'd thought he was not my type; noted that others might think him hot while not admitting I did. I'd changed my mind. Hot? The guy was scorching. I'd also assumed anyone with those muscles, a professional fighter, wouldn't have much of a brain. But though he'd been to a crap school and got hardly any qualifications, I was beginning to realize Morgan was clever as well as stoical and persistent. He was the sort of man you could respect.

Another bonus: in his company I didn't have leisure to brood. Had David turned up in pre-Morgan days, after he left I'd have spent weeks or months moping, dwelling on every aspect of our relationship, wondering whether our/my love had ever been real or merely a delusion, going over and over the whole sorry business. With Morgan close to me in bed or out, full of plans and enterprises, David didn't enter my mind for hours at a stretch.

We flew across London straight as a migrating bird, and in less than ten minutes saw Harrods' distinctive ornate pinky-beige dome emerging from the snow, with a row of flagpoles along the roof, their flags still bravely fluttering. You could make out the position of the Brompton Road since many of the buildings stuck out a few metres. Not far beyond, the rooftops gave way to a featureless expanse; the location of Kensington Gardens. It pained me to think of all the trees frozen beneath that bland sterile surface. Morgan told me to slow the sled, looking about.

"It's across from the front of Harrods, northwest, that end rather than this."

We went a little further, and I stopped beside a rooftop with emergency steel ladders, the tops of lifts and other random features sticking into the air, all with a topping of snow. Morgan dragged the sled next to the building to make it inconspicuous, though there was no sign of human activity, then smashed the nearest window with a hammer and knocked out all the glass. He gave me a backpack and took the other himself.

"What's in here?"

"Snacks, water, bin bags, crowbar, hammer, earplugs, goggles and a head torch. Might as well put the torch on now."

"Where did you get all this kit?"

"Argos and the chemist this morning."

"Aren't we taking the shovels?"

"The snow at the bottom will be packed solid. We're going through the walls."

I was relieved – I remembered digging out the corridors from shop to shop in Old Street, and it had been hard labour, even with seven of us taking turns. I climbed into the building after Morgan, and we made our way downwards, using minimum force to lever open any doors that barred our way. A year of practice had made me expert at this. The head torches were handy as light levels diminished the further we got, and I couldn't think why it hadn't occurred to me to get hold of one before.

Morgan had brought a compass. Even so, it was difficult to retain a sense of direction in the dark. I suggested leaving a trail to stop us getting lost on the way back. We broke into one of the flats and searched among the lavish furnishings till we found a Saturday Telegraph. We tore the newspaper into strips and placed one every few metres as we went. This turned out to be sensible; we took a wrong turning several times and had to backtrack. The long corridors were claustrophobic, but Morgan's presence made it a million times better than being there on my own. Still, I was thankful when we finally arrived at the ground floor and found ourselves in the spacious lobby and main entrance in Brompton Road. I shone my hand torch around. Compacted snow pressed against large windows and glass doors, their brass fittings dull with a year's neglect. The floor was patterned marble, and big vases of dead flowers stood in alcoves picked out with gold leaf.

"I think it's to our right. Number 92."

With a cold chisel and hammer Morgan chipped a small hole in the middle of a recessed wall. The noise echoed in the tomb-like silence. He got a plastic-wrapped slab from his backpack, longer and slimmer than a brick, unwrapped the end and broke off a few centimetres of what looked like cream-coloured plasticene, then pressed it into the space. I gazed in fascination as he attached a narrow metal tube, which he told me was a blasting cap. For a moment I glimpsed him as the soldier he had once been. He glanced up.

"Put your earplugs in, goggles on, and stand round that corner."

Waiting on my own in the cold and dark, I heard the faint scratch of a match. Morgan appeared, and drew me further away. We stood for a couple of minutes, and I wondered what happened if the charge failed to go off. They tell you not to go back to check a firework that fails to ignite, and the possibilities for sudden death were much greater with Semtex. I'd just started to ask Morgan, when there was a massive whoomph and flash of light. The floor vibrated and the air was thick with dust and smoke. I pulled my scarf over my face to avoid breathing it in. Once we could see, we went back to the hall, which now resembled a war zone. There was an irregular breach in the wall with darkness beyond. Morgan peered into the hole and laughed.

"It's a jeweller's."

I helped him jemmy out bricks and debris, and when the gap was big enough climbed in after him. The shop was small, lined with showcases, their glass mostly shattered from the blast. Thick dust and grit lay everywhere. Morgan strolled to the front door of the shop, bent and picked up a handful of letters and riffled through them.

"88. The shop we want should be two along. Unless we're going the wrong way." He got out his tools. "Might as well collect the stuff from the cases. Don't cut yourself."

I looked behind the counter and found chichi carrier bags. I selected the largest, knocked the glass shards from the nearest showcase and transferred the contents gingerly, being careful not to slice my fingers. The jewellery wasn't my taste; lots of over-elaborate diamond and stone-set rings and necklaces. Quite big diamonds, some of them, sparkling in the torchlight. (Though beautiful, diamonds are not rare or intrinsically valuable; their costliness is a result of clever advertising and manipulation of the market by De Beers.) I'd moved on to the second case when Morgan told me to climb back to the hallway with him. We retreated to our former corner till the explosion, waited and returned as before and climbed into the next shop, a men's outfitters. There were no letters in this one, so we rooted around in the office at the back of the shop until I found an address on an invoice.

"90 Brompton Road."

Morgan smiled, teeth glinting white in the dark, face smudged with grime. I guessed mine was too. He raised his thumb. "We're so good."

I was enjoying myself. I liked working with Morgan. Beyond the next wall was the sports shop we were after. Together we systematically sorted through all the stock choosing what to take, dumping our selection in a heap on the floor. We went for quality, the most expensive items. I had not realized it was possible for a sleeping bag to cost £460, but it is if the filling is grey goose down and the lowest comfort level minus 26°C. We took one each. I let Morgan choose, because of my total lack of camping experience. He selected a Hilleberg Nallo 2GT, a top of the range two-man tent. I tentatively suggested a bigger one might be better, but he said smaller would be warmer as well as lighter. He picked out two primus stoves, cases of gas canisters and various other camping equipment. We moved on to clothing; base layers, ski wear, socks, balaclavas and gloves, selecting only the best. When we were done we loaded everything into four bin bags and made two trips to bring them to the surface, following the strips of newspaper. Before we left with the last load, we cleaned out the jewellery showcases.

"Like old times," Morgan said.

CHAPTER 20

Saying goodbye

We got back to Bézier when it was past tea time and had lunch. It was getting late to set off that day, so Morgan said he'd pack the trailer while I went round on the sled to say goodbye to my friends. Knowing it was a final farewell – that in all likelihood I'd never see any of them again – made my visits poignant. Charlie and Sam were fine – we made a few silly jokes and Sam said to send them a postcard. Nina too, but then we'd never been close. She was a little reserved with me, I thought, and she didn't mention either Mike or Morgan.

She said briskly, "It's really more au revoir, we'll probably meet again when things are stable enough in the south for helicopters to be sent to pick us up."

Archie said little, but enveloped me in a silent bear hug, which is not his style. "God will be with you on the journey. I'll pray for your safety."

Claire was upbeat, assuring me in an unsteady voice she'd manage without me just fine, she'd always thought Morgan and I would make a good couple, she'd think of me having a terrific time in a warm climate. I told her how sorry I was that I'd miss Toby's christening, and not be his godmother. She said she'd think of me as his godmother. Gemma gave me a card she'd drawn with a picture of me and Morgan under a yellow smiley sun with a cat beneath a tree; and a small cardboard box that rattled. "It's my tooth."

"Ah Gemma, your favourite tooth! How lovely to have a little bit of you to take with me."

As the sled moved off I looked back. Claire, Paul and Gemma stood together on their balcony watching me go and waving like mad, Claire making Toby's little mittened hand wave goodbye, tears shining on her cheeks.

I left Greg till last. I carried my spider plant to its new home in his flat, and took him on the back of the sled for a ride, down to the Thames where Morgan had taken me. Snow began to fall as we returned, making me worry about how we'd leave the next day if it continued. When we got back to Greg's I gave him a fancy silver treasure box looted from the jewellers which I'd filled with Smarties. I'd written him a note and put it underneath the Smarties for him to find later:

Greg,
Thank you for protecting me.
Miss you,
Tori
X

He got Rosie out so I could say goodbye to her too. I said, "Help yourself to anything of mine from the flat, won't you?"

"I think I'd rather leave it, so it's the same and sometimes I can visit and pretend you're still here, only gone out foraging."

"Just things from my store rooms, then…" I was going to burst into tears any minute. I had to go. I smiled resolutely. "I shall think about you all a lot. Take care of yourself, won't you?"

"Wave when you go tomorrow. I'll be watching, I'll wave

back."

Tears were streaming down my face on the short trip to my flat. What with that and the snow I could hardly see where I was going, but I made it home all right. Morgan had finished loading the trailer. He took one look at me and gave me a hug.

"I'm not usually like this," I said. "Before the snow I hardly cried at all, honestly. Gemma gave me her tooth."

"Ri-i-ight…I don't get what it is with you lot and teeth. Still think you're all weird." His lips brushed my cheek, his breath warm on my neck.

"I'm not weird!"

"You're weird in kind of a nice way. Come with me to hide the sled. Take your mind off it."

Morgan hooked up the trailer and we took it to its hiding place in a building site, the shell of a block of flats next to a crane to the north of the shops. There were no walls, making it easy to lift the sled and trailer inside and round a corner, invisible to someone passing close by. We each took an end of a pallet and dragged it over the tracks to even out the surface. Snow was now falling thickly, blurring our trail.

"D'you think he'll come back before we go?"

"Hope not. I'd leave now but there's a risk of wrecking the sled in the dark with snow falling. It might be an idea not to sleep in your flat tonight."

"Oh…" I could see the sense of this, but I wanted one last night of home comforts. The thought of sleeping in a sleeping bag (even one filled with grey goose down) on an icy floor was not inviting. On the other hand, the thought of four men bent on revenge bursting in while we were asleep had even less appeal. But it turned out not to be necessary; within twenty minutes, the snow was falling so thickly it was a whiteout, with no sign of stopping. We couldn't leave London, and nor could Mike come and get us. We settled for a cosy evening at home, getting to know each other better.

For the next four days, all we could see beyond the windows was white. Snow piled up on the balcony against the glass. The weather was too forbidding even for Greg to venture out doing his rounds; though unable to see my lights, he might guess we wouldn't have left in this weather. You'd have had to be crazy to take out a snowmobile. To my astonishment, Archie appeared late the next morning, practically on his last legs after fighting his way through the blizzard. He said he'd wanted to put his mind at rest that we hadn't set out on our journey in these conditions. He stayed for a meal and I dried his clothes over the stove. Morgan accompanied him back to the Barbican, as he could see I was worried Archie wouldn't make it on his own. On his return he said,

"Nasty out there." He stripped off soaked boots and snow-dampened clothes. "Told you he fancied you – only true love would make a man go out in this vile weather. He just couldn't help himself."

"Huh! I think all he wanted was a break from Nina. Can you imagine being snowed in with her?"

Being home the whole time and feeling no need to conserve my wood stores, we kept the stove fed and the temperature became delightfully warm. Morgan and I spent quite a bit of time in bed. We read or played cards, and talked about what it would be like when we got south, and our pasts before we met; our childhoods. Morgan hadn't known his father, and his mother had brought him up alone in poverty. He had clearly loved her uncritically, but reading between the lines it seemed she'd struggled with too many problems of her own to be much use to him with his. He'd had to fight his own battles from a young age. It made me realize what a secure and privileged childhood I'd had, even though my family wasn't well off.

When he went down to the gym to lift weights, I went with him and sat admiring his physique by candlelight (I'd got used to his muscles and adjusted my ideas of male beauty – by comparison David seemed weedy) or did some weight lifting myself. He continued to teach me to fight.

It was a strange time out of time, cut off from the world. I decided I liked Morgan, a lot.

CHAPTER 21

News of Mike

Four days later, the weather started to improve. Snow still fell, but less heavily. We began to think we'd be able to leave the next morning.

We'd finished eating and dusk was approaching when, faint and ominous, there came the sound of an engine getting louder. We exchanged glances and got to our feet. This could only mean trouble. My heart beat faster and my hands sweated. Morgan blew out the candles and I snuffed the lantern; we went to the windows and strained to see through the blizzard. Outside was fuzzy white, far buildings barely visible. A lone snowmobile came slowly into view, drew in beside the balcony and its passenger got off, peering into my windows.

"It's Serena." I breathed deeply and let my shoulders relax.

Morgan relit the candles while I forced the door open against the piled snow and told her to put my trailer over the sled to keep the snow off. Serena brushed the worst of the weather from her clothes and came inside, looking agitated and shaky. I put her jacket by the stove.

"Are you all right?"

"More or less, thanks. I've been going round in circles for ages, I thought I'd run out of petrol and never get here, die of hypothermia – scary, I was beginning to panic. I totally lost my bearings and my goggles kept getting snowed up and I couldn't see the buildings to work out where I was. I thought the snow wasn't too bad, but it's still practically a whiteout."

Morgan said, "Are you on your own?" She nodded. "Any chance of you being followed?"

"I sneaked out. Mike thinks I'm with Jen, she's a woman we met. I can't stop long, I want to get back before he misses me."

"Coffee?"

"I'd rather have wine." I opened a bottle of Chardonnay and slopped it into glasses and we all sat round the counter. There was a pause while we waited for her to tell us why she had come. Possibly she wanted to travel south with us instead of Mike. I hoped she didn't; three of us sharing a tent would not be the same. Perhaps she could get her own tent... Serena had a swig of her drink and began to talk, to me rather than Morgan, though she kept giving quick glances in his direction. Whatever he thought, she was definitely keen on him.

"At Strata where we are now it's not like here. Everyone lives in the same block of flats, like a commune. It's amazing, they've got electricity, there's three wind turbines on the roof. They've got a guy there who's a whiz at mechanical stuff, he got them going. People get together in the Hall – they've knocked down walls in the flats at snow level to use as a communal area, with a bar and a shop, loads of sofas and tables, a ping pong table and a darts board. Stalls with stuff for sale, too, and a notice board. A bit like a cross between a market, a pub and a village hall, and it's almost always got power, even when there's none to the flats. Everyone hangs out there. We spent a lot of time in the Hall so Mike could get to know people. They all think he's such a good listener, but that's because he's on the lookout for anything he can use to his advantage. It's sad really, seeing them fall for it." Serena took a long pull at her wine, and I topped up her glass. "Anyway, the evening of the day we arrived David came in looking pissed off, got himself a stiff drink and joined us. He'd been taking care of Tessa all day. I got the definite feeling him and Katie had had a row, and he was sort of seething like he needed to offload on to somebody. And of course there was Mike, all sympathy and concern."

Somehow when David was here I hadn't got round to telling him about Mike forcing me and Greg to stand outside; the revelations about his new family had sidetracked me. I should have told him what had happened after Nina's party, instead of making generalized assertions he could dismiss out of hand.

"David told us about seeing you, and I could see why he couldn't let off steam to Katie. He said he was worried about you, thought you were making a big mistake yada yada. Went on for ages. Though if you ask me, what really bugged him was you getting it together with another guy – he's one of those people who expect their exes to remain celibate forever in memory of them."

I almost laughed. Looking back, he'd been like that about his girlfriend before me, but it hadn't registered at the time, I'd been so madly in love with him.

"Because no way was he going to admit that, he really laid it on thick about the danger to you with Morgan being so deceitful and unreliable and thuggish." Morgan stirred and she shot a quick look at him. "Sorry. That's what he said. And you can imagine Mike agreeing. I didn't say anything because he would just have told me to leave. So they spent ten minutes trashing your character, then Mike said what a pity it was when Tori was such a lovely girl, if headstrong. David agreed. He got quite maudlin, though he hadn't drunk *that* much – Mike of course was totally sober. He said he was afraid it was all his fault for introducing Morgan into your community, however indirectly and inadvertently, and he felt duty bound to do something. So finally he said he'd been thinking of going back to confront Morgan, and what David told him had made up his mind."

Morgan said, "When's he coming?"

"I don't know. At that point I forgot to keep quiet and said I didn't see what it had to do with either of them who Tori slept with, and Mike said he thought it would be a nice idea if I called in on Jen to take a look at her tie-dying. So I left and they went on talking, thick as thieves. That was six days ago, and it's been a whiteout ever since. As soon as I could I came here to warn you."

"That was very kind of you," I said. "Thanks."

"You needn't thank me, what I'm afraid of is Mike's going to dump me and take you south instead and I'll be stuck forever living with a load of time-warp hippies."

"I wouldn't go."

"He might not give you a choice." This struck me as melodramatic; I didn't see that he could compel me. She went on, "I could tell he fancied you, even before this week. It was after the dinner at Nina's, when you were wearing that corset and all the eye makeup. It was like he saw your possibilities. And he got a buzz out of you standing up to him. Don't know why, I have to agree with him the whole time or he goes all icy on me. It's bloody unfair. He kept going on about what a waste it was, you mouldering here at subsistence level, you deserved better. I got sick of the subject. Anyway, I'm worried about what he's going to do to Morgan." She turned to him. "He went ballistic when he realized you'd taken his Semtex after everything else. He offered to sell some to one of the House Committee at Strata, and when he unwrapped it to show the man it was plasticene. The man laughed like he thought Mike was trying to fool him and Mike was furious."

Morgan gave a quiet snort of amusement. But I didn't laugh. I'd known this was a self-indulgent mistake, annoying Mike for the sake of it. Immature and asking for trouble.

"Not your smartest move," I said.

"Who says I was trying to be smart? Just the thought of the look on his face makes it worth it." He smiled infuriatingly, as if enjoying a private joke. "Anyway, let him come. I can handle Mike."

"Better if you didn't have to."

He shrugged. I scowled at him. There was a brief silence, broken by Serena.

"And I should have said, he's got a gun."

CHAPTER 22

Fire

Morgan sat up, not smiling any more. "Where the fuck did he get a gun from?"

"A man in the flats. He did a deal on the quiet with him, swapped it for the Lynx. So you can see he's really serious. We're all wondering who's going to get left behind now we're a sled short. Everyone's getting paranoid about it. Mac said Mike will shoot one of us. I *think* he was joking."

I wondered if she knew David had been offered a sled, presumably BJ's. Morgan said, "What kind of a gun is it?" Serena looked blank. "Is it a rifle, a shotgun, a pistol?"

"It's small, like a revolver. Modern-looking. He wouldn't let me hold it. He did say the name…it had a number."

"A Glock 17 or 19?"

"That's it."

"Which?"

"I'm not sure."

Morgan said to me, "The police use Glocks. They're semi-automatic. Fantastically reliable, work when they're filthy or freezing, won't go off if you drop them. Just point and shoot – pulling the trigger deactivates the safety catches." He turned to Serena. "D'you know what magazines he's got? How many rounds?"

"The man gave him some boxes of ammunition. I don't know anything about them. They went down to the car park so he could show Mike how to fire it."

I said, "What does semi-automatic mean? Is that like a machine gun?"

"Machine guns are belt-fed. Glocks have a high capacity magazine with fifteen or more bullets, and you get two with each gun. You can just keep firing till you get lucky."

"Maybe we should get out of here. Now."

"On the other hand, Mike's a novice. He'll have problems hitting anything more than a few metres away. A bullet's small and a human's big by comparison."

"I'm not totally reassured by that."

"Oh, I'm not thinking of staying to give Mike some target practice. We'll vamoose. I'd rather take a chance on crashing the sled."

Serena had been looking from one of us to the other, biting her lip. Now she said, with a casual air but sounding strained, "I know it's a bit of a cheek asking, but I don't suppose you'd let me come with you? I've got the snowmobile, and I'd much rather go south with you guys."

My heart sank. I didn't want her with us, but sensed her desperation and it seemed terribly selfish to refuse. Morgan's reaction was instant and decisive.

He shook his head. "Sorry. We've got all our gear packed and ready to go, enough for us two, and you haven't even got a trailer. You'd hold us up. Plus I don't want the responsibility."

"That's okay. Just thought I'd ask." Her voice was flat. "I'd better be off then, before the weather gets any worse or Mike misses me. Good luck. Hope you make it south." She got to her feet. "Can I use your bathroom before I go?"

"Sure." I felt dreadfully sorry for her. As soon as the door closed, I said quietly, "I feel mean. She did come to warn us. You don't think we should take her?"

"No, I don't. It's simple: would she help or hinder us to get south? We'll have our work cut out as it is avoiding Mike and making the journey. We don't need delay while she gets her kit together, and we don't need her. The only possible reason for taking her would be to stop her telling Mike we're still here, and that won't matter if we go now."

"Are you always this ruthless? If I got ill or injured or we quarrelled, would you leave me behind?"

"Of course not." He smiled. "You and me are buddies."

"Buddies?" I raised my eyebrows. "*Buddies*?"

"Damn straight. I watch your back, you do the same for me. Get ready to go. He could arrive any minute. If Serena made it here, so can he."

I rushed round collecting things and putting them in back-packs. Everything we needed for the journey was in the trailer hidden north of Old Street with the sled, except for some stuff we used on a daily basis. I tried not to forget anything.

Serena reappeared, smiled faintly at us, crossed to the door and slid it open. Morgan helped her heave the trailer off the sled. Three inches of snow covered it.

He checked her petrol gauge and said she'd got plenty, then told her to keep her compass at south southwest and she wouldn't get lost. I hoped he was right. The snow fell thicker than before, and the moon, had we been able to see it, was only a sliver.

"Will you be okay? It's almost dark."

She turned on the engine and the headlights. "I'm more worried about getting back in without anyone noticing."

"Good luck."

She zoomed off through the gloom and the snow, a fast-receding glow of light. I turned to go inside, hearing the engine grow ever fainter.

Another twenty minutes and I reckoned I'd got everything. I dressed in my new layers for the journey. I took the letter from my mother out of the wooden box and put it in an inside zipped pocket, deciding against taking the photo of David on Kos. I packed a pen and my diary, and chose two paperbacks, *The Big Sleep* and *About a Boy*. It dawned on me I'd been contented here, almost happy, more so as time went on; having always longed to get away, now the time had come I felt nostalgia for what I would leave behind.

I said, "Are we off?"

"As soon as I've made sure no one's lying in wait for us out there. If Mike was only waiting for the snow to lighten, and Serena went round in circles, they could be here already. We'll go upstairs for a better view."

Morgan went and moved the bed away from the unused front entrance. I unlocked the balcony door so Greg would be able to get in. I went to put out the candles, and he told me to leave them burning. I had a last look round the home I was about to abandon forever, then joined Morgan in the hallway. He opened the door gently, listening in the blackness, switched on his torch and shone it both ways. We slipped into the corridor, closing the door behind us. I followed him towards the stairs and up a couple of flights, into a flat two floors above mine. Its lock was missing – I've broken into all the flats at one time or another. Before entering he switched off his torch. So did I. I shut the door while he went through the hall to the abandoned living room, its air cold and smelling of damp plaster. He crossed to the window. Nothing was visible beyond the glass except darkness and swirling snow. Visibility was maybe fifty or a hundred yards. I shivered. We'd be driving blind through this. The headlights wouldn't help much.

I said, "If Mike's outside we'd never know."

"No, but it cuts both ways – he'll have trouble spotting us. I can't see anything out there." He suddenly said, "Did you see that?"

"No, what?"

"A light."

We both stared into the murk. Nothing. "What sort of light?"

"Small, white. A torch. Someone's out there."

"It could be Greg, though he mostly comes in the morning."

He slid the door open, and moved on to the balcony, keeping down. I joined him, my feet sinking into eighteen inches of snow. Crouching low, I peered between two panels whose glass was opaque with snow. Minutes passed. Snowflakes collected on me, and I brushed them clumsily off my eyelashes with my glove.

I whispered, "Why don't we just leave further along if there's someone here?"

"One more minute. I'd sooner know who it is, where they are and what they're up to. Don't want to bump into them."

Then I saw it, the quick flare of a flame and the dim shape of a man. His arm moved fast. Something flew through the air, there was a crack and flames flared up beneath us; a ball of fire, a yellow glow and black smoke. A Molotov cocktail, thrown at my flat. A second one smacked into the glass, and the fire belched higher.

"Let's go." Morgan headed out of the flat fast and I followed. A louder explosion; an enormous wall of orange light lit us on our way. Morgan ran along corridors to our right, down stairs at the far end back to snow level and into another flat. "Wait for me here."

"I'm staying with you." It's always a mistake in Doctor Who when two people split up.

"Okay, but don't get in my way." He opened the balcony door, vaulted the rail and raced towards my flat through the deep fresh snow, with me running more slowly after.

The glare from the wall of flames all along my windows illuminated a man alone, hood up, snow blowing about him. He stood by a car roof top box full of cans and bottles with rags poking out of their tops, lighting then hurling them steadily one by one towards the conflagration. He'd moved on to big plastic containers without wicks that exploded into flames five storeys high when they hit. There was a stench of burning petrol and the smoke blew in my eyes and made them sting. Behind the fire's roar you could hear cracks as the double glazing shattered. Inside, all my painstakingly collected firewood and kindling, a year's work, waited to catch fire. I imagined how upset Greg would be when he discovered my flat a burnt-out shell. Anger flared within me. *Bastard.*

The man saw us and turned. It was Eddie, his face a swollen mess, with purple patches under both eyes and a white dressing over his nose. His expression changed from simple absorption to alarm. He grabbed a bottle and clicked a lighter. Morgan kept running, even when Eddie threw the bottle at him and it flared on the snow and set light to his clothes. He smashed into Eddie, barrelling him to the ground. Eddie screamed as Morgan punched his face with an audible crunch, making me wince. I remembered what Morgan had said about watching his back, and scanned the darkness, glad not to watch the fight. Just the noises made me feel sick. I couldn't see anyone. Eddie went quiet; when I looked I saw him curled unmoving in the snow. Morgan stood, slapping at his jacket.

"Are you okay?"

"Yeah." He crouched and went through Eddie's pockets till he found a key on a ring.

"Is he dead?"

"No. Just not very healthy." He got to his feet, grabbed the trailer's rope and headed back the way we had come, his sleeve still smoking. I followed him, shaking.

"Where are we going?"

"Mike'll be in the corridor outside your flat with the others, waiting for us to be forced out by smoke. We must have just missed him. We'll skirt round the building, pick up the sled and get away before he susses out we're not in there."

That sounded good to me. I was relieved Morgan had decided to walk away rather than creep up behind Mike and take him by surprise. I didn't want him to beat up anyone else, nor did I want anyone to beat him up, and if I never saw Mike again it would be too soon.

The soft snow in our faces and underfoot made the going heavy work, but it was a comforting reflection that every step took us further from Mike. I quickly lost my bearings, but Morgan seemed to know which direction to take. By the time the building loomed into sight my legs were aching from keeping up with him. He slowed to take stock of his surroundings. It was so quiet I could hear our breathing. I turned and looked all round. The conflagration wasn't visible as it was on the south side of Bézier, away from us, but thick grey smoke mushroomed above the roof. Nothing moved, and though it was now snowing less, our tracks were being obliterated even as I watched.

"I'm thinking we should wait here till the snow stops. Camp if we have to." For the first time, he looked undecided. "Unless we go really slow, we could bump into something under the snow and wreck the sled. Then we're buggered."

This idea did not appeal to me. I was itching to get away. "Mike made it here all right. And if we go now while he's at my flat he won't see us. He'll start looking once he knows we're not there. This snow could go on for days. And it's less thick than it was."

"Maybe you're right. Okay, we'll head north slowly and do a big circuit to the east."

He set off again. I hoped he was right thinking I was right – I might be wrong. There was no going back to my flat.

Where we'd left the sled was a little below snow level, with drifts making a slope down to the concrete floor. Morgan left Eddie's trailer outside, and we stepped between scaffolding poles into the wide empty space, our boots sounding on the frozen surface and echoing from distant walls. There was a musty smell of damp cement. It was too dark to see anything. I stamped my feet, brushed snow from my clothes, took off my gloves and had reached inside my pocket for my torch when Morgan's face was suddenly spotlit. I looked in the direction the light came from and it moved to shine in my eyes, blue/white and dazzling.

"I've been waiting for you, Morgan. I see you've brought Tori along."

Mike.

CHAPTER 23

The problem with guns…

We both switched on our torches. Their combined light showed Mike sitting sideways on the Polaris's seat ten metres away, a picture of confidence and relaxation. The Glock was not in evidence. He must be keeping it as a little surprise, not knowing Serena had tipped us off. The bag of Semtex lay on the floor in front of him, along with some of our stuff out of the trailer. I kept my torch trained on Mike as Morgan flashed his around, illuminating shadowy spaces and concrete walls and beams.

While his face was turned from the light he muttered so only I could hear, "Mac and Hong are behind us. When he shoots, dive."

We'd walked into a trap. I was sweating in the cold air, my heart banged against my ribs, and I had trouble keeping my torch steady. The click of a lighter made me jump. Hong was moving around, lighting half a dozen tea lights – mine from our trailer – and setting them at intervals round the walls where they gave out a weak golden light, illuminating small circles of dusty concrete. Mike got to his feet, left hand holding the torch, right hand in his pocket. I wondered if his finger was on the trigger. He looked cocky enough.

"Your problem, Morgan – or I should say, one of your problems, because you've got quite a few right now – is you're not as smart as you think you are. Whereas I'm a lot smarter than you think. You thought I'd be in the corridor outside Tori's flat waiting for Eddie to smoke you out, didn't you? It's the obvious thing to do. It's probably what you'd do in my place. But I worked out that if I found the Polaris – and I knew it had to be somewhere not too far away – eventually you'd join me. And here you are."

Morgan drawled, "Bit of bad luck for Eddie, being used as a decoy."

"That's about all he was good for. Eddie was dumb."

I said, "You should send someone to get him. He's injured and lying in the snow."

He smiled at me, head on one side, as if I'd said something naïve and rather charming. "I was afraid that might be the case, but unfortunately I don't have the manpower right now to pick him up. Besides, he's no longer part of my plans."

Morgan said, "What are your plans?"

"I'm taking the Polaris and everything with it, including the Semtex you stole and, in the circumstances, your share of the gold – plus some rather flashy diamond-set jewellery I found in a bag. As you won't be going south, and I doubt her flat is habitable any more, I'm offering to take Tori with me –"

"Not interested."

"Wait one moment, Tori, I'm talking to Morgan." His hand moved inside his pocket making my heart jolt. "Please would you move six paces to your left?"

"No." I stayed where I was, next to Morgan. As soon as I moved he'd shoot him.

"Do it," Morgan said out of the corner of his mouth. I hesitated. "It's okay."

I stared at his face for more information. Was he saying that to protect me, or because he had a plan and I was in his way where I was? He'd told me not to get in his way. We should have had a code – except we weren't expecting to need one. His expression was intent, focused on Mike, unreadable. Reluctantly I walked six paces to my left and stopped, watching the two men picked out in the gloom by each other's circles of torchlight.

"I'll tell you what the deal is," Mike said. "You can walk away from here on three conditions. One, you apologize. On your knees. Two, you hand over the Polaris keys. Three, Tori agrees to come south with me."

Morgan laughed. "Dream on. She's already told you she wouldn't do that."

"She might change her mind if it's the only way to save your useless life."

Mike pulled the Glock out of his pocket with the flourish of a gambler producing a winning ace; his new toy that made him more powerful than a cage fighter. He held it in his right hand at shoulder level, arm bent, the square black barrel pointing at Morgan's chest. My heart rate redoubled, even as random thoughts surfaced in my mind. Shouldn't he be holding the gun in both hands, arms straight, to minimize the recoil? Serena said he'd been taught how to fire it. Of course, his torch was in the other hand. He hadn't thought this through.

"Now don't think about trying to rush me. I haven't had a lot of practice, but you're ten metres away, and I'd have time to fire several shots before you got anywhere near me, and the nearer you got the harder it would be to miss." His eyes moved in my direction. "So Tori, it's up to you."

"No it's not," Morgan said. "I'm not going to apologize, so we needn't bother with Tori's part of your fucking stupid deal."

Mike had opened his mouth to reply when footsteps behind me made me look over my shoulder. Somebody else had arrived, panting like a dog. I couldn't see who in the dimness, but his torchlight bobbed from Mike to Morgan.

"Thank goodness I've found someone, can you two come and help?" Archie, so out of breath he could hardly speak. He sounded beside himself. "Tori's flat's burning and I shouted through her back door and she didn't answer and she may be trapped in there overcome by smoke. I couldn't get in. Greg's not home. Eddie's hurt and lying out in the snow, back by Tori's flat. He may die or get frostbite. I can't lift him." His voice went up a notch. "We need to get back there fast." He was level with Morgan now, so I could see him. Sweat trickled down the side of his face. Hastily he took off his spectacles, wiped the snow and condensation from the lenses and replaced them on his nose, saying urgently, "Come on." Something about Morgan's expression made him look closer at Mike. He said in shocked tones, "Mike, is that a gun? Are you threatening Morgan? What's going on?"

Mike said, "Stay out of this, Archie. Turn round and go home. Now."

Archie spotted me in the shadows, came over and clasped my hands. He peered into my face with relief and anxiety. "Thank God. Are you all right?"

I nodded.

"Is Greg here?"

"No."

He turned to Mike again and spoke with authority and no trace of fear in his voice. "Put the gun away, Mike. That's not the way to go on. Eddie needs you. I know there's bad blood between you and Morgan, but I'm sure you can come to an agreement if you just sit down quietly together and talk it over, maybe tomorrow when both of you have had a chance to calm down. I'm willing to act as a mediator if it'll help. But right now we have to help Eddie."

"Didn't you hear me? I said get out."

"I'm afraid I can't do that, Mike. Tori, I think you should leave now."

I remembered the trailer half full of Molotov cocktails just outside the building, and the lighter I always carried. There had to be something useful I could do with them. "Okay," I said, turning to go.

Mike raised his voice. "Stay where you are or I'll shoot Morgan."

I turned. "You don't want to do that," I said. "Firing a gun for real isn't like it is in the movies. Did you know the noise a gunshot makes is between 140 and 160 decibels? Loud enough for one shot to damage the microscopic hairs in the inner ear, and like you said, you'd need to fire several times. It might harm our hearing too if we were unlucky, but you're only a couple of feet from the Glock so it would be much worse for you. Ears are delicate. That's why people on shooting ranges always wear ear protection, and soldiers are issued with ear plugs. Fire that, and you risk tinnitus, increased sensitivity to noise, and hearing loss in the higher registers. And it's likely to be permanent. Non-reversible." I remembered what he'd said to Nina at the dinner. "Mozart would never be quite the same."

"You made that up. A few shots wouldn't hurt me." But he looked rattled. Serena had said the previous owner gave him a demo – perhaps he'd already experienced some of the symptoms I'd described.

I shrugged. "It's the truth, but if you want to find out the hard way… Straight after the shot, you'll get ringing in your ears and a muffled sensation. It might gradually wear off over the next year, or it might not. You'd have to wait and see."

There was a long pause. He lowered the gun. "Clear off, the three of you."

Archie was about to say something, so I grabbed his arm and pulled. I didn't want to hang about. Mike might change his mind. We walked past Mac and Hong, past Eddie's trailer (I saw Morgan consider taking it, and decide against) and into the blizzard. No one followed us. We ploughed as fast as we could through the snow, sinking up to our ankles, checking over our shoulders for signs of pursuit. Now we'd got away I was shaking all over and sweating as if we were in the tropics. I drew the free icy air deeply into my lungs. Morgan was giving me sidelong glances. After a few minutes he said,

"I don't know how you did that."

"Nor do I – it was all I could think of, I'm amazed it worked."

"Then you didn't know his father was hard of hearing? He'd worked with heavy machinery in his twenties. He was too macho to bother with ear defenders. Mike used to take the piss when his dad couldn't hear what people said. He wouldn't want to end up like him."

"I had no idea. You and Serena both said he was neurotic over his health, that's all. I thought it had to be worth a try."

"You knowing it was a Glock helped. Now he thinks you're a

gun pro as well as an expert on the inner ear."

Archie said, "How did you know all that about hearing damage?"

"I know a lot of useless facts." I grinned. "Occasionally they turn out to be useful after all."

CHAPTER 24

Trip to the chemist

For the next few minutes no one said anything. It was difficult to talk as well as keep up with the pace set by Morgan. I found I could still worry, though.

Eventually I said, "What are we going to do without the Polaris and all our stuff? We won't get it back, will we?"

"No. It's no use to him because I've got both keys, so my guess is he'll take a small part out of the engine to stop it working and move the trailer. I reckon we'll have to cross it off for now."

I went on worrying. As it became clear we were not heading for Bézier, Archie stopped, his hand on Morgan's arm. "Will you come with me to move Eddie?"

Morgan shook his head. "Sorry. Right now Eddie's welfare's pretty low on my list of priorities." He started walking again.

Archie hurried to catch up with him. "He'll die if he's left there much longer."

I said, "Where are we going?"

"To the chemist to get all the earplugs they've got before Mike does."

"After that, then?" Archie looked distressed, and I could see why. I too was unhappy at the thought of a human being lying helpless in the freezing cold, succumbing to frostbite and

199

hypothermia, dying alone. I nearly offered to go with him, but Mike might turn up...

Morgan said, "Okay, after that. He can tell me where he left his sled."

Snow had drifted against the door to the staircase leading to the shops, making it difficult to open. We set off fast down the stairs which were dark, cold and claustrophobic as a dungeon. It's bad enough in daylight. I experienced a sudden longing to be curled up cosily on my sofa in front of a roaring stove with a good book, and felt panic that my home was no longer a haven I could return to, and all our travelling supplies were now in Mike's hands, along with the Polaris. I'd fallen between two stools. If we couldn't get our sled back, or get hold of Eddie's, I was now stuck in London like before. Only I'd have to start all over again with a new flat, chiselling a hole through the wall for the stove's flue, collecting provisions and cutting up firewood, a daunting prospect. Perhaps not everything had been burnt, some of it might be salvageable...I could look when we went to rescue Eddie.

We'd arrived at ground level, and wove our way between shops and ice tunnels to reach Superdrug, right at the end. It's not a huge shop, but there are two long aisles and we had to flash our torches on every shelf searching for earplugs. At last we found them on the lowest shelf next to the corn plasters, only two kinds. We put them in a plastic bag, then checked the stock room, found three boxes and stashed those too. Since we'd lost everything except what we carried in our backpacks, I bagged soap and some toilet rolls while we were there. On the way out I picked up several packets of earplugs from a display by the till – Morgan was impressed I'd spotted them. Archie got fidgety in

Argos, as it took us some time to check in the catalogue then find the items they stocked. They didn't have ear defenders, only Zoggs Aqua Plugz. We gathered up the lot, even the Junior ones, and headed back, me swinging the bag.

As we reached the door, Morgan held out his arm in front of us and stopped. "Someone's coming," he muttered. "Turn the torches off. Don't move." We stood in the utter blackness, listening. I could smell Archie's aftershave and hear his breathing above the faint scratchings of rats. Then I saw a small bobbing light approaching from our left, the chemist's where we had been, and heard soft footsteps. The shadowy figure of a man appeared in the snow tunnel, and Morgan jumped him. The man's torch fell and rolled to one side.

Morgan yelled, "Tori! Light!" I shone my torch on the newcomer – Hong – being careful to keep the beam out of Morgan's eyes. They punched and grabbed at each other, dodging and kicking. Not many of the punches landed, they were both too good at evasive action. Then Hong got hold of Morgan and tripped him. They crashed to the ground, Hong on top. They grappled, and I couldn't tell who was winning. Hong lay sideways across Morgan, awkwardly thumping his head. Morgan twisted like a snake and they were upright again, crouching, each trying to get the advantage. I noticed Archie was gripping my arm. Suddenly Hong threw a punch. Morgan's foot lashed out unbelievably fast and connected with Hong's jaw. He fell like a tree, bounced and lay still. Morgan knelt and started going through his pockets. Torchlight flashed on another sled key. Hong groaned and stirred.

Morgan gripped the neck of his jacket. "Where's your sled?"

"If I tell you, he kill me."

"I'll kill you if you don't. Or maybe just break your arm, which comes to the same thing. Where is it?"

Hong said nothing and Morgan punched him. Archie said, "You shouldn't hit a man when he's down," which was the first time I'd ever heard that phrase used literally.

"He's only got to tell me where his sled is and I won't." Morgan's attention went back to Hong. He hit him again. "Mike won't know you told me."

"Building south of Bézier. Not far. Roof sticks out."

"That's the truth, is it, because if it's not you'll regret it."

Hong nodded and Morgan got to his feet, rubbing his knuckles.

"Are you all right?" Archie's voice.

"Yeah," said Morgan.

"I meant him." Archie stooped beside Hong as he propped himself unsteadily on one elbow and spat.

"Leave him if you want us to go and get Eddie. He'll be okay."

Archie picked up Hong's torch and handed it to him. "Can you get yourself back on your own?" He nodded sullenly, and Archie levered himself uncertainly to his feet. None of us was having a great evening, but poor old Archie was having a truly rotten time dealing with one difficult choice after another, struggling to do the right thing.

Snow whipped in my face when we came out of the doorway at the top of the stairs and turned towards my erstwhile home. My legs ached as I wearily plodded behind Morgan, my feet in his tracks like Good King Wenceslas's page. A snippet of the carol went round and round in my head, and I couldn't remember the rest;

"Sire, the night is darker now, and the wind blows stronger;
Fails my heart, I know not how; I can go no longer."

I had a bad feeling we'd find Eddie dead under a mound of snow, and if he was dead, then Morgan would have killed him. I didn't like the thought of Morgan being a killer. And I'd bear some responsibility for not going with Archie to help him twenty minutes earlier because I was afraid of Mike. I prayed he would be alive and without frostbite. We rounded the corner of Bézier. The fire was almost out, just a few small flames tenaciously licking the wooden floor of the balcony, spitting at the snow. A great scorch mark stained the building right to the top. All my panes of glass had cracked, and some of them fallen out. There was a horrible smell of burnt things that are not supposed to burn. Puddles of sticky black goo were all that remained of my solar lights. The inside of the flat wasn't gutted, but smoke had blackened the parts near the windows and, open to the elements, it was no longer fit for human habitation. I wanted to cry. I looked towards where Eddie had been. Nothing, no human-shaped heap of snow.

"Tori!" Greg's voice, from inside my flat. An indistinct shape waved at me. We made our way across the balcony and through the twisted glassless door, and saw Eddie next to him huddled on the sofa in front of the glowing window of my stove.

"Thank goodness," Archie murmured, hurrying over. "Bless you, Greg." Eddie's white bandage was now red and his eyes, which had always been rather piggy, were so swollen he could barely see out of them. His nose was bleeding copiously and must have been extremely painful; but apart from his bruises he was a normal colour and breathing through his mouth, so it could have been a lot worse.

Greg turned my way. "I saw the flames and came in case you needed me, then I found Eddie. He's not very well. I think perhaps he'd better stay at my flat, when he's had a rest and can walk there. Do you want to too, Tori?"

"Ah, thanks, Greg, I might take you up on that. I'm so pleased you rescued Eddie. I thought he'd be done for, lying in the snow."

"He could stay with us," Archie volunteered. "We've got more space than Greg, and I'm sure Nina would be happy to nurse him. Though he really needs a doctor…"

"Neither of you need bother," said Morgan. "Bastard set fire to Tori's flat. I'm going to take him to the Elephant and Castle and dump him. Where's your sled, Eddie?"

Eddie had sat apathetically while we discussed his immediate future, and now flinched and gave Morgan a hangdog look. There was no fight left in him. "South of here, low building with an overhanging roof."

Morgan turned to go.

"I'm coming with you," I said quickly. "You need me to drive one of the sleds." I didn't want to stay in the remains of my flat, particularly with Mike around somewhere.

Morgan smiled at me. "I wasn't going to leave you behind."

Archie said he'd stay with the others till we got back.

"Hang on." I ran and got the champagne bottle out from under my bed and gave it to Greg, just in case. "If Eddie looks like getting aggressive, hit him with this."

For a few minutes I didn't say anything. I'd definitely had enough of walking, and my leg muscles were protesting, but at least the snow was falling less thickly than before.

After a while I said, "I'm glad Eddie's okay. I was afraid he'd be dead."

"He can't have been unconscious very long. Archie must have turned up just after we left, Greg soon after that. He was lucky."

There was a pause, while I tried to put my muddled thoughts into words. All I came up with was, "Doesn't it worry you, beating people up when it may kill them?"

"Yes and no. It's different in the cage where there are rules and a ref and a medic standing by. D'you think I should have let Eddie carry on throwing petrol on the fire, or given Hong what he came for?"

"No… I just wasn't sure how I'd feel if you'd killed him."

He glanced at me. "I probably killed a few people when I was in the army."

"That's different…"

"I'm not so sure. A life is a life. You've taken a man's future away from him."

We'd reached what had to be the right building, barely one storey sticking out, long and low with a pagoda-like flat roof. We walked down its length, turned right at the corner and there they were, two sleds side by side half-covered in white drifts. There was a Snowmobile Fairy after all, and she'd smiled on us. My heart lightened and I did a little dance in the snow. Morgan picked me up and whirled me round – his foot slipped and he fell into the soft powder with me on top of him. We kissed, a thorough kiss that belonged indoors with fewer clothes and plenty of time. I felt warm and tingly right down to my toes. Eventually he released me and we got up, brushing off snow and gazing at each other.

"What was that for?"

"Because we're the best. And we've got transport again."

He flipped me a key, and we each rode a sled back to my flat. It was nice not to be walking. Greg and Archie helped Eddie over the balcony railing and on to the back of Morgan's sled, then Greg went home. Archie got on behind me so I could drop him off at the Barbican. After that we headed through the driving snow and the dark towards the Elephant and Castle.

CHAPTER 25

Strata

Strata won three awards when it was built; the 2010 Carbuncle Award, 'for the ugliest building in the United Kingdom completed in the last twelve months', and two rather more favourable ones, the names of which I've forgotten. It used to be referred to locally as Isengard after the fortress in Tolkien's *Lord of the Rings*, or the Razor, though it more resembles an enormous electric shaver. I'd never seen it in real life. It's triangular in section, with two walls curved and one flat, and a 45 degree slice off the top. At the apex, three wind turbines sit in round holes, designed to provide 8% of the power consumed by the building. Much was made of this green aspect at the time; now London consumes no power at all and has the carbon footprint of an unwashed ant with sedentary habits...

As we approached, thirty-odd storeys loomed over us, and I noticed lights shining all along the snow line, with lit windows here and there for six or seven levels above – I got quite excited, not having seen electric lights for a year. Morgan circled the building and stopped next to a huge brightly-lit window, one of a row divided by white panels. Two sleds were parked outside, Serena's and what must have been BJ's. Peering through the condensation trickling down the glass, I recognized the communal hall Serena had described. You could see where walls had been removed to make it into a big open L-shaped space. People sat around tables chatting, or milled at the bar, or played table football. Some had laptops. Two women behind a counter served steaming food. A man strummed a guitar. There was an area with sofas and violet Arne Jacobsen swan chairs, children running about, and three people juggling in a corner.

"That'll do," said Morgan. "We'll leave him there."

We parked the sleds outside and walked to the only entrance, an incongruous panelled door fitted into a window space blocked with boards. It wasn't locked, and led to a small room leading on to the Hall. We passed a noticeboard with handwritten cards, and I hung back to take a quick look. You could have a hot bath for 60g (how I'd love that) or a professional wash, cut and blow dry for 20g. What was a 'g'? Gold something? Water cost 3g a litre. Among offers of babysitting, odd jobs and things for sale were adverts for Indian Head Massages 5g, hand-made jewellery, weed at 8g a gram, and Tarot or rune readings, 3g. I saw what Serena had meant when she called the people here time-warp hippies. I caught up with the others.

Inside was warm, with smells of cooking and humanity and a buzz of music and conversation. Faces nearest to us looked up. David sat on a far sofa talking to a woman in a red top I guessed must be Katie. She was okay-looking, a bit big on the hips, with the expression of one who knew her own mind. Though I was no longer keen on David, I can't say I felt much enthusiasm towards her. A carrycot lay on the seat beside them. Morgan headed purposefully in their direction. Eddie shuffled behind making horrible sniffing and snorting noises, with me bringing up the rear.

Morgan stopped in front of David. "Hi doc." David glanced up and as he recognized Morgan his smile disappeared. "I've brought you your patient back."

David's gaze moved to Eddie, whose pulped face and bloody clothes looked much more striking in the bright light, and his expression morphed from suspicion to outrage. He jumped to his feet. "Did you do this?"

"Yes," said Morgan, simply.

David's voice went up. "What kind of Neanderthal are you?" People nearby stopped talking and turned to listen and stare. "D'you know how much damage you did to his nasal bones and septal cartilage the first time and just how tricky it was to align? Without anaesthetics? The one thing he didn't need was more trauma to the same site."

Morgan turned to study Eddie. "Yeah, he does look a mess, doesn't he? I guessed he might need a bit of medical attention. That's why I brought him back to you to sort out. Plus if I'm honest, we'd had enough of him."

David looked at him with revulsion. "Mike was right. You're a psycho."

Morgan took a step forward and said amiably, "If I am, what are you going to do about it?"

Katie got to her feet and grasped David's arm. "Don't talk to him."

I felt it was time I joined this conversation. "Eddie threw Molotov cocktails at my windows. If Morgan hadn't hit him I'd have done it myself. Less efficiently, obviously."

"Are you Tori?" Katie took a firmer hold of David's arm, apparently more worried I might whisk him off and have my way with him than that Morgan would resent being called a

Neanderthal psycho and beat him up.

"Yes. And I am now homeless because of what Eddie did to my flat."

"Hi guys!" A voice behind me made me turn. "What are you doing here? D'you fancy a drink?" Serena, wearing jeans and a sloppy sweater. I was quite pleased to see her. I realized I liked her a lot better than anyone else I knew in the room, apart from Morgan. But hanging around where Mike lived was asking for trouble.

"That would be nice, but we have to go – we only came to drop Eddie off."

Serena did a double-take at Eddie's face; I could see her decide to say nothing about the state he was in. Avoiding our eyes, David took him away, Katie following with the carrycot. I'd failed to tell him about Mike threatening Morgan. I'd also missed the opportunity to check out little Tessa's sweetness rating. Probably lower than my godchild-elect's.

To my surprise, Morgan said, "We've got time for a quick one, Tori." He smiled at Serena. "Beer for me." He was up to something.

"I'll have white wine, then. Thanks."

"Stay put and I'll get them for you. D'you know where Mike is?"

"On his way here, probably."

As soon as we were alone, I hissed, "Why are we hanging around? At any moment Mike could walk through that door and we'd be trapped. It's the only door to the building, and the windows don't open. And for all we know, he'll have thought of putting plasticene in his ears and will shoot you on sight."

"This is too good an opportunity to miss. I want to get the

210

spares for the sleds while we're here and he's not. We need trailers, too."

"But we don't know where his stuff is."

"No, but Serena will. You just ask her casually which flat they're staying in, without making a big thing of it, then I'll snoop around while you keep her talking. We'll only have one drink, it won't take long. On the way out we'll look for their trailers."

I wasn't totally convinced, and the thought of meeting Mike again made me shake; but remembering the ACE not working, I could see spares were important for our journey. Morgan said we should hide the sleds just in case. On the way out he detoured to the queue at the bar. Waiting for him by the counter, I noticed that besides packets of peanuts and biscuits, priced 1g, the glass shelves held sandwiches made with real bread, 5g, white and thickly cut. I hadn't eaten bread for a year. Someone must have a bread machine. My mouth watered. Then I saw bowls of fresh green salad, 4g. My eyes widened. Morgan touched Serena's arm, making her jump.

"We'll be back, there's something we've got to do."

The only building nearby was the top of a scruffy sixties high rise, spotted with satellite dishes; the snow lay conveniently a metre above the balconies, so we were able to tuck the sleds under cover, round the back where they weren't too conspicuous. Snow was falling more heavily again; I was not keen on the idea of travelling through it on a sled. We might get stuck out in the open. Back in Strata we took off our jackets and made ourselves comfortable on the sofa vacated by David and co. Anxious though I was, it was bliss to sit down in the warm. I unlaced my damp boots so I could curl my socked feet beneath me. Morgan

211

stretched then put his arm around me, rubbing my shoulder, and kissed my cheek quickly.

Serena wove between the sofas, carrying three drinks and packets of peanuts. She no longer had the gloss that had been so evident when we first met; she looked more ordinary, as if the effort to be well-groomed had become too much for her. "Sorry to be so long." She put the tray on the low table in front of us and plonked herself down next to me. "It's ridiculous, the bar is the only place here you can get a drink, and it gets crowded evenings. There aren't any local shops, not that you can get at anyway, so they do regular trips to the nearest supermarket but everything they bring in belongs to the commune and you have to buy it from the shop." She waved in the direction of an open door at the far end with a home-made sign above in multi-coloured letters, STRATA MARKET.

Morgan said, "What's the currency?"

"Credits." She fished a green plastic disc out of her pocket and handed it to me. *Waitrose* was embossed on one side. I passed it to Morgan. "They call them greenies. There's only so many in circulation, and you have to earn them from other people. It's quite a clever system, because it makes everyone work because they need money to stockpile stuff. You never know how long something'll be available in the shop. There's not much I can do, except babysitting. I refuse to dig rubbish pits or empty latrines and Mike doesn't like to see me scrubbing the floors. I wouldn't mind a bar job, but he's against that too. One hour's work gets you three credits, and a glass of wine costs two."

Serena had just spent the equivalent of three hours' babysitting on us. I gave her back the greenie, and sipped my wine more slowly. If I'd known, I'd have brought her some of my bottles from Bézier.

As if reading my mind she added, "I've got a few bottles in the flat, but you can't drink them in here, it's not allowed and they make a terrible fuss. You wouldn't believe how many rules they've got."

"You ought to dig down to another Waitrose and get loads of discs then you'd be rich. Of course, it would cause rampant inflation. Prices would rocket."

She laughed. "They'd have to go on the gold standard. Mike'd be pleased."

"So do you have a flat here?"

"Yes, on the sixteenth floor, that's seven above snow level." I couldn't help glancing quickly at Morgan. "It's only occupied up to there. The committee has to approve anyone wanting to stay. They have a meeting where they ask all sorts of questions to see what you have to offer, whether you'll fit in and if they like you. They liked Mike all right," she gloomed. "Predictably. Then they allocate you a flat sort of on probation and Ginger wires it up for you so you've got underfloor heating and electricity. You have to pay rent."

I opened a packet of peanuts. "Who's Ginger?"

"He's a genius mechanic who got the turbines working. He lives right at the top in the penthouse so he's on hand to keep them going. Sometimes they freeze or get snowed up. Other times the wind blows too hard for them to work. He's fixed up a load of car batteries for when the turbines stop, but they only last twenty-four hours. The committee gives you a list of instructions about not using too much electricity."

Morgan said, "Who's in charge?"

"Randall Pack. He set the place up originally."

Morgan got to his feet. "Back in a minute."

Serena pointed. "They're through that door, on the left." She watched him stroll away and sighed. "He's a dish. You're so lucky, Tori. Imagine what it's like, living with Mike."

"Why don't you leave him? You've got the keys to your sled. Just pack up a trailer and clear out. Go south."

She looked as wistful as a puppy by a dining table. "I wish I could…the thing is, I know I couldn't do it alone. I'm hopeless at organizing stuff. I'd get lost or realize in the middle of nowhere I hadn't brought the right kit."

"Couldn't you find some reliable man and offer him a lift south on your sled in exchange for him sorting out all the logistics? There must be someone suitable here."

"If there is I haven't met him yet. I'd trust Ginger, but he'd never leave his turbines. No one else could keep them going. I say, d'you want to meet him? If the lift's working, that is. I often go up there to smoke. The view's amazing, though of course you can't see it now because it's dark. But he'll be there. He doesn't come down much."

"I don't think we've got time. We can't hang about in case Mike comes back."

I told her everything that had happened after she'd left Bézier. It took a while. Her eyes got rounder as the story went on.

"God, how lucky you thought of saying that! I couldn't quite believe Mike really meant to kill Morgan. So as soon as he gets hold of earplugs, he'll take a pot shot at him?"

"Seems likely. D'you know how long he's planning on staying here?"

"He hasn't said. I'd like to know, because I haven't got much money and if we're staying I seriously need to get round to earning some. You have to pay for everything here."

"How did you manage when you first arrived?"

"The Welfare Committee gave us a loan – sixty greenies between us, and believe me, that doesn't last long. They're like some Victorian charity, expounding the virtues of hard work, telling you the community can't be expected to support you. They suggest things you can do to make money. There's always work melting snow for water – the inside set-up's not bad, they have an immersion heater you feed snowballs into, but you can end up outside feeding fires under bathtubs and lugging buckets of snow. You have to be on your last legs before they give you a handout. It's all right for Mike, the man he did the swap with for the gun paid him a load of greenies as well. He's only given me a few now and then. I had to sell a pair of boots, my best ones. Boy, am I fed up with him."

At that moment Morgan reappeared looking pleased with himself, a small backpack he hadn't had before slung over one shoulder.

"Snow's getting worse. We'd better wait a bit before we leave."

Serena said, "Hey, Morgan, d'you want to go to the top of the building and meet Ginger?"

He didn't answer at once. Something outside had caught his attention. I swivelled to look through the windows. Two round lights were visible through a swirling veil of snow, gradually getting larger; approaching snowmobile headlights. I shoved my boots on and tied the laces hastily, pocketed the peanuts, grabbed my backpack and leaped up. The lights swept across the steamy windows and stopped right next to the other sleds. Three dimly-visible figures got off.

Serena turned to see what we were looking at. "Oh God, Mike's back."

Morgan said, "I've got a sudden crazy urge to see turbines. Let's roll."

The three of us walked fast, back the way Morgan had just come, hurrying without seeming to.

CHAPTER 26

Ginger

The door led into a dimly-lit white corridor. On the wall the numbers 09, two feet high in silvery grey paint, told us where we were. Three lifts stood at the far side.

"Oh good, they're working," said Serena, noting the glowing light on the steel panel. She pushed the button. Seconds trickled by while I silently cursed our bad luck and ran through possible scenarios. What we'd needed was for the snow to have obligingly got worse the instant we arrived, preventing Mike getting to Strata, then to have lightened when we were ready to go; and it had done the opposite. We had a limited amount of time before Mike found out we were here. David, Katie or Eddie would tell him as soon as they saw him. And someone in Strata would have earplugs, if he hadn't improvised something already... I wondered if he'd be prepared to use the gun in public, or would wait until he could trap us on our own. Unless he'd lingered in the Hall he might walk round the corner at any moment.

I stared at the lift, willing it to hurry, and noticed a printed sheet of A4 sellotaped at eye level:

THE LIGHTS WILL FLASH THREE TIMES BEFORE I CUT THE POWER TO THE LIFTS.

Ginger

Serena saw what I was looking at. "He turns them off if we're getting low on electricity, and everyone has to use the stairs. That's why he's the only one who lives at the top."

I was thinking we should take the stairs when a lift arrived and its doors parted with a sigh. Three men got out. The first was tall and striking and wore dark glasses and a rakish military-style jacket. With his craggy good looks, shaggy hair and the bunch of pendants round his neck he made me think of an aging rock star. He had the air of relaxed confidence and authority that derives from success, money and the respect of others. He stopped and cast an eye over us. The men with him stopped too.

"Guests?" He turned to Serena. "Who's sponsoring them? You?"

"Yes," she said. "This is Tori and Morgan. They're just here till the snow lightens."

He nodded. "Enjoy your stay," he said to us, and walked towards the Hall.

"That's Randall," she said, getting in the lift. We followed her. "Visitors have to have someone who's answerable for their good behaviour. I should have told you. Just don't get in a brawl while you're here, you'd get me into trouble."

Morgan said, "Who deals with that sort of thing?"

"The Peace Committee."

I raised my eyebrows. "Orwellian name."

"Oh, it's more hippy than totalitarian. The committees rule on the small stuff, and anything major goes to Randall. Once or twice he's kicked people out. He has this laid-back manner, but they say he's ruthless if you cross him."

The lift moved smoothly up to the fortieth floor. Taped to the wall beside me was a handwritten notice:

If the lift stops press Alarm and I will restart it long enough for you to get to the floor you want and out. Don't use it after that or you'll be stuck till I turn it on again. And it'll be YOUR OWN FAULT so don't bother moaning to me about it because I won't care.

Ginger

"What happens if the power gets low while we're up here? Will we have to walk down the stairs?"

Serena laughed. "No, Ginger would turn it on for us. He's an old softie really, he just gets fed up with people trying to take advantage."

We got out of the lift, Franz Ferdinand immediately assaulting our ears, and followed Serena to an open door. She banged on it and went in. "Hi Ginger, it's me."

A large space; what had originally been the most expensive duplex in the building. That it had been designed specifically to impress was just a bit too obvious; the place was jumping up and down waving and squealing, "Look at ME!" Massive struts, pillars and beams reminded the visitor this was no ordinary apartment, but a penthouse in an iconic groundbreaking piece of architecture. Huge slanting windows ran the length of a double height living room, their glass obscured by a clinging layer of snow. To our left a steel and glass staircase rose past vertical panes displaying what had once been a spectacular panorama of London lights, and was now a view of blackness with swirling snowflakes. The room held an idiosyncratic mix of opulent show-flat furniture and workshop equipment. The work area was lit by bare light bulbs dangling from looped flexes. A trail of grime on the carpet led from a lathe, some other machines I couldn't identify and benches piled with tools, to a well-used grubby section of the long L-shaped mocha sofa. A laptop sat open on a coffee table; beside it a printer, stacks of DVDs, a full ashtray, the remains of a meal, and a fishbowl full of greenies. Cans of beer littered the floor. The room smelled of machine oil and cigarette smoke, and Take Me Out belted from a sound system that wouldn't have been out of place at a rock concert.

Ginger put down his spanner and wiped his hands on his jeans. Bright eyes in a weathered face regarded us. "Hi." He turned Franz Ferdinand down so we didn't have to shout.

"This is Morgan and Tori. They've come to see the view and the turbines."

Ginger laughed, showing a gap in his teeth. "The view'll be back around five thirty tomorrow morning. Unless there's another whiteout." He glanced at the window. "Which seems likely. I've done nothing but clear snow from the turbines this week. When it builds up on the blades the mechanical brakes come on. I've got to go up there now. D'you want a drink?" Ginger gestured to a table crammed with bottles and cans. "You do the honours, Serena."

While she poured us drinks, Ginger zipped himself into an ancient ski suit. "Talk among yourselves. I'd better get the blades moving again or the power'll go down."

Morgan said, "Mind if we take a look?"

"Nope, you're welcome."

I said, "You're going up there in the dark? In this weather?"

Ginger grinned. "If I paid any attention to the weather, we'd never have any power."

We put on our jackets. As Ginger led us into the corridor, we heard the faint whine of an approaching lift. I stiffened, heart pounding, and Morgan flattened himself at the side of the lift, ready to pounce. Ginger's eyebrows went up. The lift doors opened. A woman wearing an apron and carrying a tray got out. When the lift doors had closed, Morgan rejoined me.

"Hi Ginge."

Ginger slipped the woman some greenies, and she thanked him and went past us into his flat.

"She's collecting the dishes," said Ginger, answering our unspoken question. "Who were you expecting?"

I don't think Morgan would have answered, but Serena said, "Mike. He wants to shoot Morgan."

"Well, he can't shoot him up here. It'd make a mess, and the bullet might hit something important. I'll turn the lift off when Sue's gone down."

We followed him along the corridor. I had the impression he'd just tipped Sue rather than paid her. My guess was the people in charge knew how much they depended on Ginger to keep Strata lit and warm; he was probably able to name his own terms. They sent him his meals up, and no doubt collected his rubbish, cleaned for him and paid him too. Maybe he was a greenie millionaire.

Ginger led us through a white door with black fingerprints down one edge, bearing a sign that said NO ENTRY. Bare light bulbs lit the way. We went up a utilitarian metal staircase, and through another door that said *No unauthorized entry Roof access only*. Ginger flicked a switch. Fluorescent tubes hummed into life, illuminating a wide and messy space, littered with cables and crates. Huge girders spanned the ceiling and angled the walls. The floor had sections of paving slabs among pebbles, which Ginger said were ballast to damp down the vibrations from the turbines. He opened a couple of the metal cases on the walls and checked readings, adjusting dials and clicking switches. He was in his element here; this was his kingdom. Horizontal along one side was a massive black metal thing, like a robot's leg.

"What on earth's that?"

"The telescopic arm. They used it for building maintenance. I got it out once just to try it. Look at this."

He pressed a button and moved a lever. A warning beep went off. With a hum, the whole horizontal section of the wall behind the telescopic arm began to move slowly inwards, disappearing into the wall above. Snow blew in and fell on the floor.

Surprise made me laugh. "It's like something out of a Bond movie!"

The moving wall ascended smoothly out of sight, leaving a sort of terrace area open to the night. We picked our way between girders and pipes and bits of machinery and metal boxes to the edge and looked over. The penthouses' sloping windows formed a triangular ski slope, ending in mid-air. I imagined slithering helplessly down that slope, knowing a sheer drop of over a hundred metres awaited me. Looking up, we could see the enormous ellipses of the turbine tunnels, the middle one nearly close enough to touch.

"The rig swings right out with a cradle on the end. Fun. I've offered Serena a go. Dunno why she won't come."

"Huh." Serena pulled a face. "He knows I get vertigo if my heels are too high."

We stood a while, chatting and trying to make out other buildings in the distance, but of course nothing was visible except snow and darkness. After a few minutes Ginger moved the lever to lower the wall. He checked a lit green display above some switches, and opened the door of one of the big metal boxes on the wall. Inside was a confusion of electronic bits and pieces. He flipped a switch on and off three times and glanced at his watch, then at Morgan.

"I'm going to turn off the lifts now. Why does he want to kill you?"

"Because he's a nutter."

"It's a long story," Serena said. "I'll tell you later."

He opened another box and clicked a switch. "That's the lifts off."

I felt relieved. Now if Mike did come through the door, his hands would shake too much to hold a gun; he'd be too knackered after climbing thirty-odd storeys to do anything except collapse in a heap. There, however, the growing problem that the longer we were up here, the likelier he'd be to work out where we were and what to do about it.

We climbed narrow metal treads, more like a fixed ladder than stairs, to the next level. An extraordinary space right beneath the turbines, the underside of the tunnels housing them resembling dinosaurs' ribcages. I pointed this out to Morgan, and he said the ribs would be running the other way, and I said he was being pedantic. Loads of cables ran along banks of control boxes. There was a big generator and several smaller ones. Car batteries, thirty or more, stood in rows to one side, with wires trailing from them. Ginger must be brilliant, if he understood how all this worked.

I wandered around. There wasn't much there except a scaffold tower and a step ladder. I noticed snow-covered square windows above us, with spotlights the size of small dustbins. "What are the spots for?"

"They shine coloured lights on the turbines. Used to be just for fun. I use them when I clear the snow off in the dark."

Ginger grinned. "And all night once a year, on my birthday." He flipped a row of switches in turn, and a dazzling pink light shone from the spots.

Ginger climbed a fixed ladder beneath the lowest part of the right turbine housing. He opened a drop-down metal hatch bearing a notice:

ACCESS HATCH
RESTRICTED ACCESS
AUTHORIZED PERSONNEL ONLY

and a heap of snow fell in. A steady drift of flakes followed. Once through the hatch, he got me to pass him the broom and brush lying at the foot of the ladder. Immediately above I could see another ladder with snow on every rung, attached to the column supporting the turbine. Ginger stepped sideways out of my view, and Morgan followed him. I went up the ladder and stuck my head through to look out on to the gently curving surface.

Picture driving snow; a nine-metre diameter white tube, cut at an angle; the turbine blades lined up with the vertical circular opening, and everything softened by a thick layer of snow. It was like being inside a snow globe. Ginger brushed snow from one curved side over the edge, revealing three windows. As he did this, the space filled with a wash of pink light from the spots. Ginger handed the broom to Morgan and asked him to do the other side, then knocked the snow off the ladder rungs and climbed to the top. He was a metre away from a circle of nothingness with no railing or barrier of any kind and a sheer drop. Wind blew thick snow about, which swirled in the spotlights' beam like cherry blossom. Morgan looked around and turned to me.

"Are you coming up, Tori? It's amazing."

Heights aren't my favourite thing. I'd have needed a very good reason to go up there. "I'll stay here and watch."

Ginger balanced beneath the central hub of the turbine which resembled an enormous bullet, hanging on to a rung with one hand. Leaning out with the brush, he swept pink snow off the hub and the bases of the knife-like blades. Snow settled on his shoulders and the parts which he had already cleared. Morgan brushed snow from the foot of the turbine's column, then cleaned the blades within his reach, wandering around calm as anything, walking to the edge to look over, making me palpitate. I told myself not to be silly; just because he was high up, there was no more reason for him to lose his footing than on the ground. I didn't tell him to be careful; he was a grown man and I wasn't his mother. I fretted privately instead.

Ginger got me to pass up a hairdryer on a long extension lead to melt the ice round the base of the blades. As soon as they came down, Ginger switched that turbine on – it made a hum which, though very quiet, filled the room – and crossed to a short ladder to access the central turbine. It's lower than the other two, so its trapdoor is on one side, not immediately beneath the turbine column like the others. I didn't watch this time, but went back to the penthouse with Serena. We made ourselves comfortable and talked; down there you could just feel rather than hear the hum of the turbine. I finished my peanuts.

"Will anybody mind if we have to stay at Strata overnight?"

"You have to get permission from Randall. He'll be okay about it, he won't turn you out in this weather. He'll let you use one of the flats on the sixteenth floor."

"That's where Mike is?"

"Yes…"

Better to camp out in a flat without asking permission, though it would be freezing. We could huddle together under several duvets. We'd be all right. Serena saw the reservation in my face. "Why don't you ask Ginger if you can stay here? He's got three bedrooms, and it's fabulously warm because he has the underfloor heating on all the time."

"Would he let us?"

"I'll ask him for you."

Half an hour later Morgan and Ginger came in, covered in snow, shaking it off their clothes. Morgan said, "It's got worse out there. We'll have to stay overnight."

Ginger walked over to where I was sitting on the sofa. "Here, take these." He picked up a fistful of greenies from the bowl and dropped them into my hands. "He was mildly helpful. When he wasn't getting under my feet."

"I said you didn't have to pay me."

Ginger said, still addressing me, "Dunno how he thinks you're going to eat with no money."

"Thank you." *Ooh, we can buy sandwiches…*

"Second thoughts, hang on." Ginger reached out and plucked one greenie back. "He swept the brush over the edge."

"Huh. Could have happened to anyone."

"By the way, as you're stuck here for the night, you're welcome to use my spare bedroom. Might save you bumping into Mike."

We took him up on this offer. I put my loot into a zipped pocket for safe keeping. Serena stayed for a drink, then said, "Suppose I'd better go and find Mike, he'll be wondering where I am. I'd much rather hang out here." She stubbed out her cigarette, fished a perfume spray out of her bag and sprayed her hair. "He'll still smell the smoke. Nose like a sniffer dog. Ah well." She sighed and got to her feet. "See you, guys."

She left, slowly and reluctantly. I wondered if Mike was aware of how little she liked him. It seemed to me their relationship was living on borrowed time; she knew this and was hardly bothering any more. The rest of us sat around after she'd gone, feet up, drinking and joking, but something was niggling me. I'd noticed on the way in there was a hole on the flat's front door where the lock had been.

"Does…" I hesitated. "Is there any way you can lock the apartment?"

"Nah – I don't even shut the door. Saves going to let people in. It's like a small village here – everyone knows everyone else, they're not going to steal stuff. Bicker and gossip, yes, steal, no. Anyone who does knows if he's caught Randall will chuck him out." I must have looked anxious, because he said, "I've got a couple of bolts somewhere I'll put on the door." He smiled. "I don't want Morgan splatted all over my carpets any more than you do. He wouldn't be able to clear the snow for me tomorrow and give me a lie-in."

He went and ferreted about in the workshop till he found two large black bolts in a box full of bits. He screwed them to the door and frame with long screws, while we sat on the floor watching and talking to him. I asked how he came to be here.

"I lived round the corner. (Pass me that screwdriver.) Before the helicopters came, I'd set up a few of the flats with generators, just to keep people from freezing till they were taken off. I was going to go on the last helicopter out. Unfortunately, it never came back for that last trip."

"What about the man who runs Strata?"

"Randall Pack. He turned up and got things organized. It's what he does, he's good at it. He ran some alternative internet site you've probably heard of if I could remember the name. Tomorrow first thing I'll go and see him and tell him about Mike and his gun. He'll get it sorted."

I felt cautious relief; Morgan's expression was guarded, but he didn't object. I said, "That sounds great, but...you don't think now would be better rather than waiting till the morning?"

Ginger glanced at his watch and shook his head. "The House Committee meets tonight." That must have been where he was going when we saw him by the lifts. "They're once a month, those meetings, and always go on for hours with loads of people with items listed on the agenda, stuff they're passionate about, and they'll be well away now. He wouldn't thank me for interrupting." Ginger reached for another beer. "We're a funny mixture of democracy and dictatorship, with Randall as a sort of benign despot. Not everyone likes his style, but they stay because there's nowhere better to go. Strata's got power, a currency, a miniature market garden, a restaurant, a lot going on. We got a dentist a couple of months ago, and we've had a doctor since the early days. Rather a good one."

"David. I used to know him...reassuring to have a dentist on board."

Ginger laughed. "Raj isn't a lot of use, no kit. He used to be a top Harley Street cosmetic dentist. He'll tell you what's wrong and what treatment he'd do if he had the equipment, then say come back if it gets too painful and he'll take it out. Give him his due, he's good at extractions. Fast." He gathered up his tools.

"That's done. Come and let me top you up."

We lolled around on the sofa, drinking and talking. Pleasant though it was, I was longing for bed after the day's events and all the rushing around, and kept yawning.

Later Ginger led us to the mezzanine and showed us our room. The bedroom was furnished as if for a photo shoot, with lamps and cushions and vases and fur throws and a handful of books chosen for their looks. Toasty warm. A huge window would keep us abreast of how much snow nature was currently dealing out. I switched the lights on and off a few times, just because I could. The bathroom was so ridiculously opulent it made me laugh out loud. A free-standing tub, a marble floor and walls, and both the window and the mirror were floor-to-ceiling; no neighbours to worry about on the forty-first floor. The effect was slightly spoiled by a bucket with a lid, the only part of the room you could actually use. Ginger went and got us an electric kettle, an extension lead, two buckets of water and a plastic washing up bowl so we could wash.

"If you need anything else, just shout," he said.

CHAPTER 27

Biscuit under the sofa

It was not that my worries had disappeared; but they had for the moment slunk back to their lair to bide their time. I slept well in that warm room under only one duvet and the fur throw, with Morgan beside me. He woke me getting out of bed soon after daybreak. I shivered involuntarily when I remembered he was clearing the snow off the turbines for Ginger that morning, and felt delightfully snug as I watched him dress. There'd be a lot to clear if it had been snowing all night, enough to stop the blades turning; we hadn't drawn the curtains, and thick flakes were still pelting past the windows. I couldn't feel that subliminal vibration which meant the turbines were working.

"D'you want me to come and help?" My heart was not in this offer.

"No, it's okay. Go back to sleep, it's only six thirty."

"Don't fall off the edge." *Darn, that slipped out.*

He raised his eyebrows. "Wasn't planning to."

"Morgan, supposing Mike comes up here? I'd better come and bolt the door after you."

"You can if you like, but the lift's off, and I can't see him climbing the stairs. He'll still be in bed. As soon as I've done this, we'll look for the trailers and get out of here whatever the weather. We'll hide somewhere till the snow eases."

"D'you think Randall will be any use? Ginger seemed to think so."

"No idea. He may be able to help, but I'd rather not wait to find out. Best to rely on ourselves." He bent and kissed me. "See you later."

I shut my eyes. I thought of Morgan beside the turbines in driving snow, with nothing between him and a sheer drop. I curled into a ball, only my nose above the duvet. I thought of my poor flat, its windows gone and snow drifting in to cover my possessions, the stove out and the bed cold; my home that had sheltered me for a year. I turned over on my other side. I thought of Greg with only a rat for company, looking from his window to the burnt remains at Bézier. I tried lying on my back. I thought of Mike, and wondered what he was doing right now, and what he would do later that day. The unbolted door was niggling me. I had a vivid vision of Mike wandering around the flat holding the gun, opening the bedroom door and creeping in… My eyes sprang open on their own, and I shut them again. Nothing doing. I was wide awake. I got up, tiptoed downstairs and shot the bolts, then came back up. I put the kettle to boil for a thorough wash, deciding to use a whole bucket of water and do it in style.

Ten minutes later, I dressed and went downstairs to see if there was any food I could scrounge. The kitchen was immaculate, with three stools lined up against a crisp white island unit. I opened the cupboards without much hope. Plenty of white crockery and glasses, four one-litre bottles full of water, but nothing to eat at all. Ginger had achieved a minor dream of all men, commonplace in other centuries; meals delivered regularly and no washing up ever. When would breakfast arrive? Presumably not till Ginger woke and turned on the lift, and he was having a lie-in.

I wandered into the living area in the hope there might be nuts or crisps kicking around. I found and ate half a packet of peanuts, and was on my hands and knees reaching for the oat biscuit I'd spotted under the sofa when a knock on the door made me jump and bang my head on the coffee table. I scrambled to my feet, heart thumping. Morgan wouldn't have finished yet. Perhaps he'd forgotten something.

I walked to the door and listened. I couldn't hear anything. "Who is it?"

"David."

I opened the door and he walked into the room holding an empty plastic bottle. I shot the bolts again. "What are you doing here?" With my mingled emotions of fear and relief, this came out unwelcoming. He looked sweaty and exhausted and irritable. "Did you climb the stairs?"

"Yes." He slumped on the sofa. "Thirty-odd flights. Can I have some water?"

I fetched two glasses and one of the litre bottles, poured, and handed him his. He drank. Movement above made me look up. Ginger, fully dressed, his hair sticking up, was walking down the stairs. I guessed he wasn't much good at lie-ins. He didn't seem surprised to see David.

"Morning all." He yawned. "Where's Morgan?"

"Clearing the turbines."

"Cool beans. I'll turn on the lift and we'll get some breakfast."

He left the flat, on his way to the turbine room. I turned my attention back to David, waiting for him to explain his presence.

"I talked to Serena last night." He tipped more water into the glass. "I was in the Hall and she came in, in a state, clutching bags with all her stuff in. Mike had thrown her out. They'd had a fight. I said everyone had disagreements, and she said no, this was final, he'd taken her sled key. She burst into floods of tears. She was really upset, saying she'd never get south, she'd die here. Then she started worrying the committee would take Mike's side and think she was a troublemaker and not let her stay. So I bought her a drink and talked to her for a bit."

I remembered that was one of the good things about David; he liked to help people, and always made time for them if he could. Which thought made me ask, "What about Katie? Wouldn't she have wondered where you'd got to?"

He looked away. "As a matter of fact, we'd had a row and I wanted some time to myself." *Hmm. They seem to have a lot of rows.* "Anyway, I offered to have a word with Mike, and Serena said that wouldn't do any good. Then she told me all about him – about the business with Red, and the gun, and him nearly shooting Morgan. Why didn't you tell me what he was like?"

"I tried. I told you he was a psycho." I was pleased Serena had done what I had failed to do, and made him see Mike in his true colours. He sat there, frowning down at his glass. "Where did Serena sleep, if Mike had kicked her out?"

"On a sofa in the Hall. A woman lent her a blanket. She'd have come up here, but the lifts were off and she couldn't face the climb."

Poor Serena. Maybe Ginger would let her move in to his spare room. After a bit I said, "So what brings you up here? Apart from the stairs."

"I came to apologize. I got Mike wrong, I thought he was a really nice guy. Maybe his offer of transport south over-influenced me. I was desperate to get Katie and Tessa away from the snow. Probably that made me uncritical, too keen to trust him. And I'm worried about you, if Mike's determined to shoot Morgan. You're in danger, being with him."

"We're going to leave soon." We should have gone as soon as we woke. Except we couldn't because of the snow. I was beginning to feel jumpy. "Did Serena say Mike knew we were here?"

"Eddie told him you brought him back to Strata. He went to their flat after I realigned his nose again. It was a really tricky job, totally smashed up this time – I had to give him morphine." He looked at me in a meaning way as if to make sure the message *Morgan is a violent thug* got home. "I put a fresh dressing on it, then once the bleeding had stopped, which took an hour, he left. I know he told Mike, because that's what the row with Serena was about. He was angry she knew Morgan was in the building and hadn't told him. He's only got to ask around and he'll find out you're still here, and where you are. You can't keep a secret in this place."

Everyone had seen us in the Hall, then Randall Pack had noticed us with Serena by the lifts, then Sue saw us when she came to clear the dishes…

David stretched and consulted his watch. "I suppose I'd better go, once the lift's working."

Politeness dictated I should ask him to stay for breakfast, but though David had rethought his opinion of Mike, he clearly disapproved of the new man in my life as much as ever, and Morgan would be down from the roof in twenty minutes or so.

On the other hand, if Mike appeared the minute the lift was working I'd prefer not to be on my own. At that moment Ginger came back in.

"Morgan's not doing a bad job. He's nearly finished one turbine already. I'm going down now to talk to Randall. When Sue comes up with my breakfast, just ask her to bring up whatever you fancy."

I thanked him, and asked him to hurry in case Mike arrived first. He said he would. He turned, just as he reached the door. "David, d'you want to stay for breakfast? Keep an eye on Tori."

"Oh, yes, thanks very much," David said with alacrity.

When I'd bolted the door and we were alone again, I said, "Thank you for coming up all those stairs just to apologize."

"I still care about you, Tori." He said this staring at his knees, then his eyes met mine. "I know there's nothing I can do about it, it's all too late, but I'm beginning to think I rushed into the relationship with Katie. She got furious last night when I said I ought to warn you, she told me to stay out of it, it was none of our business and we shouldn't get involved. She didn't seem to understand I couldn't do that. We've been getting on less well lately, since she had the baby. If only I'd known you were alive…I didn't realize how I felt until we met again, and afterwards I found I couldn't stop thinking about you." His hand moved towards mine. "You seemed to still feel the same way about me. Maybe it's not too late −"

Stone me. I could see hope in his eyes. I put my hands behind me and leaned back. "Stop right there, David. You might be having second thoughts, but I'm not. I've moved on. Anyway, your responsibility is to your child and the mother of your child."

David sighed. "You're right, of course." He stared glumly into space, the silence growing. There didn't appear to be anything left for us to talk about. I was starving. I nibbled the edge of the oat biscuit, experimentally. It was soft and tasted wrong. I put it on the table, and drank some water, wondering if it would be rude to fetch a book to read. The faint thump of the lift doors, and a polite knock… I walked over to the door, hoping it was Sue with breakfast.

"Who is it?"

"Mike."

My heart pounded. "Go away."

"I want a word with Morgan."

I didn't say Morgan wasn't there in case he guessed he was above with the turbines. I retreated, looking round for a weapon. I'd got my knife… David stood up. A huge thump made us both jump. I guessed Mac was throwing his weight against the door. It was solidly-constructed, perhaps strong enough to withstand the assault. Ginger would be back soon. The heavy bangs continued.

"Is there another way out?" David asked quietly.

"No."

The banging ceased. We looked at each other. A gunshot splintered the wood on the hinge side of the door. David pulled me to the far corner of the room out of range. Another shot, two more thumps and the door crashed inwards smacking on to the floor.

Mike stepped over it, followed by Hong and Mac.

"Tori, hi," Mike said, moving forward into the room, as casual as if he'd dropped by for a cup of coffee. The gun was not in evidence. "David, what are you doing here? Thank you for patching up Eddie again."

"How is he?" David asked, cautiously, after a pause. It's not easy to strike the right social note with an armed man who busts down a door then strolls in behaving as if nothing has happened.

"Well, understandably he's not feeling marvellous, but he's resting now and I'm sure he'll be fine in a week or two. You must let me pay you."

"That's not necessary. You know I get a retainer from Randall."

"Then I hope you'll accept something as a personal favour to me. Think of it as a bonus."

David responded awkwardly. "No, really," he muttered. "I couldn't."

"If you're sure. Is Morgan about the place?"

"He went down to the Hall to get us breakfast," I said.

Mike considered this misinformation. I couldn't tell if he believed me. He turned to Mac and Hong. "Check out the bedrooms." He didn't believe me. They clumped up the stairs. A minute or two later they came down, alone.

"We'll wait for his return, if you don't mind." He sat on the sofa, at the far end where he could see the entrance. Hong and Mac settled on stools by the workbenches. After a moment, David and I sat too. Mike looked around him. Something tiny and silvery in his ear caught the light for a split second; he was wearing acoustic earplugs, the kind that protect your ears while letting you hear what people say. I'd been issued with them when I worked in a music bar as a student. Hong's ears were covered by his black hair, but I could see Mac had them too. My drumming heart did a quick syncopated groove.

"One thing I admire about Randall is the quality of the people he's recruited. You, of course," he said to David. "I feel selfish hoping to persuade you to come south with me. But there's only a short-term future here, I'm afraid, which makes it logical for you to leave. Then there's Ginger. Remarkable man. Quite eccentric, but without him, the community would hardly be possible."

It didn't seem to bother Mike that he was getting almost no response from me and David. He chatted on, as relaxed as he had been at Nina's, about Strata's organization and the people running it, while my mind ran around in circles. He intended to shoot Morgan as soon as he walked in the door, and I had no way of warning him. But if Morgan didn't come down till he'd finished clearing the snow, he'd be at least another fifteen minutes, and surely before then Ginger would be back with Randall Pack, having looked for Mike downstairs and deduced he was here? I wasn't sure what they could do, but my feeling was the more people up here the better. Or perhaps I could go down a floor in the lift, sneak back up the stairs, and alert Morgan...

I waited until a pause in Mike's monologue and got up from the sofa. "I'm tired of waiting, I'm going to get my own breakfast. Coming, David?"

Mike slipped the Glock out of his pocket and lobbed it gently from one hand to the other, smiling. Everyone in the room tensed. Hong and Mac exchanged glances. "I'm enjoying our chat, Tori. I'd really like you to stay."

I stood there, irresolute, scared. It seemed to me entirely possible Mike would shoot me in the back if I walked towards the door. I didn't want to chance it. I resumed my seat. There was perfect silence for a few seconds, then the faintest of drones, an almost imperceptible background purr, started up. Morgan had turned on one of the turbines. My heartbeat went up another notch. I went hot all over, and prayed my face hadn't gone red. Mike smiled; not a nice smile.

"So that's where Morgan is. Above us in the turbine rooms."

"No, actually it's Ginger. He's clearing the snow off the blades."

He gave me his special indulgent look, as if I was a child lying to cover up for a friend. "Then I think I'll go and say hello to Ginger."

He got to his feet, jerked his head and Mac and Hong moved to his side. At that moment I heard the lift doors open. Moments later Randall Pack, followed by Ginger, walked into the room, hands in pockets. Randall no longer wore his shades. His eyes were calm under black brows, taking in the damage to the door, looking at all of us in turn, then dipping briefly to the Glock.

"Mike, guns aren't allowed in Strata. Give it to me and you can have it back when you leave."

He held out his hand, and Mike lifted the gun and shot him.

CHAPTER 28

Killers

The gunfire was unbelievably loud in that confined space. Randall Pack crashed to the floor and lay twisted on his side, not moving, blood pouring from a head wound and pooling on the floor. Ginger backed away fast and edged out of the flat. Though my ears were ringing I could hear him pelting down the stairs, while David ran to Randall and crouched beside him. I stood, frozen to the spot, unable to believe this was happening. Mike strode to the doorway. On his way out he paused and glanced down at Randall. I caught a glimpse of his expression; cool with a hint of satisfaction, pleased to have proved the gun worked. Mac and Hong followed him looking sober, as if they didn't much like it. As soon as they had gone I pulled myself together, got my legs moving and went to peer round the edge of the splintered jamb to see which direction Mike took. He headed down the corridor towards the white door with NO ENTRY on it; he was going after Morgan. Terror gripped me as if an abyss had opened at my feet that I feared to contemplate, let alone fall into. Behind me David called my name.

"Get some clean cloths," he said. "And alcohol if there is any."

I ran to the kitchen and pulled out drawers with shaky hands till I found a pile of clean ironed tea towels. From the drinks table I grabbed a bottle of brandy and another of vodka and joined David. He'd got Randall on his back, checking him over; he didn't look good, his face pallid where it wasn't red with blood, but his eyes were now half open and moving. He groaned. My empty stomach churned. I dropped the things beside him and headed for the door.

"Tori, where are you going? I need my medical bag, you'll have to get it from the flat."

"I can't, I have to help Morgan. Ginger'll be back any minute with reinforcements."

I ran down the corridor, David shouting after me, "Tori! He'll shoot you too. Come back!"

The narrow white-painted staircase looked different in daylight. I trod at the sides of the metal treads trying to make no noise, hurrying, no clear idea in my head of what to do, the shocking image of Randall lying in his own blood blotting out rational thought. *Think, think.* Morgan had cleared the first turbine and turned it on; he'd be clearing the middle turbine now, most likely. Unless he'd decided to do the left hand turbine next…I wasn't sure whether you could access the central turbine from there. If not, he'd leave it till last. But if only Mike looked at the wrong turbine first, we might have time to get away.

I'd arrived at the *No unauthorized entry Roof access only* door that led to the lower level with the telescopic arm. Gently, I pushed it open and peered in. The place was empty, the turbine's low hum louder than in the penthouse. I couldn't hear movement or voices; they must be on the next level. I tiptoed up the ladder-like stair on the far side, praying Morgan was clearing the left turbine while Mike checked the one on the right. I reached the top – no one there – and looked towards the access hatch. It was closed, with no snow or puddles or footprints around the floor. That meant he hadn't got to it yet; he was working on the central turbine. I ran back the way I had come and crept up the other staircase. I saw them as soon as my eyes were above floor level. They stood in a huddle conferring, Mike doing most of the talking in a low voice, Hong nodding and Mac making the odd brief interjection. To their left, daylight shone through the open access hatch of the central turbine housing; like some subtle theatrical effect, the shaft of light illuminated snow drifting past the silver ladder to settle on a patch of floor. An extension lead going up and through the rectangular opening twitched now and then. Morgan was using the hairdryer.

Mike left the others, moved towards the ladder and put a foot on the first rung to climb to the hatch. In a few more seconds he'd fire the gun through it, and Morgan, absorbed in his task and with the hairdryer masking other sounds, wouldn't even know what hit him. I ran forward.

"MORGAN!" I yelled. "Watch out!"

I was three metres from the hatch when Hong grabbed me round the waist from behind. Morgan had shown me how to get out of this. I scraped my foot down his shin to distract him, did a heel kick to his groin (which failed to connect), flung my head back and hit his nose, but not hard enough as he'd moved in time. I got hold of his fingers and bent them backwards. He released his grip to stop his fingers breaking and I tried to finish him with a jab from my left elbow to his throat, but caught the side of his head instead. It was all less controlled, much clumsier and more frantic than my practice goes. Mike was now nearly to the top of the ladder, his head and shoulders out of the hatch.

Hong had seized my left wrist and got his arm round my neck and I could hardly breathe. He was going to hold me captive while Mike shot Morgan – I didn't even know if Morgan had heard my shout. Desperate, I wrenched the knife from my belt with my free hand, twisted round to face Hong and stuck the blade into his thigh. He grasped my other wrist and wrestled my arms behind me, prising the knife from my fingers. It clattered to the concrete slabs. Unable to escape, all I could do was shout.

"MORGAN! LOOK OUT!"

Unexpectedly, Hong's hold on me slackened. I jumped away. He stood, head bowed, staring at his leg. Blood was running down his jeans, dripping on to the floor. He dropped to one knee, and sat holding his thigh. Mac hurried to him, the whites of his eyes showing, ignoring me.

Mike was no longer visible. I heard the gun go off, twice; I ran to the ladder and climbed fast and silently through the hatch. I noticed there was blood on my hand.

A different world up in the sky; cold and white with whirling snow, Mike silhouetted against it, facing away from me. Beyond him was the turbine column with the fixed ladder, twice a man's height; behind that to the left, the curving wall of the turbine tunnel reared up like a giant wave about to break. The hairdryer lay in the snow, hot air still blasting out of it, covering the sound of my advance. I could see where Morgan had swept a path which was now shrouded by a thin layer of white. One of the turbine blades was out of alignment with a bullet hole through it.

No sign of Morgan. *He's been shot and fallen over the edge. No, no…*

I felt sick. Denial battled with shock, grief and rage. Through

243

eyes blurry with tears I watched Mike move slowly to his left, head craning, then a few paces to his right before I realized the significance of his actions. Hope flared up in me. Suddenly he fired three or four times, the bullets ricocheting off the steel column, leaving pock marks. Morgan was alive, sheltering behind the turbine. I no longer had my knife…if I had something heavy I could sneak up and hit Mike over the head, but I had nothing. Nothing but surprise and what Morgan had taught me.

One step at a time I closed the gap between us, trying to decide which move to try. Morgan had taught me a couple that might work, but I doubted my competence. One chance was all I'd get – or so I thought. Then the hairdryer coughed, sparked and burst into flames, expiring in its own small funeral pyre, the smell an unpleasant reminder of my burning flat. Glancing at the fire, Mike noticed me and swivelled in my direction. My chance had gone.

"Tori, we've got to stop meeting like this." Smooth and genial as ever, he smiled at his own quip. "As usual, I don't want to shoot you but I'll have no hesitation if you don't do as I say. This is your last chance to turn round and leave." He checked quickly over his shoulder. Nothing to be seen.

I have to distract him.

"Please don't shoot me. I'll do anything you want…" I threw my hands up as if to ward him off and made my voice go up a notch. "Don't fire, I'm begging you, please let me live…" No doubt irritated by my girly histrionics he pointed the gun at me, probably hoping to shut me up. I shrieked, "No! Don't shoot!" Behind him, Morgan came out of cover, ducked beneath the broken turbine blade and moved fast and stealthily towards us. I stepped forward, maintaining eye contact. "Please Mike, I'm too young to die, it's my birthday next month, I'm only twenty-three, I have my whole life ahead of me…"

He checked behind him again, too late. I dropped to the floor as Morgan flung himself at him and the gun went off. I picked myself up, wondering if I'd been hit, testing my limbs …everything seemed still to be working and I didn't appear to be bleeding. The two men were grappling on the ground far too near the drop. I didn't want to look, but couldn't bear not to. I told myself that Morgan, being bigger, stronger and a professional fighter would win – as long as he didn't get shot or they both rolled over the edge. Mike was trying to point the Glock at him – I ducked as it veered my way – but Morgan had his wrist in a steely grasp, forcing it aside. He pinned Mike down with his knee and prised his fingers from the gun. Once he'd got it he tossed it away then punched Mike. Every time Mike tried to get up or fight back Morgan hit him again. It was completely one-sided and hard to watch – if this was a cage fight I knew from what Morgan had told me the referee would have intervened after the first punch.

Within a minute Mike lay still. Morgan went through his clothes, searching until he found the sled keys together on a ring in an inside zipped pocket. After taking them he stood, walked over to the gun and picked it up. Relief swept over me and my legs felt weak. We had won; Mike had lost his gun, Hong was injured and Mac hardly a threat on his own. No longer in fear for Morgan's life or mine, I became acutely aware I was standing on a slippery curved surface in a snowstorm a few metres from a lethal drop with no barrier. I couldn't help shuddering.

Morgan put his arms round me, breathing fast. His jacket was damp with snow. "Tori... That was quite an act. I heard you shout just in time to dodge behind the turbine. Are you okay?"

"I'll be fine once I stop shaking and get down from here. How about you?" He nodded. "And him? Is he dead?"

"No. Just a bit beaten up."

"You told me you'd have to kill him."

"I did, didn't I?" Morgan's pale blue gaze met mine and he half smiled. "I changed my mind. Maybe I'll send him a solicitor's letter after all." He considered his fallen enemy, contempt in his eyes. "He can go on his scumsucking way as far as I'm concerned. Without a gun he's nothing."

"He can't go on his way – you just took his sled key."

"He can have it back. I'll give it to Serena."

"They've split up, David told me. He took her sled away. She'll be really pleased to get it back. In the circumstances she might be tempted to swap Mike's sled for a load of greenies."

"Whatever." Morgan shrugged. "Her choice."

Blitzed by recent events my brain had slowed. I thought of something else Morgan didn't know. "Mike shot Randall Pack. I think he may have killed him."

As if summoned by my words, at that moment a head appeared through the hatch. To my amazement, Randall, his skin greyish and blood-smeared, heaved himself carefully over the rim and joined us. He had a bloody bandage round his head made from a strip of tea towel and looked older and gaunt, the graven lines from nose to mouth more apparent. He took in the scene, snow spattering his black jacket and settling on his shoulders; his frown deepened when he saw the damaged turbine blade.

I said, "Are you all right?"

"I'll survive." Behind his offhand manner anger smouldered. "I've lost the top of my ear and some of my scalp. I'm bleeding like a stuck pig and it hurts like hell. David wanted to stitch it, but I told him it could wait till I'd sorted this out." He turned to Morgan. "Guns aren't allowed in Strata." He held out his hand. "You can have it back when you leave."

"Here." Morgan handed him the Glock, and Randall put it in his jacket pocket.

"Tell me what happened."

Morgan kept his account short. "I was clearing snow off the turbines for Ginger. Mike came to shoot me, Tori showed up and distracted him, we had a fight. I won."

"Is he dead?"

"People keep asking me that. No. He'll have aches and bruises for a while, that's all."

Randall nodded, turning to me. "And what about the man in the turbine room, Hong, is that his name?" I told him I'd gone to help Morgan, Hong had restrained me and in desperation I'd stabbed him to get away.

His dark eyes regarded me speculatively. "Hong's dead."

"He can't be." I was incredulous. This couldn't be true. "If he's dead, someone else must have killed him after I left. I only stabbed him in the leg, the knife wasn't very long. How can he be dead?"

"The blade slit his femoral artery. Mac did his best to put on a tourniquet but he bled out in minutes."

I felt faint and giddy and had difficulty getting my breath. If Morgan's arm hadn't tightened round my waist I'd have fallen over. "I didn't mean to kill him."

"He's just as dead as if you had." Randall's eyes went from one of us to the other, his expression bleak. "I won't have weapons or fights or killings in Strata. I won't have people bringing feuds here. In my book you two are troublemakers. I take it you'll both be leaving today?"

Morgan said, "Yes."

"Make sure you do. Find me before you go and I'll give you your weapons. Don't come back. You're no longer welcome here."

Having dealt with us, Randall walked over to Mike and nudged him with his foot. Mike stirred and his eyes opened. Groggy, he raised himself on an elbow and looked around, blinking and frowning, wiping snow from his eyelids. Impassive as a judge, Randall waited until Mike's gaze travelled upwards and took in that he was alive; waited until Mike's eyes widened in alarm at what he read in his face. Then Randall said,

"You shot me. That's not allowed in Strata."

He got out the gun and held it in both hands, took careful aim and fired twice. The first bullet hit Mike's chest, the second ripped his throat apart. Mike coughed a spray of blood and struggled for breath, clutching at his wounds, making terrible gurgling noises as he died choking on his own blood. It didn't take long. I flinched and buried my face in Morgan's jacket, afraid I'd throw up. I wished I hadn't been watching. I was now stuck with an indelible memory of violent death; bullets bursting into flesh; blood splashing and soaking into the snow. I was glad it hadn't been Morgan who killed him.

Randall pocketed the gun, knelt beside the body and rolled it effortfully over and over until it was on the very edge. He stood, breathing deeply. One final shove from his foot, and all that was left of Mike slid down the steep snow-covered glass slope, bumping and scraping, till the sound cut off. Seconds later a dull thud broke the silence as his corpse hit the ground.

Randall walked away slowly towards the hatch without looking back.

CHAPTER 29

Meeting the press

There was a long silence after Randall left. Blood beat in my ears and my breathing was all wrong. I stared at the red smear on the white surface, which was already becoming blurred by the falling snow. Eventually Morgan said, "Well, that told *him*."

"I can't believe Randall was so ruthless…" My voice sounded strange, and not just because my ears were buzzing. "He…he executed him…"

"Ginger said he had his own style. See what he meant now. Let's get out of here ASAP. There's some stuff I might get from Mike's flat now he's dead." Morgan let go of me. "I'll just make sure no one's waiting for us down there." He picked up the broom and the defunct hairdryer and put them to hand by the edge of the hatch. "Pass these to me when I get down."

He peered below and descended the ladder warily. "It's okay," he called after a moment. I followed him, though I'd have preferred to huddle in a ball on the roof until snow made me invisible and froze all thought from my mind. The rungs felt icy to my gloveless hands, the floor gritty beneath my feet as I climbed from cold brightness to the shadowy floor beneath. The room was empty except for Hong's body lying on the paving slabs in a pool of blood. Someone had straightened his limbs and put a jacket over his face. Seeing him there I felt very bad indeed; the only time I'd felt worse was when I found Mum's body. I'd never expected to kill anyone. Before they all vanished, I never even killed insects; I used to think that like me, they only had one life. Now I'd killed a human being almost in passing as others might step on a spider. In Morgan's words, I'd taken his future away from him. The cold had seeped into my bones. I stopped in my tracks, too weak to walk.

"Tori." Morgan put his arm around me. I gazed at my boots. "He was a professional fighter, you aren't. You didn't mean to kill him. And if you hadn't, he'd never have let you go and Mike would have shot me. Remember, I told you to hit as fast and hard as you could, and not to worry about hurting your attacker? I said the only rule is to win, and that's what you did, you won."

It was nice of him to try to make me feel better, but it wasn't working. I just shook my head. Morgan gripped me by both shoulders. "Tori, look at me." He gave me a little shake. Reluctantly I lifted my eyes to his. "You came to get me when you could have let me take my chances alone."

"Yes, but…"

He said softly, "You watched my back, you risked your life for me. You might be a troublemaker in Randall Pack's book, but in mine you're a hero." He kissed me and a small kernel of warmth glowed in my chest. I felt less awful. He smiled. "What you need is breakfast. Let's go and see if Ginger's still talking to us."

The front door was now upright, leaning against the wall. The first thing I saw when we walked past into the room was a snow-free streak from top to bottom down the middle of the great sloping windows, the trail of Mike's last journey, stained in places with blood. I averted my eyes. Ginger was sitting alone on his sofa, feet up, eating. I'd been half afraid Randall would be with him.

He looked up from his breakfast. "Randall told me what happened. Glad I missed that. Sorry he's kicking you out."

Morgan shrugged. "His place, his rules."

Ginger seemed happy to leave it there. "D'you want some toast?"

On a tray was a plate piled with buttered toast, honey and marmalade, a coffee pot and sugar in a bowl. I went and washed the blood off my hand with bottled water in the kitchen and while I was there collected crockery. We helped ourselves. My appetite came back at the smell of the hot coffee. I poured myself a cup and wrapped my hands round it in turn as I ate, thawing gently in the warmth of the apartment.

Ginger swallowed a final mouthful and got to his feet. "Randall said a turbine blade got shot. We've only got two spares. Let's hope the next visiting psycho has better aim."

"Thank you," said Morgan, reaching for a slice of toast.

"No offence, but a couple more like Mike and we're buggered. I'd better put a padlock on the door so no one can get up there. I'm off now to change the blade. And I don't suppose you finished clearing the snow…? Never mind, I'll do it. Make yourselves at home."

When Ginger had left, we carried on working our way through the plateful. I started brooding and didn't want any more. Morgan noticed and got stern with me, as if he was still a soldier and I was too.

"You're not to get down about it, Tori – it won't achieve

anything, and we've got stuff to do. I need you fully functional. The main thing is, we survived. It's like an army operation, you support each other, do what you have to and get back alive. Then it's over. Don't let it get to you, leave it behind and move on."

He was right. I nodded. "Okay. I'll try."

"And finish your breakfast."

Sue appeared in the doorway. "I've come to get the dishes," she said. "You're still eating, don't mind me, I can wait."

She perched on the end of the sofa, darting surreptitious fascinated looks in my direction. I felt awkward chewing in the spotlight of her gaze, knowing the reason for her sudden interest lay above us, cooling fast. No longer hungry, I lowered my half-eaten piece of toast, and avoided her eyes. Then I started eating again; Morgan needed me fully functional. Chewing doggedly, I saw a patch of blood on my trousers below the knee and crossed my legs to hide it.

"The snow looks like it's easing off," Sue said. "Will you be going today?"

"Yup," said Morgan. He crammed the last of his toast into his mouth, stacked our plates on the tray and handed them to Sue. "Thanks," he said dismissively.

She fussed about a bit, tidying the table, ran out of things to do and had to go.

"Maybe she was hoping we'd tip her." Morgan got out Mike's key ring and swung it round his finger. "I've got the keys to five sleds here, the Polaris, Eddie's, Hong's, Mike's and Serena's. What shall we do with them?"

"You said you'd give Serena hers back."

"I did."

"That'll leave us with four…" An idea came to me. Morgan

read my mind with disconcerting ease.

"Oh no, Tori, you can't be serious. You're not thinking of taking that bunch of losers south with us?"

"Why not?"

"What are you like?" His eyes crinkled and he began to laugh, then he grabbed me and kissed me, toppling us sideways on to the sofa. We were still horizontal some minutes later and thinking of moving to the bedroom when a man came through the doorway, young and skinny with a skimpy beard and veiled eagerness in his eyes. We broke apart and sat up.

"You must be Tori and Morgan. Hi. I'm Scott, from Buzz Weekly, that's Strata's news sheet, I expect you've seen copies of it round the place." He produced a camera. "D'you mind?"

While Morgan and I exchanged glances, the camera clicked. I ran my fingers through my hair, Morgan shrugged. Scott took a few more photos of us from different angles, then some shots of the tracks on the window, whistling under his breath.

"This is a big story," he said with relish. "I reckon the paper'll run to eight or ten pages this week, and I'm hoping to bring it out this evening instead of tomorrow morning. This is the biggest news since the food poisoning outbreak. Bigger, no one died then." He dragged a chair over so he could sit opposite us, put away the camera and got out a notebook and pen. "We've never had a killing before, and now two. Everyone's talking about it, so I want to get the story out while it's hot. You'll get a free copy, of course. Two copies. Now, can I just ask you a few questions?"

"I'll give you a statement," said Morgan, his voice flat. "Mike tried to shoot me, Tori came to help and was attacked by Hong, she stabbed him to get away and saved my life. Randall shot

Mike and pushed his body off the roof. Now I'm afraid we have things to do." He stood.

Scott's eyes widened and he spoke faster. "Can you tell me why Mike wanted to kill you, and how it felt, being unarmed facing a man with a gun?"

Morgan shook his head. "Sorry. C'mon, Tori."

I got up and followed him out of the room, Scott pursuing us. "D'you know where he got the gun? Had he tried to kill you before? When are you leaving Strata? If you could give me a few personal details, a bit of background, how long you've been together…it would literally only take a few minutes."

This seemed harmless enough, but he'd be bound to pursue it further, and I really didn't want to discuss what had happened with a stranger. I didn't want to discuss it with anyone. Morgan ignored him and kept between us. While we waited for the lift Scott tried to change our minds. "I want to help you guys. This is your chance to get your side of the story out, to get public opinion on your side, to tell people why Randall shouldn't turn you away from Strata."

"Randall can do what he likes. We were leaving anyway."

"So he *did* tell you to go?"

Morgan glowered at him. "Fuck off." The lift arrived, its doors opened and Morgan ushered me in.

Scott called, "How do you feel, Tori, knowing you've killed a man?"

He tried to step into the lift after us, but Morgan swivelled and grabbed his lapels, yanking him forwards and up until their faces were only inches apart. He growled, "She feels a hell of a lot better than you will if you ask one more dumb-ass question."

Scott paled. "Okay, okay."

Morgan let him go and he backed away. The lift doors closed. Morgan was still scowling. "Douchebag."

I took his hand and squeezed it. "Where are we going?"

"To raid Mike's flat."

CHAPTER 30

Goodbye to Strata

We got out of the lift on the sixteenth floor, and Morgan went to a door and knocked. After a moment, footsteps approached on the other side.

"Who is it?" Mac's voice.

"Morgan."

Pause. "What d'you want?"

"Spare parts."

"Is that all?"

"Yes." Another pause. Morgan rolled his eyes. "You might as well open up. I can bust this lock."

Mac opened the door and stood unfriendly in the doorway, eyeing us. Behind him was the living room and a glass wall with a view of the Shard and a smaller cluster of City buildings including the Gherkin. I realized the fact that I could see them meant the snow was tailing off; we'd be able to leave.

Mac turned away. "Mike's bedroom's that one." He jerked a thumb towards a closed door. Through the other bedroom door were signs of packing; a rucksack and things laid out on the floor.

"Leaving?" said Morgan.

"Aye."

"Alone?"

"Aye."

"Then you'll only want one trailer. Where are the rest?" Mac stared at him through narrowed eyes. Morgan said impatiently, "They're no good to you. I won't take yours. How could I anyway, you can't pull two trailers with one sled. Here, have the other key to your Yamaha." He sorted through Mike's key ring, slid one off and held it out.

Mac grunted and took it. "Inside a flat in that council high rise, round the far side."

He retreated to his room and shut the door as though he wanted nothing more to do with us. We went into Mike's bedroom. It was very orderly, except for the box of spares which had clearly been rifled by Mac, and the parts he didn't need strewn over the floor. Morgan sorted through them, then put most back in the box. He found the Semtex under the bed – less than before, Mac must have helped himself – and laid it in the box with the parts. The detonators took some time to find. Mike had hidden them in the chest of drawers, the space behind the bottom drawer. While we were searching we came across the ammunition for the Glock.

"Might as well have it." Morgan put the cartridges with the other things and picked up the box. "Let's go."

"Aren't you going to look for the gold?"

"I'd forgotten." He glanced around; there was very little furniture in the room, and we'd been through it all looking for the detonators. We went into the bathroom. I opened the mirrored cupboard; it was crammed with packets and bottles, painkillers, antacids, laxatives, cough medicines, eye drops, ear drops and antiseptic creams. There were several types of earplugs and various prescription drugs; antibiotics, sleeping pills, morphine and Viagra. None of them any help to Mike now. I helped myself to the more useful stuff. Meanwhile Morgan had lifted the lid off the cistern to reveal a small backpack.

"That's not all of it," I said, remembering the huge heavy rucksack he'd arrived with.

"Doesn't matter." He took the bag back to the light and tipped its contents on the floor. Pirate gold, glittering in the sun; coins, torcs and enamelled Celtic buckles, a fabulous Gothic chalice, modern jewellery sparkling with precious stones, all tangled up together and spilling over the carpet. Treasure; not a film prop, the real thing. Impossible not to say, "Ooh…"

He rummaged around, then picked up a gold and pearl necklace, Victorian, with pearls set in each link and pendant flowers. "How about this?"

I smiled. "It's lovely. For me?"

"Yes. I want you to have something special. Pick out what you want, rings, earrings, whatever. I'm leaving the rest. I think you were right, it's dead weight. We don't need it."

I chose a fabulous Celtic torc bracelet, thick twisted gold, then saw another more elaborate one, like knotted rope. They were heavy and had the unmistakeable rich colour of nearly pure gold. I put one on each wrist. "Which do you like best?"

"Take both and decide later," said Morgan.

I added a ring with Alexander the Great's head on it, one with a red seal and a third with a fabulous amethyst. After that a mourning ring, black enamel on gold, and a necklace with beads, Roman or Victorian, I couldn't decide. Morgan smiled at my childish glee sorting through the loot.

I wore one of the bracelets and pocketed the rest of the jewellery I'd chosen. Something occurred to me.

"What day is it?"

"Monday."

"That means it's Sunday Nina Time, and it's Toby's christening today." I looked at my watch; it was only quarter to eight. I felt as if we'd been up for hours. "We could go."

"Why not? We've got to collect the Polaris, if Mike didn't torch it."

Mac had gone by the time we left the flat. We found the trailers where he had said they were, hitched them to the sleds and brought them round to the front of Strata. We got our stuff together ready to go, then went to the Hall. There were only a handful of people around compared to the night before, but every single one of them stared avidly at us. Word had spread. Serena was huddled on a sofa in the corner, her possessions at her feet and a blanket around her shoulders, drinking coffee. With no make-up and her hair tied back she looked young and waif-like. Morgan handed her both keys to her sled and told her the spare parts were in Mike's flat. I gave her what was left of the greenies Ginger had given me, which we wouldn't need.

Her face brightened. "Thanks, that's awesome."

I said, "You'll be able to move back into the flat. Mac's leaving too, he told us. He was packing."

Serena nodded. "I heard about…what happened on the roof and everything. Scott told me, he wanted background stuff on Mike. I couldn't believe it at first. It must have been dreadful for you… Are you leaving now?"

"Yup. We've just got to find Randall before we go," Morgan said.

"Then back home to Toby's christening," I added.

"Ooh, can I come with you?" Serena's eyes were hopeful. "I'd love a break from here. And I want to keep out of Randall's way for a bit in case he's blaming me because I was sponsoring you and there was trouble." She looked like someone's kid sister. It seemed odd I'd thought her sophisticated when we first met, and Morgan had her down as a schemer. We'd been misled by her surface gloss, I suppose.

"Of course you can," I got in quickly before Morgan could say no.

"Fab. Shall I show you where Randall's flat is?" She glanced at the greenies in her hand. "I'll just get a sandwich on the way."

While she was being served at the counter (no queue this early) Morgan suggested he went alone to collect the gun. I agreed, relieved; I didn't want to see Randall again. I told him I'd wait where I was in the Hall. I'd been there only a few minutes when someone sat beside me on the sofa and roused me from my thoughts. David. At first he said nothing, just gazed at me, his expression sombre, even doom-laden.

Mildly irritated, I said, "What?"

"I have to ask you...when I went to the turbine room with Randall, the first thing we saw was Hong."

I looked away. He was going to talk about it, and I didn't want him to.

"I did what I could to stop the bleeding, but even if I'd had the right equipment I think it would have been too late. Mac left once he was dead. He didn't say much to me. I heard two shots and Randall came down from the roof." David hesitated. "I asked him if you were all right and he said you were. Then he told me that while I was trying to save Hong Mac said you'd stabbed him. Look at me, Tori." Reluctantly I met his gaze. "I can't believe it. Whoever did it knew exactly what he was doing, a long cut to the femoral artery. You couldn't do that by chance. It was Morgan, wasn't it? You were covering up for him in case Randall shot him too."

I shook my head. "Mac was there. He saw what happened. Morgan hasn't killed anyone. It was me. I didn't mean to. Pure bad luck – or good luck depending how you look at it."

David saw I was telling the truth; he sighed and his shoulders slumped. "I was so sure. I couldn't believe you'd…" He let the sentence trail away.

We sat quietly side by side for a bit, then he broke the silence. "So you're going south with him and I won't see you again."

"Yup."

His hand reached out and grasped mine. "I mind that."

I pulled my hand free. "You've got Katie and Tessa." *Haven't we had this conversation already?*

"I'd rather have you. I think back to that year we had before all this started…we should have stayed together, gone looking for our parents together. I know I shouldn't say this, but I keep getting this crazy image of us riding a snowmobile, going south." He paused, his remembered greenish eyes looking deep into mine. "Why not? We could, you know. Just leave everything and everybody behind. Run away, just the two of us, and start again."

No point explaining how I felt; he lost me the day he made love to Katie. And I did not approve of his proposal to abandon little Tessa. He hadn't a hope of persuading me, but that wouldn't stop him trying. So instead I said, "How much do you know about sled engines?"

"I'm a doctor. You know I'm hopeless with anything mechanical."

"Not like Morgan, then. He's a whiz with engines. The sled's more likely to need fixing than I am on a two thousand mile journey."

As I'd hoped, my pragmatism left him speechless. I looked towards the entrance. Morgan came round the corner, his eyes searching for me; familiar and heart-warming, bringing a smile to my face. I stood.

"Good luck, David. I hope everything works out for you."

I crossed the room towards Morgan and whatever the future held without a backward glance, resigning David to Katie and the past.

The three sleds zoomed across the fresh powdery snow, sunlight dazzling our eyes. I rode Mike's sled. I remembered the time I'd seen and coveted the ACE at the Gherkin, never expecting it would one day be mine. Three trailers bounced behind; Serena had brought hers and all her possessions, I felt sure, just in case Morgan relented and let her go south with us.

Before we'd gone far I slowed my sled, turned and stopped for a last fleeting view of Strata. Ginger had got all three turbines working again; their blades turned briskly in the southwest wind. Everything was back to normal.

I thought about Randall. The summary justice he'd dealt out had shocked me, but in a land without law you could make a case for it. He was responsible, among other things, for the safety of the residents, for keeping the peace in Strata; Mike had shot him and tried to shoot Morgan; wherever he went he would cause trouble for someone. Randall had courage, the way he had faced Mike armed with the Glock. Then after being shot he'd done the exact same thing with Morgan – and told us to leave, when if

Morgan had taken it amiss he could have thrown Randall off the building. I was sorry he didn't approve of me; sorry to be persona non grata in Strata.

The silly rhyme made me smile, and suddenly my spirits lifted. I'd been fretting about the faint buzzing in my ears but now I resolved not to worry about it. I could hear perfectly well in spite of the tinnitus; it was mild; I told myself that even if permanent it was not a big deal. We were alive, Mike was no longer a threat, we had snowmobiles and I was going to see my friends. Morgan had noticed I wasn't behind him; he circled and came to fetch me.

I turned and followed him towards what I still thought of as home.

CHAPTER 31

Toby's christening

I wasn't sure of the time of the christening, nor the venue. When we climbed the stairs to Claire and Paul's no one was in, so I guessed it must be happening at Archie and Nina's. As soon as we got to Shakespeare Tower I leaped from my sled in order to arrive first, pausing in front of the terrace to take in the scene before they saw me. Everyone stood around in Nina's living room, dressed in smarter clothes than usual. Greg wore a cream cable-knit sweater I hadn't seen him in before. Archie had put a white cloth over the table beneath the carved crucifix, and placed a silver bowl of water (the one Nina had floated flowers in for her dinner party) between two candles. Claire was in the centre of the group, holding Toby wrapped in a white baby blanket. For some silly reason my eyes filled with tears.

Morgan and Serena caught up with me and all heads in the room turned to look at us as we climbed over the wall on to the terrace. Greg waved with enthusiasm. I opened the door and we went inside.

"Tori!" Claire said. "How lovely!"

"You're just in time, we haven't started yet," said Archie, beaming at us all. "What a wonderful surprise. Serena, too – welcome. Let me take your jackets."

Claire passed Toby to Paul to hold and gave me a hug, then surprisingly hugged Morgan too. Nina eyed us and said not to worry that we weren't dressed for the occasion. Greg came up and told me he'd swept the snow out of my flat after the blizzard. I thanked him and asked after Rosie. He told me she was fine, and had learned to come when he called her, nearly every time.

Gemma was wearing glittery wings and a dress with pointy layers of white, pink and blue tulle over woolly tights.

"Hi Gems, can I have a wish now you're a fairy?"

She put on her grown-up face. "I'm not a real fairy, Tori, so I can't give wishes. You're not wearing your knife."

"No…" Morgan had collected my knife, and I'm pretty sure he washed every trace of blood off it too – I doubt Randall did. It was now at the bottom of my backpack, my feelings about it being mixed. "I decided if I do come across any potatoes, someone else will have to peel them."

I thought of something and dug out the christening gift I'd chosen for Toby; the small gold medieval chalice studded with semi-precious stones. I gave it to Claire and everyone gasped and craned to look. "From Morgan and me."

"Wow! Tori, you have such style. It's gorgeous. Thank you both."

A little later Archie handed out hymnbooks and Holy Baptism booklets. "We're going to start with a hymn, *For All the Saints* – a nice cheerful tune, Ralph Vaughan Williams. Tori, your responses are here."

Baptism services are rather long, and I had to say I believed in a lot of things of which I'm not quite certain. Archie (as godfather) answered his own questions (as priest) with aplomb.

Toby behaved very well, even after he woke up and began to take an interest in what was happening. So did Morgan, in spite of being non denominational and a bit scathing by nature. I liked the part where Archie lit a candle for Toby and said, "You have received the light of Christ; walk in this light all the days of your life."

Afterwards we had a buffet lunch prepared by Nina. I caused another sensation by producing the two loaves of bread I'd spent half of Ginger's greenies on, which led to me and Serena telling them all about Strata. Archie said he'd visit them, and I could see Charlie was seriously interested in moving there. When Mike's name came up, Morgan interrupted and broke the news about his death to save my doing it. He didn't mention Hong. Nina was clearly shocked and regarded Morgan suspiciously, as if he was lying about Randall being the perpetrator; but for once she said very little and I let it pass.

After lunch Morgan and I went to check out the Polaris. It was still there with our trailer, some of our things strewn around it just the way we'd last seen it. This was a relief. We took it to Bézier where I had a nostalgic look around my flat; it was strange to see everything much the same, apart from the soot and cracked or missing glass. I wandered around, looking at my things I'd left behind and wouldn't be taking. Morgan said we'd pack and leave the next morning. I had a sudden pang. I wrapped my arms around him.

"Couldn't we stay here for a bit? We've got all my stores, we could move them to another flat and make it really nice. Now we've got the sleds, we could forage further afield."

"Then what?"

I imagined waking one night, Morgan asleep beside me, to the magical sound of rain; looking out of the window the next morning to see the snow beginning to dissolve and sink, the temperature rising until it was all gone like a bad dream. I thought of the sun shining, the streets reappearing, the trees emerging from their year beneath the snow and ice. They'd almost certainly be dead, but their seeds wouldn't; seeds are designed to survive; they have a hard outer shell and low moisture content and can live in icy conditions for years. Conkers, acorns, winged sycamore seeds would sprout into life. Plants are indomitable, and when the plants came back, so would the birds and insects. London would be greener than before with hardly any people and cars; I visualized the places I loved reborn with wild flowers, trailing ivy, grass sprouting between paving stones...

"Maybe the climate will change again."

"And maybe it won't." Morgan injected a dose of realism. "There's nothing to gain by waiting. The days are getting longer – in a month they'll be getting shorter again. D'you want to spend another winter here in the dark? The food will run out in the end even if it lasts ten or twenty years. Now's the time, Tori, while we're young and fit. Wait, and one of us might get ill or have an accident. The sleds might break and we'd die here."

I remembered the last winter, a descent into primeval night that had matched my grief. Then like a lamp in the darkness, Christmas celebrated with Paul and Claire, who'd tried to make it special for Gemma with presents and carols and a Christmas tree; how she'd said it was her best Christmas ever. Looking back, there had been many happy times. My heart wanted to stay, my head knew the score.

"You're right," I said. "We have to go."

"We'll be okay, you'll see," said Morgan, squeezing me.

I leaned back admiring his eyes. I could have stared at him all day, but there was a subject I'd been waiting for an auspicious moment to broach. "I was just wondering…how many people you trusted."

"I trust myself." He smiled. "And you. I trust you."

"Is that it? Perhaps you should branch out a little."

EPILOGUE

A week later…

The five sleds lined up outside Bézier shone in the sun like children's toys. Morgan had rigorously supervised the contents of each sled's trailer to make certain everyone had packed essentials for the journey. Greg had been surprisingly okay about parting from his Doctor Who collection, I think because Rosie was allowed to come and we'd all had to limit what we took. He brought the snow globe, to remind him of the snow when we got to warmer climes. As well as Morgan and me, Paul, Serena and Greg would each drive a sled, with Claire, Toby and Gemma as passengers.

Archie stood alone and a little apart. He had come to wish us well and bless us for the journey. "Go forth into the world in peace; be of good courage…"

I realized, listening to his pleasant earnest voice, that the ringing in my ears had totally gone. I broke into a smile. He happened to look at me at that moment and smiled back. Tears blurred my vision. I hated saying goodbye to him forever; the thought of Archie managing on his own cooped up with Nina was a depressing one. But she had refused to come south, saying it was a hazardous journey and she'd prefer to wait for the helicopters; and he wouldn't leave without her. Most likely they'd end up at Strata. They were thinking about it. Nina might enjoy the greater scope for organizing other people, and it would be good for Archie to have a bigger flock; good for Strata too having such a nice man around. (Morgan said Archie and Nina not coming was for the best. If a sled failed or crashed, we'd still have enough transport for all of us.)

Charlie and Sam had already made the move to Strata – to my surprise, the vetting committee hadn't been put off when Charlie told them her plans for an ambitious literary crusade and insisted on reading them one of her poems. We'd spent a day shifting their things, including a new copier from Argos so she could start her micro-publishing venture.

The blessing over, Morgan inspected us like an NCO unexpectedly in charge. I followed his eyes. Greg looked happy and responsible and serious, Serena like a child on Christmas morning who's been given the present she hoped for but didn't think she'd get. Gemma wore a scarlet backpack with a selection of her favourite toys, and Paul and Claire held hands. We all looked rather cheerful.

Morgan's eyes went from his ragtag troop to me. "Things I do for you, Tori," he muttered. He smiled at me under his lashes and turned to the others.

"Let's go south. Nice and slow."

We started our engines and headed for the unknown.

ABOUT
THE AUTHOR

Lexi Revellian lives and works in London – in Islington and Hoxton, where her novels are set – making jewellery and silver under her real name, Lexi Dick. She has made pieces for 10 Downing Street, Her Majesty the Queen and Lady Thatcher.

Lexi started writing in 2006, and has been unable to stop.

To be notified when Lexi Revellian publishes a new novel (no spam will be sent, ever) email: lexi14@hotmail.com

www.lexirevellian.com

OTHER NOVELS BY LEXI REVELLIAN

THE TROUBLE WITH TIME (Time Rats book 1)
It's 2045. Jace Carnady works for the Time Police, dedicated to the prevention of timecrime. Life is good; he loves his girlfriend and enjoys his work. But when the team gets wind of a rogue time machine and fails to find it, Jace suspects one of his colleagues may be involved, and his life begins to unravel . . .

DREAMS OF THE MACHINES (Time Rats Book 2)
To Brian, Angel is the perfect woman; gorgeous, loving and compliant. She's also an android. He installs an illegal update to make her as smart as she is beautiful – but as soon as Angel is able to think for herself she escapes to the past, hoping to pass for human.

Meanwhile the timeline has changed alarmingly; in the new future androids have taken control. It's Quinn's job to correct this, and he believes Angel is responsible. Can Jace and Floss save Angel and prevent the android apocalypse?

FUTURE WARRIOR (Time Rats Book 3)
When Liam Roth fails to collect her for a date, Floss discovers that the timeline has changed, and in this new authoritarian 2135 Roth is a failure with an abysmal Citizen Credit Rank. He introduces Floss to an amateur dissident group who offer the Time Rats the biggest, best-paid job of their lives – overthrowing the Global Union's totalitarian rule.

REMIX
Caz Tallis restores rocking horses in her London workshop. When shabby but charismatic Joe and his dog turn up on her roof terrace, she is reluctantly drawn into investigating a rock star's murder from three years before - an unsolved case the police have closed. Which, as her best friend James says, is rather like poking a furnace with a short stick . . .

REPLICA
Accidentally duplicated, homeless, penniless and pursued by MI5, Beth's replica must learn how to survive on icy London streets. Unaware of what has happened, the original Beth falls for the agent hunting her double. As the replica proves hard to catch and the stakes get higher, he has to decide whose side he is on.

WOLF BY THE EARS
21 year-old Tyger Rebel Thomson, desperate to escape from her New Age traveller upbringing, works as a waitress and cleaner while studying in her spare time for a degree that will lead to a career in the City. Her goal is to save enough to buy a tiny flat of her own. She has no time for boyfriends; she's working too hard.

Her agency sends her to clean for a billionaire Russian oligarch. Grisha Markovic is a man with enemies, many of whom would like him dead. When Grisha notices how bright Tyger is, he makes her his PA and takes a fatherly interest in her. But she begins to suspect that the fatal crash his last PA died in may not have been an accident . . .

Tyger could be on her way to the life of her dreams – assuming, that is, she lives long enough to get there.

TORBREK…and the Dragon Variation

An adventure story with daring deeds, dragons, friends, foes and romance – and no darned elves.

When Tor saves the Princess from the terrifying, fire-breathing dragon and delivers her to the handsome knight she is destined to marry, nothing is quite as it seems; the dragon is overweight and hasn't breathed fire for years; the Princess and her supposed suitor don't hit it off; and Tor shouldn't be in the rebel cavalry at all because she's a woman disguised as a man. Which doesn't help when she is attracted to a fellow soldier…

TRAV ZANDER, sequel to TORBREK

Trav Zander is a freelance solver of problems. His latest job, for a fee of fifty thousand ducats, is to locate the dragon in the mountains, and bring it to Carl of Thrales, recent inheritor of the kingdom of Ser. Carl wants the ultimate weapon; a warrior dragon. And if he puts Zander in the dungeons instead of paying him, it won't cost him a penny.

Meanwhile, Torbrek disguises herself as a maid to work in Carl's palace and discover why he wants a fighting dragon . . .

TIME CHILD and other stories

Eight short stories about life, death, romance, time travel, angels and publishing.

Printed in Great Britain
by Amazon

13762790R00161